Abolish the Rose

Alanna Irving

atmosphere press

For the five-year-old
who wanted to be a story-writer
because being a shopkeeper
involved too much maths.

The question of common sense is always "What is it good for?"—a question which would abolish the rose and be answered triumphantly by the cabbage.

– James Russell Lowell

I'm sitting on the patio, contemplating the garden over the rim of a cooling cup of tea. Summer is ending, petals are fading and falling, orange is claiming more and more ground over green. Shadows invade earlier and earlier each day.

I'm bored.

Boredom doesn't sit well with me; I'm not good at doing nothing.

The idea of relaxation, of nowhere to rush to and nothing to get done—it sounds lovely. I thought I'd leap at the chance, but the reality seems to just put me on edge.

It's not a problem my husband has. He's been retired for almost two years, and loves it. He gets up and spends an hour or two reading the paper, doing the crossword, tidying the kitchen. Then he takes the dog for a walk, sometimes stopping in at a friend's or at the library, and after lunch and a nap, he spends the afternoon in the garden. I have to admit, his work pays off. The lawn is clearly defined, there's a functioning vegetable patch and flowerbeds with actual flowers. The patio has been cleared and furnished with a table, chairs, an outdoor burner, some decorative pots.

He tried to teach me to garden. He was very patient as I hacked away at his delphiniums. But I couldn't find it in myself to care. I couldn't see the point.

The dog comes bounding through the open back door to greet me, a triumphant return, panting joyfully and sniffing around the legs of my chair in case something has changed in the half-hour she was away. The sounds of my husband drift out from the kitchen, keys on the counter, the shuffle of newspapers, the clink of a mug.

I give the dog's back a good tousle as I stand up, and step into the cool of the kitchen.

'Hi,' he says, reaching out to see if the kettle is still warm enough for another cup. 'Look, I picked this up, thought you might be interested.' With his other hand, he slides an A4 sheet of paper across the table towards me.

The university in town is running a new programme of evening classes. I run my eye down the list. *Philosophy: Pre-Socratics to Modern Day, Quantum Physics for Beginners, Introduction to Programming*. A selection of languages, French, Spanish, German. And some more craft-orientated, *Learning to Sew, Interpretative Art, Memoir Writing*.

I raise an eyebrow. 'Are there that many people who want to write memoirs?'

He shrugs, abandoning the kettle and going over to peruse the fridge. 'I think memoirs are interesting. An insight into the experiences and the people that have shaped someone's life, the meaning they give their own memories, how they choose to tell their story.'

I flick the edge of the paper with my finger. The experiences that have shaped my life. The people. *Robert. Peter. Michael.* 'I don't think anyone needs to read about my life,' I say, putting the sheet back down again and starting to unstack the dishwasher. 'I've had to live through it once, I think that's enough.'

My husband frowns. 'What about art? You used to draw,' he says.

I shrug, feeling my back ache as I bend down to cupboards. 'I did, once.'

Michael.

Robert.

Peter.

'Well, think about it,' he says, taking a clean plate from the stack I'm holding, putting his sandwich on it and heading towards the stairs. 'I think you'd enjoy it.'

I stick the leaflet on the fridge, to humour him. For the next few days, it catches my eye whenever I pass. *Interpretative Art. Memoir Writing.* I shake my head, to myself. Surely I have better things to do with my time.

Week One

'What's the function of art?'

Eamonn twirls a paintbrush through the fingers of one hand. Long, dextrous fingers, like a pianist, or a magician. I think he would be good at sleight of hand.

'Does it need a function?' Mild-mannered Niall. Nobody answers. Eamonn raises his eyebrows, leaving the question open to the floor.

'It's a form of expression.' Alberta, the housewife.

Eamonn resumes his pacing, a casual stride back and forth. Exaggerated turns.

'Good. An expression of what? What do you try to convey in your art?'

'Pain.' Becca. Even her words seem aggressively thin and spiked. 'It's a way of releasing all the anger in the world.'

'I don't paint because I'm angry,' Alberta says. 'Art isn't pain, art is beauty.'

Tutting from the two university students.

'That's the patriarchy, teaching you the only value is in beauty.'

'Art doesn't have to be beautiful. The world isn't beautiful.'

'So is art supposed to reflect the world? Imitate reality?' asks Morris, leaning his head back into the basket of his two hands.

'I like pictures that tell a story,' says Alberta, determined to be a part of the discussion. 'Where it's not just static, you can see or you can guess what's going on, or what has been going on.'

Eamonn is smiling at the floor, nodding his head in time with the slow beat of his footsteps. At the end of his lap he looks at me.

'What do you think?' he says. 'Camille? Why do you paint?'

A beat. The class looks at me.

I shrug.

'Passes the time.'

It always seems to start with childhood. *Did you have a good childhood?* they ask, *a happy childhood?* And, of course, it's always the cause of later symptoms. *Had a troubled childhood.*

My childhood was fine. If anybody asked me that—and I can't remember anybody doing so—I'd find it strange, almost irrelevant. When I think of myself as a child, and then my adulthood—they're two different lives.

I grew up in the suburbs in the sixties and seventies, the only daughter of a nurse and an engineer.

I grew up baking with my grandmother and helping out at cake sales. I had shiny shoes and socks pulled up to my knees. I played with the boy next door and learnt French with the maid over the road who used to babysit us. I struggled with my times tables and recited my history dates for my father when he came home from work and sat on the sofa and I brought him tea, or a whiskey if it was cold and raining.

My mother was a beautiful woman, tall like me, and she loved to dance. Whenever she was home, the wireless was on, even if she was just cleaning. In the evenings we'd play cards, the three of us, and on the weekends my mother and I would go visiting friends or for walks in the park, and when I was allowed to watch television she would sit behind me and stroke my hair and absent-mindedly twine it into plaits. I was always in awe of my mother's hair. She worked hard, and often long hours during the week, but she always had immaculate hair, perfect mahogany curls.

I enjoyed my childhood, in my little suburban cul-de-sac. I grew to adolescence and began to explore the world further; I went out with my friends instead of my mother, I went to bowling alleys and concerts and tea shops, and sometimes on Saturday mornings, my mother and I would curl up together on the sofa with mugs of cocoa, and talk in a low murmur while we listened to the rain scurrying across the roof and waited for my father's heavy footsteps on the stairs.

When I was eighteen, I was accepted into university, and I moved away from home, trying out independence for the first time.

And that's where I met Michael.

'Wasn't it Shakespeare who said "the object of art is to give life a shape"?' Morris asks. I have been wondering when the quotes would start to appear—throw in some artistically-placed flat caps and some expensive pseudo elbow patches and we could pass for an intellectual group of academics. Though perhaps this is unkind to Morris. He's easy-going and harmless; it doesn't sound pretentious coming from him. Something about his pose, leaning back even though he's on a stool, ankle on knee, arms braced against shin.

'Actually, no,' Eamonn says, smiling. He's clearly glad someone has made this mistake so he can correct them. He's stopped pacing and is perched on the edge of his battered wooden desk, one foot flat on the floor, the other bent and swinging. 'Commonly misattributed. Those are actually the words of the French dramatist Jean Anouilh—' impeccable French pronunciation '—in *The Rehearsal*. But a valid point nonetheless.' He spreads his arms. 'What do we think of that? "The object of art is to give life a shape." Agree, or no?'

There's a pause, a silence slightly too long. A classroom where nobody knows the answer, nobody dares to volunteer a guess. Some meaningful facial expressions, people trying to look pensively cerebral. *Can we get on with the painting already?*

'I don't know if I'd say art gives life a shape,' one of the students says, a little nervously, perched forwards on her stool. 'It's more that art is shaped by life.'

Eamonn nods, intensely interested. 'Go on.'

9

'Well, when we create art, when we represent something, the way we represent it will be influenced by our judgements and our values, which essentially come from our own experiences. So it's, like, a representation *through* our own personal filter.'

'Or at least through society's,' her friend says. 'Because basically all our values are dictated by the media.' This one is Emmi. She's pretty, with high round cheeks, oversized black-rimmed glasses, and very fine straight hair cut to her jawline. There's something mixed-raced, maybe Asian, about her eyes, completely smooth under her lower lashes. She's wearing an oversized shirt buttoned right to the collar, very tight burgundy trousers and brown leather brogues with fringes. I'm not sure quite what the desired image is exactly, but she's trying very hard to be a part of it.

'What if you did the opposite,' Morris says, recovering easily, 'and you deliberately created art that flies in the face of social norms and values, to make a statement, be anti-establishment.'

'Yeah,' says the first student, Rosaline, nodding enthusiastically, 'but either way, the art, whether it's depicting or contravening social norms, it's still shaped by them, shaped by life.'

Alberta is nibbling her lip gently. I think she wants to say something, and Eamonn thinks so too. He looks at her but doesn't say anything, smiling benignly. He's a gentle teacher.

'Maybe it just means art allows you to look at life and reflect on what's been going on, take a step back. See it from a different angle. One of the things I like about painting is that you can lose yourself in what you're doing and forget about the housework, the kids, whatever's happening day-to-day. It's kind of the time I take for myself, and I feel like it gives me time to sort things out in my head. Think things over. Understand, almost, what's been going on in life. Give it a shape?' She shrugs and blushes.

Probably not the right pastime for me, then. If I wanted to brood over the past I'd have taken the damn *Memoir Writing* class. The last thing I want is time to think about my life.

I met Peter in the supermarket.

Robert was six; I was twenty-eight, and fraying at the edges. I couldn't get used to the stares and the whispers, the frustration, the resignation, the unbearable ache of *it's not fair*.

I was feeling particularly numb that day. We'd had an appointment with the audiologist in the morning, and Robert had refused to cooperate. My ears were ringing from the tantrum, my knees were throbbing from tiled floors and angry trainers. He was skipping now, waving his arms wildly, and singing at the top of his voice. I was too exhausted to run after him, to explain that we had to *walk nicely*, even to bribe him to be quiet. He was throwing things into the trolley, everything that had his favourite colours (red and blue) on the packaging. I leant on the trolley handle with my forearms, dragging my feet, my eyes unfocused, strands of hair escaping and floating around my face, wearily putting back everything he wasn't allowed—which was most things. 'Let's try him on a wheat-free diet,' the doctor had said. 'It might clear up some of his localised symptoms.' As though it wasn't hard enough to get him to eat anyway.

People stared as he went flying past, and then their eyes would inevitably, inevitably swivel round to me. Occasionally there was pity in those eyes, but on this day I saw nothing but cold, harsh judgement. Parents hurried their children away. One mother even covered the eyes of her three-year-old daughter and turned her into the next aisle, away from Robert. I felt my head drop down onto my arms. Everything was heavy, everything was an effort. I just wanted to hide from the world.

I was in line at the deli counter, my ankles crossed, watching Robert rifle through packets to make sure they were all facing the front, turn cans around so they were all at the same angle, line up boxes so the patterns on the packaging all aligned, singing *Baa Baa Black Sheep*. He didn't mean to be so loud, but he couldn't hear well, didn't realise he needed to control the volume.

'Excuse me. Excuse me?' I jumped. A young man with sandy hair and glasses was leaning towards me. 'I believe you were first.' He gestured towards the counter.

'Oh. Er. Right. Sorry. Thanks.' I ran a hand over my hair and moved forwards to speak to the server. Robert ran over and began walking his fingers across the glass, singing *Itsy Bitsy Spider*. The only words he knew to the song were the words "itsy bitsy spider". The woman weighing out the ham frowned. I sighed. I'd learnt to recognise them, the ones who'd take issue. This one was heavy-set, middle-aged, hairnet too tight across a sagging forehead.

'Can you ask him to stop that please?' The same tone,

every time. *It's your fault. You created a faulty child and you can't even control him.*

'He's not doing any harm,' I said wearily.

'He's dirtying my glass.' *Your glass?* I wanted to say. *Well excuse me, I didn't realise I was dealing with the Queen of the Deli Glass.*

'Robert,' I said ineffectually. Then, more sharply, 'Robert! Stop that. Come here. Hold my hand.' Robert hummed to himself. I crouched down and pulled him around to face me. It looked harsh to manhandle him, but he had to watch me speak or he wouldn't hear. 'Robert, look at me.' I gave him a shake. 'Look at me!'

He looked at me, twisting his shoulders back and forth. He was playful now, the doctor's visit forgotten.

'Come on, Robbie,' I said more softly. 'We're going to the checkout now. You can help me put everything on the belt in the right order.' He loved the conveyor belt at the check-outs, but it was risky. If he focused only on our shopping it was fine, because he could tessellate every item as he placed it on the belt. If he got distracted by someone else's shopping, things could get messy. People didn't like him interfering with their arrangements; they didn't want their groceries tessellated.

I waited, watching him. He smiled, docile, and took my hand. I breathed a sigh of relief, took the ham from the deli lady, who was still frowning, and tried to steer the trolley with one hand and Robbie with the other. It didn't work terribly well, but Robert decided he'd like to help, and we found a comfortable if slow-moving partnership with him between my arms in front of me, pushing the trolley with me.

'They can be a handful, can't they?' I jumped again. It

was the same sandy-haired man, at the check-out next to mine. He was smiling, at Robert.

I was instantly wary.

'Yeah, they can be.' Non-committal answers. I didn't have the energy for anything else.

'How old is he?'

I wasn't used to people taking an interest, not this kind of interest. 'Six.'

'Ah, wonderful. He's a beautiful boy. Very happy.'

I couldn't deny that. Nobody in the supermarket could fail to notice Robbie's *joie de vivre*.

The man smiled, kindly. 'It isn't easy bringing up a child with... difficulties.' His eyes flicked down, just for a second, to my hands as they fumbled with my purse.

I tried to blush, nod and say something dismissive all at once, and found I couldn't. He smiled again. His left canine tooth was a little bit slanted. It was cute.

Robert tugged on my sleeve, and I turned around to pay the cashier. The sandy-haired man picked up his shopping, only two small bags.

'Well, lovely meeting you,' he said politely, and I turned and smiled. I wanted to say thank you, thank you for treating me like a human being, thank you for acknowledging me, but Robert was pestering me and the cashier was still holding out her hand and I couldn't get anything out before he'd turned and walked away.

The students interest me the most. Two of them, nineteen or maybe twenty. Studying things like "Business" and "Fine Art". So young, they feel things so deeply. They cling to their convictions with a sort of desperation; they let their doggedness define them. I think back to myself at that age, and I wonder if I miss it.

I thought we would be painting bowls of fruit, maybe go on a field trip to do a landscape. I'm not bad at drawing. The picture usually looks like what it's meant to look like. Copying I can do. And I'm not bad at cartoons either, basic people or animals. But Eamonn doesn't give us anything to copy, he just wants us to paint. From the inside. Release ourselves, express ourselves. I gaze at him with an interested expression fixed on my face and concentrate on not letting my eyes roll.

In the last week of my first term, snow started to fall rather romantically all over the university. I had one more essay to turn in, but the words just weren't coming. My room, which had to be all packed up and bare again in five days, was as full as it ever was, my things strewn all over the place. The window, which looked out onto an utterly unromantic brick wall beyond an alleyway, afforded only a glimpse of the outside world, a portal of blue in the top corner slowly being obscured by white. I tilted back on my chair, balancing on two legs, and leant my head as far back as it would go, trying to refocus my mind.

There was a knock at my door, and I looked up to see my friend Chloe put her head around it.

'Making any progress?'

I let my arms drop dramatically. 'None at all. It's hopeless.'

She came in and sat on my bed. 'If you're not getting anywhere, you may as well come to this mixer with me.'

She bounced, grinning.

I twisted round and rested my chin on the back of my chair. 'It's a faculty mixer. I'm not in your faculty.'

She put her hands on my shoulders and her face close to mine. 'But I really want to go, and I really don't want to go on my own.'

'Why do you want to go anyway? Aren't these things supposed to be really dull?' She hesitated just a second too long, and the penny dropped. 'You want to go chat up a boy, don't you?'

She grinned. 'Pleeeease, Cam? This is a great excuse for me to talk to him, but I'm really really nervous.'

I glanced back at my essay, the expanse of blank paper, the pile of books towering over it. I groaned. 'Fine, let's go. What do I wear?' I stood up.

'What you're wearing is fine, it's not fancy or anything.'

I looked down and wrinkled my nose. 'Fine, come *on*, then.'

'Thank you, thank you, thank you!' she said, leaping up. 'Let me just go check my make-up.' I grabbed my coat on the way out and pulled the door shut behind me.

'Well? Is he here?'

'Yes,' Chloe hissed, not moving her lips.

'Where?' I looked around to where she was looking.

'Don't look, don't look!' She grabbed at me.

'OK, OK. Are you going to talk to him?'

'Yes. Eventually. Look natural.'

I smiled. 'I am being natural. You're the one freaking

out.'

She tossed her hair. 'You're right. OK. I can do this. He's in a group, I can break into a group. Completely casual.'

'Absolutely. You can do it. You look great.' I meant it, too. She had long red hair and large blue eyes and a generous sprinkling of freckles. She always looked great. 'Go get him.' She raised her glass of wine to me and sashayed away. I raised my own glass at her retreating back and turned to grab a handful of novelty-shaped cheese biscuits.

I surveyed the room, crunching. I didn't know anybody else on Chloe's course, and I felt superfluous. Somebody came up to the table next to me to pour another glass of wine. I leaned over without really looking at them.

'At what point can we talk about things other than work?' I said.

The guy looked up, surprised. I wondered if he'd just give me a weird look and walk away. 'Excuse me?'

I was already regretting trying to strike up a conversation. 'You know, at a faculty gathering, you all have one thing in common, your subject, so everyone talks about that to start with. I was just wondering when the conversation moves on to other things.' Still he stared. 'You know, hobbies, interests, popular culture. The meaning of life. Pursuit of happiness.' The man put the cork back in the wine bottle and picked up his glass.

'Actually, I think you've got it the wrong way round. The drunker these Fellows get,' he indicated the lecturers scattered around the room, 'the louder they are going to argue about their particular theories in their particular field of study. You should have gone in there with the popular culture while everyone was still sober.'

'Ah, I've misjudged it,' I said. 'Tactical error.'

'Well, you'll know for next time.' He smiled politely. 'Are you a first-year?'

'Yes, but not actually in this faculty. I'm studying History.'

'An intruder? You've infiltrated and you're stealing our biscuits?' He was obviously joking, but he said it with such deadpan sincerity that for a moment I stared at him in horror. Then he grinned, and I burst out laughing.

'What about you, do you belong?'

He inclined his head. 'Intermittently. Third-year Politics and East Asian Studies. I have Mandarin super-visions here.'

'Very impressive. I've never been to East Asia.'

'You should, it's a wonderful place.' He began to move away. 'Excuse me.' And he went back to his friends. I stuffed the rest of the biscuits into my mouth.

Chloe was my this time deep in the middle of an animated group discussion. I tried to catch her eye to signal that I was going, but she didn't notice. I drained my glass, put it back down on the table, and made for the door. Before I left, I glanced back at the man, the third-year East Asian Studies student. He was deep in conversation, and he didn't look up.

'Now, we're going to move quite quickly through the first half of term. We'll be exploring some different techniques and different materials and tools we can use for different effects, so we'll be working on a different painting each week. Of course, this means you won't necessarily finish them in class, but obviously you can do so in your own time.' *Obviously*. 'Second half of term, I want us to focus on something more ambitious. A project. It doesn't have to tell a story necessarily, though of course it could do, but we want to explore the idea of some kind of narrative, a progression. So you can maybe be thinking of a starting point for your project, keep your mind open to unexpected fountains of inspiration you can base your masterpiece on. You won't necessarily have a clear idea of what it will be yet or what it will physically look like, but you can begin to shape your narrative.'

He likes the word "necessarily". You can hear the faintest hint of an accent in there—*necess-AIR-ily*—American or Canadian maybe.

I glance around the room, somewhat glumly. I'm looking for an ally. Someone I can share my cynicism with. But everyone is wide-eyed and earnest, they're lapping it up. I sigh, wondering why, however hard I try, I always seem to be the odd one out.

We had to clear out Dad's study. I was on my knees on the floor, tired and cross and headachy, going through the cupboards and drawers to try and throw away as much as we could, trying to make room.

I drew out some photo albums, which I laid aside to keep without looking at them. Then there was a box folder with my name on it—school reports and crayon drawings and certificates. And at the bottom, my sketchbooks. Three of them. I flicked through them. I'd dated each drawing.

From almost a whole book of horses when I was ten to actual considered artworks when I was fourteen or fifteen, after which my social life and school work started to take over. I paused over a picture of a woman looking back over her shoulder. The proportions of the face weren't quite right but it wasn't bad. I closed the books, put them in the pile to be thrown out, and reached for the next drawer.

I try and joke around with the girl next to me. She's young, somewhere in her thirties I would imagine, skinny in a way that looks pinched and old. She wears four or five necklaces of different lengths, and long fingerless gloves that reach up past the elbow. She hunches over her easel and her brush moves so fast it's almost feverish. I look down at the brush in my own hand, my blank canvas. Nothing is coming to me. Not for the first time, I wonder if I was simply born without imagination. Or had it stamped out of me, over the years.

'How do you have so much to "express"?' I whisper, trying to convey the air quotes with my voice because my hands are full. She glances over. One eyebrow twitches.

'I paint my pain away,' she says, a refrain I would come to hear a lot from her. 'It helps me release. Haven't you ever experienced pain?'

I think about it.

'When I was six,' I whisper, 'I fell off a climbing frame and broke my arm. The bone was sticking right out, you could see it. I screamed and screamed and screamed.' I smile fondly at the memory—the other kids frozen in shock around me, no one daring to come near, several others joining in my scream at the sight of the blood and the broken white bone. The grown-ups rushing over and my head spinning, the disappointment later that, drugged up, I hadn't paid attention to the fact that I was in an ambulance. The triumphant return to school, the proud cast, the awestruck gazes.

The girl shakes her head at me, and turns back to her canvas, a splattered black hole of moss green, bruise blue and mud brown. She thinks I don't understand. She pities me.

It was a game of Frisbee. An ordinary Saturday afternoon. We barely even noticed he was out of breath. It was such a normal thing, hardly worth registering. We were all running around. It's just that we stopped panting, and he didn't.

All the things that could have happened to him, all the things that could have gone wrong, the problems that we faced and struggled to overcome, and this, this game of Frisbee, this was what took him from me.

It was just galling.

Eamonn's footsteps behind me make me jump. He's circling the room.

'Does anyone want to share with us what they're painting? The story behind it?' Silence. He laughs. 'That's OK. We haven't really gotten to know each other yet. Don't worry, I won't ever ask you to share something you're not comfortable with sharing. But I want us all to think of this as a safe space for self-exploration and expression, OK?'

Safe space. There's that urge again, the eye-rolling. I have to focus on keeping them still in my head, like stones. The effort almost makes me laugh.

The classes are two and a half hours long. After an hour, Eamonn makes us get up and walk around the room.

'Reconnect with the space,' he says, 'come back to reality, ground yourself. It'll give you a fresh perspective when you come back to your work.'

'Ground myself,' I mutter to no one. 'What does that even mean?'

'He has a distinctive approach, doesn't he?' asks Morris, who has fallen into step with me. As people always do when told to move around, we all seem to have taken up a circuit of the room. 'Bit different from our generation.' This is generous, I know. He's at least ten years younger than me. 'I know it's not everyone's cup of tea, but you have to come at it with an open mind. You never know what might fall in there.' Morris is tall but has a relaxed stoop to his shoulders. He smiles at me and I feel a flutter of something foreign, something girly and long-forgotten, and I shake it off immediately. I find myself watching him as he settles himself back at his easel. Attractive in a shabby sort of way. Shame about the ponytail, really.

I pick up my brush and twirl it on the clean surface of my palette. The bristles fan out, a perfect circle. I wait for inspiration, but she is slow in arriving.

'Do you know what somebody asked me at my art class?' I ask my husband over breakfast.

'What's that?' He is reading the paper, completely obscured apart from the shiny bald spot at the top of his head and his long-distance glasses perched on top of it. His short-distance glasses will be on his nose. He refuses bifocals.

'Have I ever experienced real pain?' I say, pausing for effect. 'Can you imagine? Do you think I could get to sixty-two years of age and never have anything happen to me?' I bring the mugs over to the table. He lays his paper down, not taking his eyes off it, and stirs his tea. I always add sugar and stir it, and he always stirs it again. I tried not giving him a spoon, but he would get up, fetch one, sit down and stir his tea. I decided it was a comfort thing, the action, the routine, and not a comment on my tea-making abilities. In years to come, when I'm old and senile, this is the sound I will remember, metal clinking on china, the sound of breakfast with my husband. I sip my coffee, black and strong.

'Imagine that,' he says.

I move the butter closer to my plate and pick up my knife.

'You look ridiculous with two pairs of glasses on,' I say.

'Mhmm.' His tone doesn't change, and won't, all morning, not until he's finished the sports section. He isn't really listening, he's on autopilot. I sigh. The dog comes and lays her head in my lap, and I absentmindedly scratch the back of her ear with the handle of the butter knife.

'As though you can only produce great art from great pain,' I continue blithely. 'I know I'm more pragmatic than most, but some of them are verging on hippies. It's such a stereotype, the tortured artist.'

My husband crosses one leg over the other, puts his

23

spoon down and raises his mug with one hand, and turns the page of his newspaper with the other. He will hold this pose until he has finished the left-hand page, then take a sip of his tea, fold the paper in half and eat his breakfast while reading the right-hand side of the page.

'At least he's consistent,' I tell the dog. She gazes up at me with her soulful brown eyes. I give up and turn the radio on.

Later, I look at myself in the mirror and wonder what it is that they see when they look at me. An old lady, no doubt, a has-been, a by-gone. What could I contribute to any pertinent discussion? How could I possibly relate to modern-day life?

Have I ever experienced pain?

'The problem is,' I tell the dog, 'it's a generational thing.' I look back from the dog to my own face. Was I once beautiful? 'I wonder when people started thinking they had a right to be happy.' I think of my parents. Hardworking and honest. For them, it was important to be a good person, to do your job, take care of your family, to contribute to society. That was what you worked towards, and happiness was just a by-product. A bonus. It wasn't deserved or expected or demanded. Had my parents been happy? I like to think they had been. I stretch the skin of my cheeks with my hands. Have I been happy?

Have I experienced pain?

'*You don't have to do this, Millie, you have a choice.*'

'*Ms Addison? I'm afraid I have some bad news.*'

'*I'm going to have to ask you to leave the room.*'

'*Camille, I can't do this without you.*'

Oh yes, pain is something I'm well acquainted with. I run my fingers through my hair, fluffing it up, and remove non-existent lipstick smudges from the corners of my mouth.

When did my eyes start looking so watery? I remember them as vivid blue, cornflower blue my father used say, but now they are limp and fading. My skin is weary, sinking down and folding in on itself. I pull it taut with my hands on either side, my lips stretching. Whatever beauty I had is long gone now, I suppose. Decaying, like the rest of me.

'Come on,' I tell the dog, 'you may as well come with me.' I kiss the top of my husband's head as I leave.

Week Two

In the second class I sit next to Alberta. She's a fifty-two-year-old housewife suffering—as she keeps telling us—from empty nest syndrome.

'Adrian, my oldest, is in his third year at Warwick,' she boasts, and I can almost see her fluffing her feathers, 'and Heather went off to Durham this September.' She wears a lot of headscarves and headbands and other assorted headwear, which sort of jar with the rest of her image, but in a good way. In a very *her* way.

I find I like sitting next to Alberta most. She is by far and away the most talented of the group. Her paintings are of things, as opposed to Becca's abstract shapes and splodges of colour. She paints landscapes, trees, beauty. She shies away from praise though, it makes her uncomfortable.

'My pictures are too static,' she says. I have given her a compliment, not knowing yet that she likes to be unrecognised. 'I want it to tell a story, I want people to look at it and think about what's going on.' She shrugged.

'I don't know. It's stupid.' The phrase grates on me. It sounds like a line from an American sitcom. *It's stoo-pid.*

But Alberta I like. She seems shy, she's like a child trying to discover herself.

'I've been a wife and a mother for so long,' she says. 'And don't get me wrong—' American phrase again '—I love it, but now the kids are grown up, I want to find out who I am on my own again. I mean, not on my own, I'm still married, but Jonathan works all day, and I have to be by myself, I have to have things for myself now. Does that makes sense?' I nod, but she doesn't need me to say anything. 'Do you have children?'

I look down, unscrewing the paint.

'No, I don't,' I say. 'No children.'

I wish I could say I looked into the cot and felt nothing.

I was very aware of the noises around me. Beeping and whirring and the squelch of a mop in the corridor, the undercurrent of murmuring voices and shoes tapping or squeaking or scuffing. I was alone in the room, I remember, though I don't know where everyone else was. A nurse would enter in a minute or two and ask if I wanted to hold him, but for that minute or two, it was just him and me.

I looked at him.

He was small and red and a little crusty round the edges. His tiny limbs moved jerkily, as though separate entities from him. His mouth opened and closed. I didn't know what newborns were meant to look like. His head seemed very large and heavy—but wasn't that normal? His ears were a little small, I supposed. His eyes were very small, and far apart, squinted into deep creases. One of his hands stretched out towards me, like a miniature high five. I looked at it, tiny lines and tiny nails and tiny knuckles.

I looked down at him and I hated him.

As a child, I had a new dream every week. I wanted to be an astronaut, a chef, a ballet dancer. None of them were really serious. For a while in primary school I insisted I was going to be a nurse when I grew up, but that was only because I wanted to be like my mum. I wanted to impress her, to make her proud of me. I never really had the temperament for a caring profession; too impatient, too rough, too squeamish. In the early years of secondary school I toyed semi-seriously with the idea of being an illustrator, but, having no idea how one would go about earning a living illustrating, decided that success was too unlikely, and probably I wasn't good enough anyway. When people asked, I would shrug and scuff my toes on the floor and say I didn't know what I wanted to do after school.

I was smart enough and well-off enough to go to university, and it seemed a good way to put any career decisions off further. Out of my little gang of schoolfriends, only myself and my best friend Maria were aiming for higher education—the rest went to work in a dress shop, as a nanny, or got engaged. Maria and I sat at the back of our class and looked at hairstyles in magazines and tried to meet the others for coffee or a cigarette or to discuss wedding dresses, but the times never seemed to work out.

We stayed behind after school to do our homework together, and watched the boys from the boys' school down the road play rugby on the sports field.

History was my best subject, and my most encouraging teacher, and so I applied to do History, not really knowing where I could go with it, but not really caring too much about that either. I had no destination in mind, but my horizon was limitless.

Maria wanted to be a nursery-school teacher, had been decided on it for as long as I'd known her. Her path was as clearly mapped out for her as mine was hidden from me. We said a tearful goodbye at the end of our last summer as we set off in different directions, promising to write and visit and keep in touch. The promises were empty, and they broke easily.

Our mid-way perambulation. I find myself falling into step with Eamonn.

'You know,' I say after a beat. 'Sometimes, I'm not entirely sure if you're running an art class or a therapy session.'

Eamonn smiles benignly at his boots.

'Does it have to be one or the other?'

I got pregnant, once.

I'd had my suspicions for a while; I'd done the maths. My husband—though we weren't married yet—had to go away, for a funeral, and was going to stay on for a fort-night to help out his family. I took the opportunity, when

I was alone, to make an appointment with the doctor. I was in the shower when my hand strayed to my abdomen. Was it a phantom swelling I was feeling? I imagined the baby, a perfect human in miniature, an entire tiny future-person beneath my fingers. I wondered if it was something I could do, raising a baby. Again.

First, I thought I could. I felt those maternal feelings I'd always heard of rise in my breast. I imagined a child of mine and his, to love and raise and be a part of us.

And then I knew it was stupid. We couldn't afford it, the time or the money, and—though it was the hardest thing for me to admit—I didn't want to. I had spent my early twenties being kept awake by a crying baby, and now, as a more mature thirty-something-year-old, I didn't want to shackle myself to that, again. I wanted to move towards independence, not away from it. I didn't want to lose myself, sacrifice myself, again. I didn't want the exhaustion and the worry and the mess, I didn't want any of it.

But I wasn't imagining it. It was happening. I knew there were options, I knew I could get rid of it—but I also knew that I wouldn't. Leaning against the sink, I saw my mother looking back at me from behind the fogged mirror. I couldn't do that to her. And could I do that to him, my boyfriend, my one-day-to-be-husband? Could I deny him the chance of being a father?

I wondered how I was going to tell him. Would he be excited? Would he be angry? Anxious? Was this something he wanted to do with me? Would I dare bring up the idea of adoption? I couldn't bear to spark hope in him only to snuff it out again.

Sometimes, just sometimes, I caught myself daydreaming about a little girl, a daughter. Our daughter.

It happened in the night. Four days before my appointment, I was woken by stabbing pains in my lower back, and lay there for a moment, clutching the edges of my mattress like I was going to fall off. Another cramp shot through me and I cried out, then bit down on my pillow and prayed I hadn't woken anyone.

I sat on the toilet and squeezed my eyes shut and tried to breathe through the pain. I tried not to think about what was happening, about what was leaving my body. I was being emptied, and the void hurt.

I took a shower afterwards. Red ran down the insides of my legs and pooled around the drain. I let hot water drip down my face and stood there until it was over. Almost over. It didn't completely stop for days. I stripped my bed and scrubbed at the stains until my hands were raw. I cleaned the bathroom. I bought new sheets. I didn't attend my appointment. When two months had passed, I knew I was sure. There was no baby.

I still didn't tell anyone. I couldn't find the words. There was nothing to be done about it now, anyway. There was no point in telling my boyfriend, giving him the pain of losing something he hadn't known he had. I fed Robert and cared for him and cooked for my father and saw my boyfriend and went to work, and life carried on.

My overwhelming feeling was relief, and I was scared of being judged for it.

I try painting Beijing this week, watercolours. Everyone does floaty lakes and misty rivers and willow trees in watercolours, I want to try iron skyscrapers and neon lights and the scream of traffic and the smell of soy sauce, just to see if it could work.

I try to remember the view from our tenth-floor flat. I can't seem to get enough greys. I need gunmetal grey for the buildings, dove grey for the smog, stone grey for the streets. The lights look superimposed, out of place, not part of the picture. I can't get them to look right. The more I try to add to it, the less it looks how I want it to. Eventually I give a voiceless wail of frustration and crush my brush all over the middle of the picture, a blue blotch, and toss it aside. I've given up. I can't paint China.

Eamonn corporealises. I groan out loud this time. 'Don't ask me to tell you about this one, Eamonn, it's a mess. I gave up.'

Eamonn turns down the corners of his mouth and nods. 'Shame,' he says, 'I think it's good. Abstract cityscape, no? Nicely layered.'

I shake my head and pull my sleeves back down.

'If you say so, mate.'

We were on our way to some event, and now when I think back on it, I can't for the life of me remember what the event was. It was black tie, I remember that, and I was wearing a full-length purple dress and a—fake—diamond necklace around my throat. Michael was in a tux with his hair slicked back. He had his camera with him, and before we left he had me strike some poses. I felt like a princess, like I could walk among the clouds. I was the luckiest girl in the world.

'You look a million dollars, Millie,' Michael said, kissing my cheek. I couldn't stop smiling. The phone rang. 'That'll be the car,' he said, reaching for it. I gave a little wriggle of excitement, pulled at the neckline of my dress to make sure it was in place, and wiped any lipstick smudges from the corners of my mouth. 'Hello hello,' Michael said into the phone. His face changed abruptly. 'Oh, hello. Yes, she's here, hold on.' He held the phone out to me. 'It's your mother,' he whispered.

My excitement dropped several degrees. Why would my mother be calling? It must have been mid-morning in England, a Friday—wasn't she at work? My parents and I wrote to each other, regularly—long-distance phone calls were expensive. I knelt on the sofa so I could reach the handset. The skirt of my dress rode up and creased.

'Mum?'

The distinctive crackly static. Then, after a moment, 'Hi, Camille, honey.' She sounded faint, but there was something strange in her tone. I pressed the receiver into my ear, looking down in concentration.

'Mum, what's wrong? Why are you calling?'

'Oh, nothing dear, I just—fancied a chat, you know.' The breath she drew in was shaky. Was she—crying? I gripped the back of the sofa with my free hand. Icy fingers clamped down on my chest.

'Mum, what's happened? You're scaring me.'

'I'm sorry, Millie, I shouldn't be bothering you. You're probably off out on the town, aren't you, on a Friday night, the two of you...'

I resisted the urge to shout. 'Mum, has something happened? Is it Dad?'

'I'm afraid your father's... not here...' Her voice, already faint, grew fainter. And then, quite clearly, sobs.

The ground fell from under me.

'What do you mean not here? Did something happen?' I looked wildly up at Michael, who was frowning at me concernedly, questioningly. My mind raced with scenarios— Dad couldn't be *gone*—and my eyes darted around the room, desperately seeking some remnant of the happiness I had been lost in a moment ago. A lifetime ago.

'No, nothing's happened, your father's fine,' Mum said in a rush. She took a deep, shuddering breath. 'I'm sorry, I shouldn't be calling you like this. But your dad walked out and I felt so alone and—I just wanted to hear your voice, sweetheart.' My brain couldn't comprehend what I was hearing, had no frame of reference to contextualise it. I had seen my mother grow misty-eyed at films, but to be crying on the phone to me? My parents were grown-ups, for heavens' sake—they were my *parents*. They were my resource of calm and comfort and reason and support.

'Millie?' Michael stepped forward. I shook my head at him, helpless.

'Something's happened,' I whispered. 'She said my dad walked out? I don't know what to do.' Tears started to prick in my eyes, and absurdly I worried about my make-up smudging. Michael crouched down next to me and put a concerned hand on my arm.

'What do you mean, walked out?'

'I don't know. Mum,' I said into the phone, twisting around so that I was sitting on the sofa. 'Mum, I'm here. Tell me what's happened.' Michael glanced at his watch.

I stopped hearing the static. My body sagged. My mother was distraught and apparently abandoned and Michael was concerned about being *late*? I stared at him limply.

'I'm really sorry, Millie, they'll be expecting me,' he

34

whispered. He twisted his lips together. 'Or should I call and say we can't make it?'

'Mum, hold on,' I said, and put the receiver on my shoulder. 'It's fine, you go,' I told Michael. 'I don't think anyone's hurt, they've just had an argument or something. Dad's never done anything like this before.'

'I can send the car back for you if you want to come later on.'

I hesitated. I had been so looking forward to the event —but I couldn't leave Mum like this. Something must be seriously wrong for her to be calling the other side of the world in tears. I shook my head at him. 'You go, I'll be too worried to enjoy myself, I need to make sure she's OK. I'll pay for the call.'

Michael shook his head. 'Don't even worry about the cost. It's family. Look, I'll go and show my face, I'll get back as soon as I can, and you can explain everything to me. We'll make sense of it.'

I nodded, feeling the tears rise again. He kissed the top of my head as he stood up.

'I love you, Millie.'

I gave a weak smile as he reached the door. 'I love you too.' I brought my knees up to my chest, nestling into the corner of the sofa, the beautiful dress crumpling around me. 'Sorry Mum,' I said back into the phone. 'I'm here. Tell me everything.'

Bank holiday.

Dad had Robert for the day; I was having lunch with a friend. Not a friend, exactly, a woman I had met through a support group. She had an autistic daughter. She wasn't someone I would have chosen, in another life, to spend my time with, but I couldn't afford to be choosy. And at least she understood how suffocating it could feel, how much you could sometimes need to just get away from it all. Even if the furthest you could get was a coffee shop.

She was talking about how they were thinking of hiring a behavioural aide for her daughter, and I was picking at my sandwich and resisting the urge to knead my temples. I wanted to say that for me, "getting away from it all" didn't involve talking about the children, because that made it the same as every other of my days.

I couldn't help but feel churlish. The ugly, petty part of me deep down inside felt aggrieved, felt like I deserved it less than everyone else. Robert wasn't my child. I didn't even ask to be a parent, much less this kind of parent. The urge to stamp my feet and scream *it's not fair* didn't rise to the surface like it once had, but there was still a deep-seated anger, and it was only made worse by the fact that I couldn't do a thing about it.

'Are you OK?' my friend said. I looked up, trying to pretend I had been listening.

'Yeah, yeah, I'm fine.' I smiled. She leaned forwards.

'It's hard, isn't it?' My smile tightened. I didn't want to talk about how hard it was, I didn't want her sympathy, I didn't want anyone pretending they knew how I felt. What I'd given up. 'I'm just going to run to the loo,' I said, pushing my chair back. 'Be right back.' I kept the smile on my face as I walked away.

I rearranged my hair in front of the mirror in the bathroom, then hoisted the smile back up. Time to make my excuses and leave. I could walk around the streets a little by myself before anybody expected me home.

I returned to the table and sat down briskly, pushing my plate to one side and sitting upright to make it clear I was ready to get the bill and leave.

'Excuse me.' It was the man at the table behind me. 'Sorry, your chair's just—' he gestured at the floor, where my chair leg was pinning the hem of his coat to the floor.

'Oh, I'm sorry,' I said, awkwardly, trying to shuffle my chair in and up, half-standing, and catching my foot, and stumbling.

'That's OK, thanks,' the man said, laughing. Then he looked at me again, bending down. 'Hey,' he said, and I looked up at him properly for the first time. 'From the supermarket, right?'

Sandy hair, glasses, slanted tooth. I was taken aback, more by the fact that he recognised me. I pushed my hair behind my ear.

'Right, hi, the deli counter.' I waited for him to leave.

'Where's your son today?' I felt myself getting a bit annoyed. Who strikes up a conversation with someone on the basis of *I once saw you in a supermarket*? But his face was open and honest and calm. Genuine. I smiled awkwardly, flustered.

'Actually, he's not my son,' I said, not knowing why. Usually I made a point of not getting into details with strangers. Nothing specific. 'He's my brother. Half-brother.' I tried to gauge his reaction without staring, my eyes flicking to his face and back down again. No surprise, no calculation, no judgement. Just honest interest.

'Oh, wonderful,' he said. 'So he's with his parents today then.'

'Yeah. With my dad. His dad. Well, sort of.' Too many words. *Wrap this up, Camille.*

37

He saw that I was feeling uncomfortable and smiled again. He was very softly spoken, and his laugh was soothing. 'I'm Peter,' he said, and held out his hand. I tried to take it and caught my plate, making it bang on the table. Embarrassed, I jerked my chair back and snatched at flying lettuce leaves. I felt colour flood my face and cursed under my breath.

'Sorry, sorry,' I said, trying not to flap. I flapped.

'It's OK, it's OK,' Peter laughed. I stood up, made an exaggerated gesture of smoothing myself down, and held out my hand.

'Hi, Peter, I'm Camille.'

Peter smiled, and shook my hand.

'Hello Camille.'

Chloe and I were walking home together, via her faculty building so she could hand in an essay. The Fellows' pigeonholes were in the lobby, but she asked me to wait a minute so she could check something in the library.

'Just one sec, I'll be really quick,' she said, and disappeared around the corner. I crossed one leg over the other and spun around in a slow circle. I studied the photographs of all the faculty members on the wall. It was after five; people were starting to trickle out, slowly, back to colleges and dinners and beds or bars. I stood aside to let two girls with satchels pass, and I saw Third-Year-Politics-With-East-Asian-Studies enter the lobby, deep in discussion with an older man, his supervisor presumably. They paused, clearly about to go in different directions but not yet finished with their conversation. I ducked my head and tucked a strand of hair behind my ear, wondering if he'd notice me. I kept stealing glances at him but he didn't look my way.

I drummed my fingers on my thigh, wondering what was keeping Chloe. East Asian Studies and his teacher finally parted ways, and he turned to go, digging in his bag as he went. A piece of paper wriggled free and fluttered to the ground. I stepped forward to retrieve it.

'Hey,' I said. 'You dropped this.'

He turned around, looking distracted. His hair was longer than when I'd seen him before Christmas, and sort of rumpled. It suited him.

'Oh, thanks,' he smiled as he took the paper from me, and I knew he'd turn away again without a second thought if I didn't say anything.

'Third-year Politics with East Asian Studies, right?' I said quickly, and he looked confused. 'We met last term, at the mixer. I was the imposter. Stealing biscuits.' I started regretting the words. Of course he didn't remember me— we had a five-minute conversation almost two months ago. I wouldn't have even registered on his radar.

'Oh, right,' he said. 'Well, no biscuits right now, I'm afraid, they only come out for special occasions.' I laughed, and we both knew it was fake. He gave an awkward nod, and left. I rammed my knuckles into my forehead. *Idiot.*

'Who was that?' Chloe asked, coming over.

'Guy I met at the mixer last term. He clearly didn't remember me, though.'

'He's cute.' She grinned wickedly. 'Might we be interested?'

'We might,' I said, taking her arm as we left the faculty. 'But I think we might have just blown our chances by acting like a complete fool.' Chloe laughed. 'He is hand-some, though, isn't he?'

With about fifteen minutes to go before the end of class, we start packing up. I wash the inky residue off my hands at the sink, and watch disapprovingly as Morris casually wipes his on his jeans.

Eamonn is discussing Van Gogh with Becca.

'I mean, yes, he only sold one painting in his lifetime, but that's actually because he just *wasn't very good*,' he says conspiratorially. 'Not for his time, not compared to his contemporaries.'

'I thought he was supposed to be "ahead of his time",' Becca says, gathering the boxes of paints in her arms. Eamonn raises his arms in an exaggerated shrug.

'Ahead of his time, bad at marketing,' he says, and smiles his Eamonn smile. 'Reasons or just excuses?'

'How many paintings have you sold?' Becca's tone is uncertain—you can tell that if Eamonn had been her friend, she'd have been openly taunting—not maliciously, but provocatively—but even though we're all adults there's still a hierarchy here. Eamonn's our teacher, a "real artist". Even Becca wants to show some respect.

Eamonn begins bringing the canvases down from the easels. 'More than one,' he says with a mysterious grin.

Niall squeezes past me to get to the sink. He smells faintly of oil—perhaps he's a mechanic.

One of the students—Emily? The one with shorter hair —is still seated, staring at her canvas with displeasure.

'I'm so bad at this,' she mutters to her friend.

Rosaline glances over. 'It's fine, Emmi. It's good.'

But the comment only seems to disgruntle her further.

'Anyone fancy the pub?' Morris asks the room in general. Everyone hesitates. We're a comfortable class, we have a good atmosphere. But are we friends beyond the studio? It feels like a big decision.

I catch Alberta's eye, and then she surprises me by saying, 'I'd be up for it.' She seems surprised herself, so used to fading into the background. I feel absurdly proud of her, trying to build herself a life outside the family home.

'Yeah, sounds good,' Niall says.

Becca shrugs. 'OK.'

I think of the load of washing in the dryer that will need putting away, of an inviting cup of peppermint tea in front of the ten o'clock news. I think of chit-chat over a pint—what everyone's finding hard about the class, how good Eamonn is, job description, marital status, who's watching the new drama on BBC 1. Like university students in their first week, cut adrift in a new city, searching desperately for a bond they can cling on to.

I decline, politely. Emmi and Rosaline have already left. Eamonn says he has to lock up the studio but he might join them for a drink or two. They are discussing directions to the nearest pub and I try to slip out unnoticed.

'Bye, Camille,' Eamonn calls. 'See you next week!' I turn and wave at him as unobtrusively as I can, clutching my bag to me with the other hand and feeling ungainly. Did I imagine it, or did he wink at me? The air is cold as I stride towards the car park, and I feel it sharp against my flushed cheeks.

I loved him. I did.

It's just that I also blamed him for stealing thirty-three years of my life.

Week Three

We are using oils.

Eamonn circulates. After a while I become aware that he's standing behind me, and my brush hesitates.

'Tell me about this,' he says in his melodious voice. I can feel my shoulders starting to rise reflexively, and then I look over and see Morris. *You have to come at it with an open mind.*

'It's my honeymoon,' I say, looking back at my painting. 'We just went for a walk and came across this beautiful waterfall in the middle of the woods. I can't remember exactly what it looked like, but I've tried to get the general shape, and, I suppose, I wanted to capture the mood, very relaxed and serene and... pretty.' The word sounds lame on my tongue.

Eamonn nods his slow nod.

'That's wonderful, Camille,' he says. 'That's really wonderful.'

43

Dad was waiting for me when I climbed down, limp and exhausted, from the coach. Time had passed agonisingly slowly. The packing, the waiting—dear god, the waiting—the airplanes full of recycled air and plastic food, stale coughs and dazed stupors, and finally the coach from Heathrow. I leaned my forehead against the window. Signs in English. Cool, overcast skies. A driver who called me "luv" and coins I knew instinctively without having to squint. My heart ached with familiarity. I hadn't realised how much I'd missed that deep, innate sense of belonging.

My body was crying out for rest, but as the motorway sped by beneath us, my mind grew more and more taut. It didn't feel like going home, it felt like going into the unknown. I wasn't going to see my parents, I was going to see two adults with problems they didn't know how to face, and I didn't know how I was going to face them either. I didn't know how to shift from being a child turning to her parents for answers to an adult sharing in their adult crises. I didn't feel ready. I still wanted them to take care of me, I wasn't ready to take care of them, to see them in all their human vulnerability. I wanted the journey to end, but I wasn't ready to face what awaited me when it did.

I had planned to get a bus, the same bus I used to catch home from school years ago, from the centre of town back to my parents' house. By the time I dragged myself off the second plane and onto the coach, the plan had changed to forking out for a taxi. When I raised my head to see Dad standing there, leaning against a lamppost with his arms crossed high on his chest, a wave of relief crashed over me so hard it almost took my knees out from under me. His face, as overcast as the sky above him, broke into a ragged smile when he saw me. I staggered into his arms. He smelt of salt and vinegar crisps and wood shavings, the same smell he would bring into the house after an afternoon in his garden-shed workshop when I was a girl. I clung to him like I was still a child, and he patted my back like he understood everything I wasn't saying.

'How was the trip?' Dad asked as I retrieved my backpack from the haphazard pile of luggage the driver was building on the pavement.

'Long,' I said, grunting the bag over my shoulder. Dad glanced at his watch. It was four o'clock in the afternoon.

'Shall we get cracking, or do you fancy a cuppa?' I had been desperate to see Mum for the past three days, but I looked at the stubble on Dad's chin and the shadows under his eyes, and suddenly I was afraid of it.

'Cuppa,' I said. We went to a café and ordered a builder's brew and a fry-up. I sipped my tea and savoured being able to banter with the server.

'Manage to sort everything out OK?' Dad asked gruffly.

I shrugged. 'The school wasn't happy with me leaving, but they couldn't exactly stop me.'

'And Michael?'

I shrugged again, biting into a sausage. The pause stretched on too long. Dad kept his eyes fixed downwards.

'How's—' I started to say, and then choked on a piece of toast. 'I mean,' I reached for a drink, swallowed. 'Have you gone back home?'

Dad sighed, looking defeated. 'It's such a mess, Cam. And she shouldn't have dragged you back from China, it's not your problem to deal with.' I thought about reaching for his hand but I picked up my mug again instead.

'Don't be daft, of course I need to be here.' I tried to

catch his eye but he was still looking down, and I was shamefully relieved he didn't look up. 'I'm glad she told me,' I said firmly. 'This isn't the kind of thing you want to hear about afterwards.'

The house was deafeningly quiet when we entered. The front door creaked into the still air like I was entering a deserted museum. Or a mausoleum. I felt like I should be seeing dust motes catching the light—but of course there was no dust in my mother's house.

'Hello?' I called. Dad was behind me. I walked into the hall and dropped my bag on the floor, as I had a million times before when I was a schoolgirl with a schoolbag.

Mum appeared at the top of the stairs.

'Darling, you're back!' And she came down towards me. She was wearing a loose shirt, but even so, you could tell she was thicker than normal. She hugged me and I felt the swelling, firm and decisive. Unavoidable. But her hair smelt the same as it always had.

Dad coughed from behind me.

'Shall I put the kettle on?' Mum asked, in a voice that tried to be bright but was strung just a little too thin. 'Are you hungry, Millie?'

Dad shook his head. 'We've eaten,' he said, and then went into the living room and turned on the television. Mum and I looked at each other. Her face was a little pasty. For the first time since setting off from my flat in Beijing, tears rose in my eyes.

'Oh, Mum,' I said, and held my arms out to her again

like I was a child and it was me who needed to be comforted.

'What happened?' I said to her, when we were both sitting on the back step with cups of tea. 'You had an affair?'

She shook her head, her eyes wide and shining.

'It wasn't an affair,' she whispered. 'I didn't even want it to—I never meant for it—' I waited for her to say more but she didn't, and then the realisation crashed over me.

'You mean he—' I struggled to put it into words, struggled to even comprehend the concept as it pertained to my mother. 'It was—who was he?'

'A colleague,' Mum said to her knees, shaking her head. 'He was drunk...'

'Why didn't you tell Dad?' Tears began to fall, raindrops in tea.

'It was my fault,' she whispered, 'I should have—I didn't—'

I put my cup down firmly on the ground, got up and crouched in front of Mum. I took her cup, too, put it to one side, and held both of her hands in mine. The time for prudishness was long gone.

'Mum, did you want him to?'

She shook her head, eyes down.

'Then it wasn't your fault.' I shook her, gently, to make her look up. 'It wasn't your fault.'

I told her to go in and talk to Dad, properly. I stayed out on the back step, arms folded across my belly, watching the wind ripple the leaves and the tea cooling beside me.

I was on a date with another man when I saw him again. Not a boyfriend, or anything, just a chap from one of my lectures who'd asked me out for a drink. We were in a pub, at a small round table by one of the darkened windows, sipping glasses of red wine. The guy was nice enough, but I was bored. I can't for the life of me remember what we talked about. I was watching the level of wine in the glasses slowly recede and wondering how low it had to go before I could make my excuses and leave. I was wondering what excuse I could give for leaving.

'Another round?' he said, and I realised I had erred in willing the tide down too quickly. *Give him an excuse. Tell him anything. Extricate yourself.*

'Why not.' *Damn.* 'Let me get this one.' And I hopped off the stool and darted away before he could stop me. I leant against the bar, savouring a few minutes of peace. The pub wasn't heaving, but there weren't many empty seats. I tapped the toe of my shoe absentmindedly, not making much of an effort to catch the bartender's attention.

'Well hello there.'

I turned around. East Asian Studies had appeared by my elbow, looking rather dashing with his hair swept back and a scarf around his neck. *A scarf, inside?*

I smiled. 'Hi.'

'You know, I'm not sure there are any biscuits here you can steal either.'

I leaned in conspiratorially. 'No, but I've got my eye on those pork scratchings.'

He laughed.

'What can I get you?' the bartender said to East Asian Studies.

He looked at me, and pulled out his wallet. 'What's your poison? If I may be so bold?'

'House red, please,' I said to the bartender. 'Um, two glasses.' Regretfully, I indicated my date, who was tracing his finger through the condensation on the window.

'Ah, do excuse me,' East Asian Studies said, artfully whisking his wallet out of sight again. 'I didn't realise you were with your boyfriend.'

'He's not my boyfriend,' I said quickly. 'Just a—friend.' I handed a note to the bartender.

'And he makes the lady pay?'

I tossed my head. 'Oh please. Don't be such a patriarch. I am an independent woman, and I'm quite capable of paying for my own intoxication.'

'But not your own cheese biscuits.'

I tucked my change away and picked up the two wine glasses. 'Don't be barbaric,' I said.

'Of course,' he said, clutching his heart dramatically. 'What was I thinking. Never make a woman pay for her own cheese biscuits.'

'Well quite,' I said, raising my glasses to him, and walking off in what I hoped was a dignified yet sultry manner. As I sat down again I glanced back over at him, and found he was still looking. I think I may have blushed, but fortunately he turned to place his order at the bar, and I don't think he noticed.

A while later—almost finished with glass number two and determined to get away before number three—my date excused himself to go to the bathroom. I reached down under my chair and dug around in my bag for a tissue or a mint—I can't remember what—and when I resurfaced, there was a packet of pork scratchings on the table, and a napkin with a note scrawled on it: *Not trying to be patriarchal, just gentlemanly. Michael.*

A warm glow I had never experienced before spread through me, from deep in my stomach all the way outwards, making my toes tingle. It was such a bizarre gesture, so ridiculous and so utterly romantic. It pulled the corners of my lips up in a huge smile and I couldn't bring them back down again. I felt stupid and flushed and fluttery and happy. I tried to compose my face but I couldn't stop myself searching the room for him. The pub had filled up, and I couldn't see him—maybe he was in a different room, or maybe he had left. I craned my neck—he had to be here, I had to have some way of contacting him again. My mind raced with similar silly gestures I could do to reciprocate, and then I saw my date coming back. I stuffed the scratchings and the napkin into the pocket of my jacket and tried to smile nonchalantly. I didn't hear a word of what he said for the rest of the evening. My heart was pumping loudly and my head was full of Michael. *Michael.*

'That's so cool, painting your honeymoon,' Rosaline says. 'You must have such rich experiences to draw on for inspiration.'

I like Rosaline. It's a beautiful name. She has a beautiful nose too, smallish and very slightly upturned, dainty. Her eyes are green and stick out a little, looking surprised or just intently interested, and her hair is long and dark and curls into very tight natural ringlets. She parts it at the side and pins the long side up by her ear to keep it out of her face. It suits her. She's tall and quite shy, and holds herself like she feels awkward about taking up too much space.

'I think that's just a way of telling me I'm old, honey,' I say, leaning slightly closer towards my painting as I try and dapple the light through the leaves.

'How long have you been married?'

My eyes flick over to her. She's engrossed in her painting, but for once I understand, it's nice to chat while we work.

'About twenty years.' She nods, and out of the corner of my eye I see the surprised down-turn of her lips. 'People always expect it to be longer,' I say with a half-chuckle, 'just because I'm old.'

'No, no, I wasn't saying that—'

'We were together for a few years before that. But I suppose we did marry late, for our generation anyway.'

'Emmi, my friend,' Rosaline gestures with the handle of her brush to the girl across the room, 'she wanted to do this class because she's just been through a break-up. She says it's good to let the feelings out. Kind of like what Becca was saying last week, right?' She leans back a little, bites her lip, skimming her painting with a critical eye. 'I'm not sure I agree with all of that,' she says, reaching for more paint. 'Art is pain, and everything. Art can just be a pretty picture. I dunno. I'm not really into the deep meaningful stuff.' I'm happy to let her ramble. I reach for a flat brush and attempt to blend my colours together. I find it hard to balance so close to the canvas, to angle my wrist to get the brush in the right direction. My stool slips, and suddenly there's a yellow splodge in my blue waterfall. I curse quietly.

'The beauty of oils,' Eamonn says, 'is that they're forgiving. They won't dry for three days, plenty of time to correct mistakes.' He stands beside me and shows me what I should do to fix it. 'This is definitely not one we'll finish in class,' he says. 'But whenever I'm in—and I come in most days—you're welcome to use the studio to work on your pieces.'

He moves over to Niall, who is still sketching.

'Try and move on to the paint, now. It's not about creating perfection, it's about seeing what you can do with different materials.'

Rosaline is mixing paint, delicate little strokes on her palette.

'Have you ever been heartbroken?' she says.

***

Once, in spring.

Robert was about eighteen months old. It was unusually warm for May, and we were out for a walk in the park; Dad, me, the pram. For the moment, Robert was quiet; we could hear the birds singing, smell fresh air instead of stale vomit and baby food. We walked in slow silence, luxuriating in it. I felt the breeze play across the tight skin of my cheeks and lips. Too many nights falling asleep over the kettle as it boiled.

We passed by an ice cream van, and Dad bought two Mr Whippy cones with flakes and strawberry sauce. Robert twisted, wanting to see, and Dad bent down to let him lick a little ice cream off his finger.

'Oh, what a beautiful baby boy!' Two American—they *would* be American—ladies, late fifties to early sixties, drawn over by the sight of the pram. Dad looked up to see who had spoken, and they peered round him to see the baby. I stared sadly at my strawberry sauce. The expressions, taken aback; the tone of voice, suddenly uncertain. Poor Robert. But the Americans, to their credit, didn't say anything. They carried on the conversation as they normally would have.

'Is this your grandson?' One of them asked kindly. They weren't to know. Dad looked at me.

'Er, no, actually,' he said, drawing himself up.

The ladies' eyes went from him to me and back again. 'Oh, I see, er, well, it's a lovely day for it.' They began to move away.

'This is my daughter,' Dad said loudly after them. 'And this is the son of my late wife.'

'Dad,' I said. 'It's OK.' I put a hand on his arm, made a polite face at the two women, gesturing that they should move on. I willed Dad to let it go. Those poor women hadn't known what they were letting themselves in for. But something had snapped inside Dad, overflown, and it had to come out.

'Do you want to know the full details? How he was conceived? His exact diagnosis? How my wife died?' More people were staring, including the ice cream man, cone poised and ready. 'No? Then why don't you mind your own business and stop sticking your noses and your—

your—*assumptions* where they don't belong.'

He took hold of the handles of Robert's pram, and I put my arm around his shoulders to guide him away, and we walked home like nothing had happened, pretending we couldn't feel the stares boring into our backs.

People in group situations tend to gravitate towards the same seat, I've noticed. Maybe it's a British thing. It's not that we become particularly attached to the chair, it's that we fear offending someone by taking theirs. But Eamonn (maybe it's the American in him) insists we take a different seat every class.

'A slightly different perspective,' he says. 'A new environment, even just in some small way. A different fall of light, different shadows, maybe more of a draught or closer to the heater, just to keep things fresh, remind us of where we are.' Sometimes I think inside his mouth is a random word generator. He has a very soothing prosody to his voice, low-toned and rhythmic. He has trendy hair, longish and grey. A silver fox.

I was on my way back from a job interview at the local council when I saw her. Or rather, she saw me. I was walking with my head down, watching the pavement, blending into the wet grey and the hardened spots of chewing gum as far as I was able, twisting my shoulders to avoid people going in the other direction. The stiff skirt was digging into my waist, and the taste of long years of prospective office life was souring in my mouth. Suddenly a pair of red kitten heels passed me, stopped, and said, 'Camille?'

I looked around, and found myself face-to-face with Maria, my childhood best friend. I was so shocked to see her I could only stand and gape.

'Maria,' I said eventually, feeling my face colour and my throat creak. 'Oh wow. What a surprise. You look great.'

She did, too. She was tall, as she had always been, and slender now. Her hair was blow-dried, her eyebrows plucked, her lips painted, and her figure taut in a tailored dress. As she squealed and drew me into a hug, I smelt her perfume.

'What are you doing here?' I asked weakly as she released me. I suddenly felt very small and very young, next to this glamourous *woman* that had somehow morphed out of my friend. The friend that had stolen cigarettes and lipstick from her older sisters for us to try, who had announced one day that I needed to start shaving my legs, who regaled me with the details of her first kiss while I listened enraptured.

'Oh I'm just up for the weekend, visiting my parents,' she said. 'Are you, too?'

'Um, yeah,' I said, dropping my gaze again. I was acutely aware of my ill-fitting shirt, my clunky shoes, the hair I had run my fingers through too many times.

'Well, I also have an ulterior motive,' Maria said, holding her left hand up to her chest. 'We need to start thinking about wedding venues!' Her knees bent like her whole body was squeezing with excitement. The ring was ostentatious—not my taste at all, but to my horror it brought tears to my eyes.

'Oh wow, congratulations,' I said, trying to sound genuine and fighting the urge to flee. Maria's *isn't it wonderful* face faltered.

'Are you OK?'

'I'm fine, I'm fine,' I said breezily, brushing a hand over my eyes. 'You've just caught me—well, by surprise, I wasn't expecting to see anyone.' I gestured vaguely down at my clothes as though that explained it. 'I'm sorry, I don't know why I'm getting so flustered.'

Maria squeezed my arm.

'We *must* catch up,' she said. 'I can't believe it's been so long! I haven't seen you in—what? Six, seven years? Fore*ver*.'

'I know, crazy,' I mumbled. She spoke differently from how she did when we were younger. I wondered if she was a teacher at some upper-class institute for offspring of the very posh. Of course she was a teacher, she was always going to be a teacher. I decided wildly that her fiancé must be a doctor.

'OK, I'm sorry, I didn't mean to ambush you,' she rattled on. 'I have to go, I'm meeting my fiancé, but you're at your parents', right? I'll call you. Unless—do you want to come? Meet him? Have lunch with us, it'll be so fun!'

Dismayed, I stumbled back a few paces. 'Oh, no, I'm sorry, I can't. I really have to get back—'

'OK. But I'll call you, yes? We'll go to tea, there's so much to catch up on!'

I waved clumsily, kept on stepping backwards, needing to avoid another hug. 'Absolutely. Yes. Sounds great.'

Maria's perfect face creased with concern. I rounded a

corner and leant against the wall in relief. My breathing was shaky. When I got home, I unplugged the phone.

I was surprised when he called.

I suppose I shouldn't have been. I mean, if somebody asks for your number, it's a fair assumption they're going to call you. But it hadn't registered. I supposed I had lost my social nous.

'Hi there,' he said when I answered. 'It's Peter.' I hesitated a beat too long. 'From the café. And the supermarket.'

'Yes, right, hi,' I said. 'How are you?'

'I'm well, thank you, how are you?'

'Yes, fine.' I waited.

'So, I saw that the central library is having an afternoon for children with learning disabilities, you know, stories and activities and things, loud as you like, and parents, obviously, well, or—' he swallowed. 'I wondered if it would be the kind of thing your brother would... enjoy...' I put my head on one side and smiled, bemused. I wasn't quite sure what he was trying to achieve, but I was willing to see where it would go.

'Yeah, that sounds interesting. Actually we were already planning on going.'

'Oh. Right.'

'Yeah, it's a support group we belong to, they do activities like this every now and then.'

'Great. Um.'

I decided to throw him a bone. 'But maybe we'll see you there?'

'Yes. That would be great. I mean, to see you. Both.'

'Well it was your idea. I'd hate for you to miss out.'

He laughed awkwardly. 'Well anyway. I wanted to mention it to you, and maybe I'll see you there, let's say that.'

'Thank you, that's very sweet.'

'Great. See you on Saturday. Maybe.'

'Maybe.'

'I'll let you go.'

'Bye.'

I put the phone down and shook my head slightly in wonder. Funny man.

The library was chaotic, and loud. There were other kids like Robert, a handful with autism, one in a wheelchair. But the staff were great, two of the normal library staff and three special-needs teaching assistants. They read stories, they sang songs, they got all the kids making arts and crafts out of paper and foil and string. For once there was shouting and running allowed in the library, and a special section (the sci-fi shelf) for being quiet, with bean bags. There was a table at the back where the parents had put cakes and biscuits they'd brought in, and a kettle for tea and coffee.

Dad didn't often come to the support group meetings, but he had come with us that day. It was nice to see him sitting with Robert at a miniature table with his knees around his ears, making his own craft concoction, nodding knowingly at the chatter of the other little boy next to him. He looked relaxed, for once.

I saw Peter come in, hovering awkwardly at the door. I smiled, and put down the book I'd been flipping through. I got up and went over to the food table, shuffling the plastic spoons in their cup and rearranging some muffins on a plate. Peter came over.

'Well hello.'

'Hi there.'

He drew an exaggerated circle on the floor with his foot. 'So... you might have guessed. I don't have a child with a learning disability.'

I looked at him sideways. 'I suspected you might turn up alone.'

He smiled. 'Well I just really wanted to make friends with—sorry, what was his name?'

'Robert. He's over there, with Dad.' I pointed him out.

'What is it—is it OK if I ask what he has?'

'Down Syndrome,' I said. 'Cup of tea?'

'Yeah, sure. Thanks.'

'You know if you're here, you're going to have to lead a round of Simon Says.'

'I am?'

'It's the rules.' I handed him his tea.

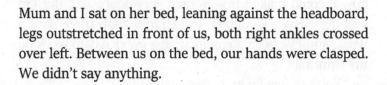

Mum and I sat on her bed, leaning against the headboard, legs outstretched in front of us, both right ankles crossed over left. Between us on the bed, our hands were clasped. We didn't say anything.

Week Four

Alberta and I meet for coffee. The wind is brisk but we sit outside because the dog is with me. She sniffs around every table leg, takes an interest in a passing Pekinese, then settles herself under my chair. It's Tuesday of week four; class is on Thursday.

'She's lovely,' Alberta says of the dog, but she doesn't get too close.

'So how are you coping *sans enfants*? House not too quiet?'

She makes a circle with her thumbs and forefingers and places them around the rim of her cappuccino cup. 'It's definitely different,' she says with a smile. 'I can see how it could make some women very depressed. But I'm keeping busy. I volunteer at a charity shop three days a week, and I've been going in almost every day to work on my paintings.'

'You can just go in there on your own?'

'Well Eamonn comes into the University most days. If he's not lecturing, he'll be in his office or the studio, sometimes the library. I just go find him and he lets me in and leaves me to it.' She shrugs and smiles, a secret, teenage smile. 'Sometimes he helps me, gives me extra tips. I'm really getting my money's worth for this course.'

'I bet you are,' I say, and my tone makes us both laugh.

'No, no, he just—it's nice, sometimes we spend the whole afternoon painting together.'

'That explains why your paintings are so much better than everyone else's, I was wondering.'

Alberta blushes demurely. 'They're not better, they're just more finished, I have more time, I—'

'Alberta, learn to take a compliment.'

'Bertie, please, everyone calls me Bertie.'

'Really?'

She wrinkles her nose. 'I know it's not very feminine. I always wanted to be an Allie, I think that's so pretty. But Bertie sort of stuck. My husband calls me Bertie.'

'Is he missing the children?'

'I think so, but he doesn't say. Says it's nice to have some peace and quiet. Actually, we're going up to see Heather at the weekend.'

'How is she getting on at Durham?'

'Oh she loves it, got a really nice group of friends there. Finding the work a bit stressful I think, very different from school. Much less hand-holding.' I nod sagely. 'I've already been thinking about Christmas,' she says, 'it's going to be so lovely to have everyone home again.' I roll my shoulders to ease the stiffness. I'm expecting Alberta to carry on about her children as mothers often do, but she trails off and stares deep into her cup. I dip my head, trying to catch her eye.

'What?'

She sighs lightly. 'It's true what they say, you know,' she says, 'it does feel so empty without them. It just makes me realise—oh, but it's awful to say.'

'What is?'

'It makes me think I haven't done anything with my life, I've just wasted it all being a mother and a housewife.'

I shift uncomfortably. 'Who says being a housewife is a waste? You've raised two beautiful children.' I've never seen her children but I know this is the right thing to say.

She nods, reaching up to fiddle with the end of her headscarf. 'You're right, I know. I was never really cut out to be a career woman, anyway.' I can't think of anything to say. 'Besides, you're never done raising kids, are you?' she says brightly. 'I had Adrian on the phone last night asking how to work the fuse box, really they're hopeless on their own. They'll be keeping me busy for years yet.'

At home the next morning, I tie a scarf around my head, just to try it, but I feel ridiculous and return it to my neck.

It was the scarf that made it all possible. If it hadn't have been for that scarf, so incongruous in a warm and steamy pub, I might never have seen him again. It was purple and white—the colours of King's College. I considered trying to befriend the porters in order to wrangle Michael's surname out of them, but I couldn't be sure they'd be friendly, and in such a big college it was unlikely they'd even know. I sat in lectures for days after the pork scratchings episode, gazing into the middle distance, tapping my pen, and wondering how I could get in touch with him and what I would do when I did.

At dinner in Hall, I asked my friends if any of them knew anyone in King's, or in third year, or both.

'I know someone at King's,' Anna said, 'but he's a first-year Chemist.'

'I think my sister knows someone in third year doing PPE, but he's at Magdalene,' from Patricia.

'OK, look, we need some serious sleuthing here,' I said. 'Chloe is my year at his faculty, but he's only half based there.'

'I have supervisions at King's,' Eloise offered. 'And I hand my essays in there, so I have access to the pigeonholes.'

'OK, that's promising. If we can find out his surname, I can leave him something in his pigeonhole.'

'What would you put in his pigeonhole if you knew it?' Anna said.

'I don't know. I was thinking maybe a packet of cheese biscuits, and a note saying something like, "don't worry, these are stolen", or something. I'm not sure.' I blushed.

As it turned out, Patricia's sister's friend did know a third year at King's called Michael.

'There's a guy who goes by Mike, but she's pretty sure he studies sciences.' I shook my head. He had written *Michael*. 'Then there's a Chinese guy called Michael—' again, a no, '—and then there's the head of the college debating society. Tall, skinny, brown wavy hair, battered satchel?' she asked.

'He's not that skinny,' I said. I could definitely imagine him debating.

'Well if it's the same guy, his surname is Preston.'

'If it's not, someone is going to get a very unexpected

surprise in his pigeonhole,' Anna smirked. I felt the excitement shiver in my stomach again.

'OK, is this too forward?' I asked, showing them the note. Giggles all round.

'Oh my god, Camille, you're so brave,' Anna said. 'I don't think I could be that brazen even in writing.'

'I think it's good,' Chloe said. 'Nothing wrong with a girl knowing what she wants.'

'You'll put it in his pigeonhole?'

Eloise tucked the folded piece of paper assiduously into her diary. 'If I can find a third-year pigeonhole for an M. Preston, I will deposit this note.' She grinned. 'Even my part in your life is more interesting than my actual life.'

I clapped my hands and gave a little bounce. 'When's your next supervision?'

'Thursday.'

'OK. I hope he likes it. Oh god, what if he thinks it's stupid?'

Pork scratchings can only sustain a girl for so long. Dinner sometime? Camille.

I was in line to pay for my lunch on Thursday when my heart dropped through my shoes like a lead ball. I whipped around to Patricia.

'Oh my god, Patty, what have I done? He's going to think I'm so strange! What kind of girl asks out a boy she doesn't even know? He's probably not even interested!' Patricia laughed.

'Relax, Cam, it's fine. If he doesn't want to see you, no harm done. You'll probably never see him again.'

'What if he does want to see me? How is he going to get in touch with me?' She reached across me for cutlery.

'Isn't that part of the fun? It's so romantic. I'm crazy jealous.'

'I'm so nervous I think I'm going to be sick.' I was alternately elated and terrified. 'I think I might have to have two puddings to calm me down.'

'You really like him, don't you?'

'Don't be ridiculous, I barely know him.' I looked at her sideways, and we both grinned. 'I think I really, really do.'

'What's Down Syndrome?'

We were sitting in a room I came to think of as the Bad News Room. It seemed to serve no function except to shut off the rest of the world while the doctor told you the worst. There was a low wooden table with a box of tissues, and a water cooler by the wall. I stared at my hands, and at the thin, faded carpet beyond them.

The phrase wasn't new to me, but I didn't have the energy to dredge up where I had heard it before, what it had meant, what it was doing here, now, in this doctor's mouth. I was so tired. We had been at the hospital for days, through the delivery, through the news, through the grief counselling and the form filling, and now this. I wanted, powerfully wanted, my own bed in my own room. I wanted to crawl into my mother's arms and have her hold me and tell me everything would be OK, to fall asleep next to her on the sofa and hear her voice when I woke up.

Tears dropped from my eyes, blurring my vision. I was looking down and I wasn't blinking: the tears didn't roll down my cheeks, they just fell straight onto my thumbs as I clasped my hands in my lap.

'It's a genetic condition caused by the replication of a chromosome.'

'What does that mean?'

'It means he's going to have some differences, in the way he looks, the way he develops, the way his mind works.'

'He's disabled?'

'Well, we try not to say that exactly. We don't know how severe it will be. He may be able to live an almost completely normal life.'

The silence was hollow. I think the doctor was expecting more questions, but—and this sounds harsh—it was hard to care that much about what he was saying. How could we think of anything but what had been taken from us?

'Typical physical signs are slanted eyes, a flatter bridge of the nose, a single crease on the hand instead of the normal palm lines, and a large space between the big toe and second toe. He may have problems with speech, hearing or vision, and cognitive development.'

I wanted to put my hands up and cover his mouth and stop him saying all these things. I didn't care, I didn't want to know.

'There's also a high risk of heart conditions, so we'll be monitoring him very carefully for the next few days. Moving forward, you'll want to be looking into some support groups, build up a network of people in a similar situation. Behavioural therapy and speech therapy might be something to look into as he grows up, but for now all you'll need is to keep in close contact with his doctor.'

He seemed to know he wasn't going to get much more out of us. He stood up. 'I'll leave you to process,' he said, and he left.

I glanced sideways. Dad was gazing at the opposite wall, unblinking. There was a stoop to his shoulders.

'I—' I began, and then didn't know how to carry on. He turned to me.

'How are we—?'

'I don't want to keep it,' I said.

———

Week four, pastels. I'm sitting next to Niall, a quiet, thoughtful man, young to my eyes but probably late forties. He's very close to his canvas, smudging lines with his thumb. He'll be smudging them with his nose if he's not careful. Eamonn is circulating.

'Tell me about this, Niall,' he says. That's always his phrase, *tell me about this.*

Niall steps back and brushes his hair off his face, leaving a fine white smudge on his forehead.

'I was thinking about freedom,' he says. 'My nephew always does these smudged lines when he's trying to show something moving fast. So I've done this sort of bird, he's supposed to be flying. I was thinking sort of, freedom from fixed boundaries between colours, freedom of movement, kind of thing.' He tilts his head on one side as he speaks, gesturing with his hands around the painting. On the pretext of reaching for the cloth to wipe my hands, I lean over to take a look.

The picture is OK, very simplistic. Background of white

and blue and grey smudge of bird. I can see what he's trying to go for, making it look like the bird is flying, all the smudges out in one direction, backwards.

'That's wonderful, Niall,' Eamonn says. 'That's really wonderful.'

When we break to stretch our legs, I make a beeline for Alberta.

'Hello, Allie,' I say, and she laughs. 'How are you?'

I take a peek at her painting, even though she demurely tries to bat me away.

I am genuinely impressed by Alberta's art. In oil she created an autumnal landscape in the rain, in the foreground a path disappearing off to the right, a streetlight illuminating the raindrops and leaves glistening in oranges, reds and salmons. In pastel she has made a Japanese garden, the lightest of aquamarines and mints, and pale pink cherry blossom. By the end of the class, an ink figure walks over the pastels, a girl picking her way through the gardens, just the back of her, long plait down her back, hand resting on a tree trunk as she passes.

'Where is she going?' I ask.

Alberta smiles and shrugs. 'Anywhere you like.'

I like to think she is meeting a lover, the hand on the tree showing she has just glanced behind her to check nobody has seen because it is a forbidden love. And I am surprised at my own imagination.

Even after all that, he outdid me.

It was about two weeks later. I was having some trouble with a supervisor I didn't get on with, and had spent the morning talking to my tutor and my Director of Studies and was feeling generally quite strung out and tense. I had an essay due in four days' time—for a different supervisor—and I hadn't even started the reading list yet. Typically, it was one of those reading lists that was full of journal articles, so I couldn't get any of them in college. I had to go into the faculty and make photocopies if I didn't want to sit and read them there in the library.

I was wandering the shelves distractedly, my reading list held loosely in one hand and the strap of my bag in the other. I found the shelf I needed and ran my finger along the spines, searching for the right issue. *411, 412, 413... 415.* I sighed in frustration, scanning the whole shelf. Why could nobody put things back in the right order? Then I caught sight of issue 414, shoved in carelessly at the end of the row. I grabbed it, and flicked through the pages to the article I needed.

Tucked in there, right into the spine, was a note. I recognised the handwriting from hours of lying on my bed staring at a paper napkin.

Saturday, Fitzbillies' at 7? Michael. PS I hope you thoroughly research this essay.

I laughed out loud, not even noticing the scandalised looks from people hunched over desks. I pulled the note out and let the book fall back on the shelf, and literally pressed the paper to my chest. I did a little spin. My deadline was still looming, but I knew I wouldn't be able to stand still long enough to wait for the photocopier. I grabbed my bag and ran out of the library, desperate to tell someone and to decide what to wear on Saturday.

I caught the bus to town, not wanting to walk in case my shoes started to pinch. On the bus I began to panic. In my room, in front of my mirror and my friends, my dress felt glamorous and my hair, carefully pinned and curled, coquettish. But now—I looked down and spread the material through my fingers. Was it too much? Should I be playing it more casual?

I wondered what I would say when I saw him. How should I greet him? A handshake, a hug? A kiss on each cheek? Would he be waiting outside, or would he be sitting at the table? Oh god, what if I got there first? Where should I wait for him?

I felt queasy walking towards the restaurant, almost physically ill. My stomach clenched and rolled. What was this feeling? Fear? Why was I so nervous? *Calm yourself, Camille.* He was expecting someone cool and confident, sassy enough to invite herself out to dinner. I ran my fingers along my lower lip-line in case of lipstick smudges.

I turned the corner and there he was, standing outside Fitzbillies', wearing a large black coat and his hair slightly tousled by the wind. His hands were in his pockets and he was swaying his shoulders slightly from side to side, as you would when you were bored or not sure what to do with yourself. He saw me and turned, the light from the window lighting up one side of his face. He broke into a huge grin and came towards me, bringing his hands out of his pockets.

'You got my note!'

'I did, but I have to confess I haven't actually finished the essay, so I probably shouldn't be here right now.'

It looked like he was going for a hug, but I think he was actually going for a kiss on the cheek. I ended up leaning in too far and there was a clumsy, awkward moment. We mumbled *sorry*s and uncomfortable chuckles and I blushed furiously and we stood facing each other on the street.

'You look great,' he said. My hand went to my hair automatically, but as it was pinned, there was nothing to tuck behind my ear.

'Um, thanks,' I said. Should I tell him he did too?

He stepped to the door and held it open for me. 'After you.'

'Thanks,' I said again, going in. *You have to say more than just "thanks".* We were shown to a table, and sat down. *Right, we're all settled, you can bring out the personality now.* 'So how—oh, thanks—' the waitress poured us both glasses of water and handed us our menus. *Jumped in there too early.* 'Thank you. How did you manage to get the note in the book? How did you even know which book?'

'Ah,' he said mysteriously. 'I have my ways.'

'It was Chloe, wasn't it?'

'It was. Actually, first I went up to completely the wrong redhead, and she had no idea what I was talking about. I think I may have scared her.' I laughed, somewhat inelegantly as I'd just taken a sip of water. 'But once I found the right girl, she managed to sneak a look at your reading list, and here we are.' He reached for a piece of bread.

'What if somebody else doing the same essay got the book before me?'

'Then I'd be sitting here with somebody else,' he laughed. 'It was a flawed plan, I admit. It was either going to go very well or very badly. Looks like I got lucky.' He was gorgeous when he smiled. His eyes crinkled up. 'The more important question is, how did you find my pigeonhole?'

I raised an eyebrow. 'I too have my ways.'

'I'm not going to lie, I was a little alarmed that you knew my surname.'

I ran my finger around the base of my wine glass. 'That's not all I know,' I said, trying my best to sound sultry.

'Should I be scared, or...?'

My straight face cracked into laughter. 'No, I'm lying, that *is* all I know. My friend's sister's friend found you— it's a long story.'

'Friend's sister's friend? Wow, you had a whole operation going.' He caught my eye. 'You must have really wanted to find me.'

I blushed and looked down, then up again. 'I can't ignore a man who bought me pork scratchings,' I said. 'That would just be rude.'

'Well, quite.' He picked up his menu. 'Have you been here before?'

'Not to eat,' I said. 'The bakery does the best Chelsea buns in Cambridge, though.'

'No, no, the *only* Chelsea buns in Cambridge. Worth speaking of.' Our eyes met again, and we smiled. My stomach fluttered again, only this time it didn't make me feel so sick. This time I liked it.

He walked me home afterwards, all the way to my college.

'You don't have to,' I said. 'It is really far.'

'No, I want to. To be honest, there's a rumour going round that Girton doesn't really exist, so I kind of want to see for myself.'

We walked slowly, taking our time over each footstep, talking. He told me about his dissertation, and I told him he was exactly the kind of person who should be at Cambridge.

'What is that supposed to mean?'

I looked up at the stars that were becoming visible as we left the centre of town. 'Anyone who can talk with that much passion about something, especially something so—'

'Pointless?'

'Specific. That's what institutions like this are for, the pure joy of academia.'

'Aren't you passionate about history?'

I shrugged. 'It's OK.' It was getting quite cold, and I wrapped my arms more tightly around me for warmth.

'Here,' Michael said, shrugging off his coat.

'No, don't be silly, I'm fine.'

'No, take it, I was overheating anyway. I'm like a radiator.'

'Are you sure? It's such a cliché.'

'Yeah, clichéd for a reason. I look like a gentleman, and I can stop wishing I hadn't brought such a heavy coat.' He held it out for me.

'Mmm,' I said, wriggling into it. 'Warm.'

'Now will you put your hands down?'

'What?'

'You had your arms crossed, which makes it very difficult for me to hold your hand.'

'Well nothing worth having comes easy. You have to work for it.' We grinned at each other. I let my arms swing self-consciously for a while, then settled into a normal gait.

'Are you any good at constellations?' he asked, tilting his head back.

I glanced up again. 'Not really. I know the big dipper. That's about it.' He reached sideways while I was looking up and took my hand. The tips of his fingers were cold. He gently interlaced his fingers with mine. I looked over at him and smiled shyly. He smiled back, and gave my hand a little squeeze.

'There it is,' I said, when we reached the college gates. 'Told you it exists.'

'So it does.' We slowed to a stop and he pivoted to face me. He took my other hand, and held them both.

'Good thing too, or I'd have nowhere to sleep tonight.'

'Miss Addison, I had a perfectly lovely time with you this evening.'

'And I with you.'

He stepped closer. 'I'm glad you had half the university track me down.'

'Some people would call that creepy.' He was very close. My heart was thumping with anticipation. I was sure he'd be able to hear it.

'It was a little creepy,' he whispered. 'But I kind of liked it.' He filled my whole field of vision, above me in the dark.

I've heard people talk of fireworks at a first kiss, but that's not how I'd describe it. When he kissed me it felt like sparklers, tingling all the way to my fingertips. I went light-headed. He pulled away slowly, lingeringly, and my eyes stayed shut. When I opened them, he was smiling down at me.

'Can I see you again?' he asked.

'Of course. You know where I live now.'

'A million miles from Cambridge.'

'Are you in the faculty tomorrow?'

'Yeah, I have lectures all morning.'

'Can I meet you at lunchtime?'

'Sure.'

He smiled, and kissed me again. 'I'll see you there.'

I moved away, letting go of his hand at the last possible moment, swinging my arm. I watched him go, watched him turn and wave three times before he was out of sight. I stretched my fingers out and turned in a full circle before slowly dragging my feet inside, bringing with me the delicious tingling in my stomach. I thought about every detail of the night, and it fastened a smile to my face that I couldn't scrub off.

Eloise stuck her head out of her door as I fumbled for my key. 'How did it go? Was it amazing?'

I leaned against my door.

'It really was,' I said.

Every Sunday, Mum would put on her navy suit and pearls, take her best handbag out of the wardrobe and catch the bus to church. When I was little, I would go with her. I'd sit cross-legged on the floor at the foot of my bed while Mum sat on the bed and brushed my hair and parted it with a comb and twisted it into two plaits. She would get the box of ribbons down from my shelf and let me choose two, and tie bows around the ends of my plaits. Then, hand-in-hand, we'd walk down the road to the bus stop.

One day when I was twelve or thirteen, I asked Mum if I could go out with Maria and her mother on Sunday instead of going to church. Mum was ironing, and, without stopping the slow, steady sweep of her arm, she paused, just for a moment.

'Is that what you want to do?' she said. I was sitting at the table, swinging my legs, drawing.

'Yep.'

'OK then.'

And that Sunday I didn't go to church.

It didn't strike me as a big deal at the time. I stopped going to church on days when I had something else to do. And then, I stopped going to church even when I didn't have something else to do. Eventually, Mum stopped asking if I was coming, and she walked down the road to the bus stop alone.

So when this thing happened, this awful thing, I had to say it.

'Have you thought about—not keeping it?'

Dad looked up sharply.

'Camille.'

'It's a valid option.'

'No, it isn't,' Mum said, in a stronger voice than I'd heard from her since my return from China. 'It is most certainly not an option, and I don't want to hear you mention it again.' I looked desperately from one parent to the other.

'Why put yourself through it, after everything you've already gone through? When you don't have to.'

'I do have to, I—' she ran a hand through her hair, her perfect curls long gone, greys speckling her temples. 'It's not my choice to make.'

'It's your body. And at your age, you know how risky it can be. Please, please think about this.' She took my hands and squeezed them to her chest, trying to make me understand.

'I have to believe that God won't give me more than I can handle. I have to believe that this is His plan for me, and I don't have a right to change that.'

My patience was beginning to fray. 'How can you say that, after everything that's happened? What kind of god would put you through all that? Please just give yourself a break, you don't deserve this.'

Mum gave up, let me go, turned and began to put the plates on the draining board away.

'Mum, I'm serious. Do you really want to have this child, knowing where it came from? Would you even be able to love it?' Mum slammed a plate down on the counter, making Dad and I jump.

'Stop it!' she shouted, breathing hard. 'Just stop. After everything he's done to me, everything he's made me, I will not let him make me a murderer too. I cannot, I will not do that.'

'OK,' Dad said, going up behind her and trying to massage her shoulders. 'It's OK.'

She brushed him off. 'I am not a murderer.' And she vanished upstairs.

I tried to admire her for her strength and resolve and faith, but I couldn't find anything but anger for her stubbornness. There was a way to put this all behind us, and she wouldn't take it. I looked at Dad.

'Are you really OK with this? Raising that child with her? Pretending it's yours?'

'No, Camille, I'm not,' he said flatly. 'But I'm not OK with abortion either, it's a sin. It's wrong.'

I shook my head. 'Dad, I'm trying to see a way out of this, and I'm trying to see it get better, but this way—it's always going to be part of this family, that baby is going to be living proof of what happened.'

'Maybe it will be OK,' Dad said. 'Maybe we can build something beautiful out of something horrible and disgusting and painful.'

'She's forty-five. You're forty-seven. How can you do the parent thing all over again?' My dad sighed as though from the very depths of his soul. He looked so old and helpless—too old for forty-seven—and I hated that. Dad looked as lost as I felt.

'I don't know, Cam. I don't know how we're going to do it.'

'Niall's a very Irish name for someone with such a Northern accent,' I say absentmindedly. Niall laughs.

'Camille—' he says it with an exaggerated French accent, *Cam-eey,* 'is a very French name for someone with such an English accent.' He reaches for a dust cloth to wipe his fingers on. 'My mother's parents were Irish. I'm a born and raised Scouser.'

'I knew there must be some Irish somewhere in there.'

'What about you?'

'Oh I'm not continental at all. My mother's favourite flowers were camellias. And she thought Camille was more refined than Camilla.'

'Yeah, I can see that, it has a certain class about it.'

I look down at the array of colours in front of me, debating which to use next.

'Apparently it was either going to be Camille or Genevieve. Either's nice, I suppose.'

We wanted to name him after Mum, but there wasn't much we could do with Annabelle. Her maiden name was Robertson: we called him Robert. We gave him Dad's surname. It was just easier that way. I carried on calling Dad, "Dad", and Robert picked it up from me. There never seemed to be a good time or a good reason to address the issue, so we didn't.

I have, and I always have had, the greatest respect for my father for what he did for Robert. I'm not sure I could have done the same in his situation. There were times when I almost couldn't do it. There were times, at night, that first year, during the screaming and the pleading and the crying, when I thought I couldn't go on. I never—not once, not ever—thought about harming him, but I used to hope—and nobody knows this—hope that he wouldn't make it through the night. It would make everything simpler, it would just be best for everyone. And I would pull the duvet over my head in shame.

Week Five

I'm sitting next to Emmi. She's very young, early twenties, Rosaline's friend. She actually goes to the university, they both do. She's studying Business Administration and Marketing, one of those new-fangled degrees that don't mean anything to me.

People at that stage, students, young adults, really make me feel my age. Make me use old-sounding words like *new-fangled*. I would love to be that young again, when everything is possible, when you stick to opinions that have no basis with illogical ferocity, when everything is to be protested and injustice is all around, when you feel everything so deeply that the smallest success can buoy you for days and the smallest hurt can rip you apart.

Or maybe I'm just being sentimental. I don't really want to go back to that.

I haven't spoken to Emmi much, or at all, and I'd like to, I'd like to get the full set. I like the idea of the seven of us, complete strangers, bonding together over an *Interpretative Art* evening class.

But I'm struggling to find something to say. Forty years is a big gap to bridge with words.

'Have you had any ideas about what you'll do for your project yet?' I ask, trying to keep my tone light and worrying that I sounded like a grandmother. Emmi glances up at me.

'I was thinking about doing something inspired by my grandpa. He passed away earlier this year.'

'Oh I'm so sorry,' I say automatically.

'It's OK, it wasn't unexpected. But he was really great and I really looked up to him and think it would be nice to do something in his memory.'

I am genuinely impressed. 'That is a lovely idea.'

'I think so. I'm not sure what exactly it will be yet, though.' She chews her lip absentmindedly. 'How do you put someone onto a canvas? I don't want to just paint *him*, I want to paint *who he was*.'

I am beginning to worry about the second half of term. Everyone seems to have these great ideas germinating, and I have nothing. I can barely come up with enough creative expression to last me one two-and-a-half-hour session a week, let alone a whole six weeks.

'What would you do, to paint something in memory of someone?' says Emmi. I wonder if she's been reading my face while I was lost in worry. 'Or, how would you paint someone you look up to? Do you have anyone like that?'

I keep my voice neutral.

'My dad,' I say. 'My dad is inspiring to me.'

'In what way?'

'He's the strongest, most selfless man I know. Not many people would have done what he did.'

'What did he do?'

I've forgotten myself. I'm not here to unburden my secrets onto adolescents. I'm not quick enough a thinker to come up with something to distract her, so I knock the paintbrush-washing water over, and Eamonn bustles over to clear it up and make sure everyone's art is unscathed. He touches my arm once everything is mopped up.

'Everything OK?' he says quietly. I nod, and he winks at me, and when I look back at my canvas I've forgotten what it was I was trying to create.

I sat in the waiting room with my father. It was a small, square box lined with fraying blue chairs. An old TV set crackled in black and white in the top corner, but nobody was paying any attention to it. A very young man—he looked barely out of his teens—sat in the centre of two sets of parents, looking decidedly green. A heavy-set man with a few days' stubble was falling asleep in one corner and jerking awake again. Other people may have come and gone, I can't remember them now. I think an elderly Spanish woman came in at one stage, and I feel like she was the mother of the man with the stubble, but that can't be right, I'm sure he was there alone.

Dad was in very good spirits, considering. He brought the paper with him, and read aloud to me, *listen to this, Cam*, or, *can you believe this*, or, *here's something interesting*. We did the crossword and I dredged up interesting facts from my degree to tell him. He always had a pencil behind his ear, that's something I remember about him from childhood. I don't think his job was always as hands-on as he'd have liked it to be, and he spent his spare time drawing and designing and fiddling with bits of wood in the shed at the bottom of the garden. The pencil was there in the waiting room with us, in its familiar spot behind his ear, and he'd take it out and chew it, and spin it through his fingers, and put it back, and take it out and put it back facing the other way. As time stretched on, the tension rose, in both of us. He chewed a bit too hard and the pencil snapped in his mouth. He spat out splinters and graphite and pulled faces that made me laugh. He stuffed the pieces into the pocket of his jacket and took the paper cup of water I fetched him. We shared a smile, and then his face grew taut again. His hand wandered to the empty space behind his ear again and again. After a while I reached out and took his hand and held it in my lap. They were large hands, square, dry and calloused, already showing signs of age. I stroked my thumb over his knuckle. His hands weren't my hands. I had my mother's hands, narrow and bony, though she bit her nails and I kept mine tidy.

We sat like that until the doctor came to get us. I'd slipped into a sort of waking doze, and this sudden vision startled me. I jumped, and my heart gave such a lurch it was physically painful. But the doctor was smiling as he beckoned us, and if there was something lacking in that smile, I didn't notice it until later.

'It's been tough,' he said, 'but I think we're pulling through. She's resting now, but you can come and take a peek.'

She was lying there, curls dark and limp against the pillow, face still shining with traces of sweat. She looked drawn. She looked old, too old to be doing this. I smoothed her hair back from her face, and looked at the lines around her eyes and down her cheeks. Dad leaned over and kissed her forehead.

'Well done, sweetheart,' he whispered. 'Well done.'

'Mr Addison? Miss Addison?' The doctor drew us aside and clasped his hands together. Even now I wonder if that's the pose he always used to deliver news like this. At the time, all it did was make me realise there was something missing.

'Where's the baby?' I said.

'We're just—cleaning him up,' the doctor said. Unease in his voice? 'I have to tell you, we have some concerns—' The activity around my mother started to intensify. Were there more people, or did they just get closer, faster, more urgent? Her face was suddenly pale, too pale. Was there noise? My ears were registering nothing but pressure.

'I'm going to have to ask you to leave the room.' A nurse, in front of us, ushering us towards the door. My mother was getting smaller and smaller. My feet were moving but I couldn't take my eyes off her, I think I was reaching out to her. Dad struggled harder than I did, the nurse raised her voice, I clutched at his arms.

Outside, we watched through the tiny window in the door. Then a patient was wheeled down the corridor on a bed and we were hustled out of the way. When I looked back, my mother had been taken out of the room by another door.

Internal haemorrhaging, they said. A risk with older pregnancies. Nothing more they could do.

My father stepped backwards, and backwards again

like he could step back through time. He stepped against a chair and sank down into it. The same blue chairs as in the waiting room. His eyes were wild and staring, and then he—crumpled. From the inside out. I watched his heart break, and the rest of his body caved in around the wreckage.

He cried. I had never seen my father cry. I had seen him angry, but I'd never seen this kind of outpouring of emotion. I sat down beside him. I wanted to draw him to me, to hold him, but I couldn't touch him. I wanted to fetch my mother, I needed her to take care of the two of us, and then I cried too.

It wasn't dignified. It wasn't elegant. The two of us sat there and bawled. It was loud and shuddering and messy. I don't know how much time passed. Eventually there was nothing more to come, no more tears, no more noise. I don't remember stopping, but then there was silence. A raw, wrenching pain in my chest. A nurse came with two cups of water and asked us something, but it didn't register. Dad was staring at the ground, not seeing anything. He reached and fumbled for my hand, and I held it.

That moment took every ounce of my concentration. And the next one. I don't know how long we sat there, but each successive moment was the hardest thing I'd ever done. Everything I was, was straining to survive, straining not to fall apart under the weight of this. One moment at a time. Moment after moment after moment. Somehow, it worked. Somehow, forty-odd years later, I'm still going.

Eventually, though, we had to face the subject of the baby.

I'm casting about for inspiration, with limited success.

Landscapes haven't been working for me. As much as I admire Allie's creations, I can't get mine to look right. They look infantile. What else can I paint?

I look around the room. Emmi and Rosaline are leaning in towards each other, whispering, laughing. Niall is leaning away from his canvas, brush in hand, biting his lip, eyeing his work critically. Morris is lost in concentration, almost invisible behind his canvas. Allie is bobbing her head to music only she can hear, flicking from palette to canvas and back again, a smile on her face. She's in her element. Becca is painting, but not with the deep concentration of Morris or the cheerful contentment of Allie.

I keep looking at Becca. She's almost opposite me, on the other side of our semi-circle. She's early- to mid-thirties, maybe older and looking well for it. She's very pale, still suffering from the odd bout of angry red acne. The skin on her hands looks very dry. She has thin lips, an aquiline nose, brown eyes and platinum-blonde hair aggressively straightened. It's cut just above her shoulders, feathery, different lengths, which I suppose is trendy. She always wears her fingerless gloves that reach to her elbows, and I wonder not for the first time if they hide something. Scars? Drug tracks?

I reach for a lighter shade of paint, and sketch out the outline of a face. I try and study her as a subject of art, without letting her know I'm watching. High cheekbones, jaw slightly forwards. Square forehead. I spend twenty minutes trying to make her eyes the same shape, and eventually give up in frustration. I glance at the clock. Half an hour until our mid-way break.

I mix up an unevenly-stirred batch of creamy colour, and paint over everything I've done, a block almost to the edges of my canvas. I don't look up at Becca anymore. Rosaline is painting but Emmi is still leaning over her shoulder, finishing some scandalous story or other. I get the sense Rosaline is annoyed at the distraction.

After our five-minute stroll around the studio, I sit down and I paint Becca again, this time without looking. I paint her and I think about her sharp, pointed wit, the anger I've sometimes seen in her eyes, the nervous way she flicks her fingers against each other. Her high-pitched laugh, unexpectedly loud, her confident stride, the outline of her throat as she swallows.

I don't even notice when Eamonn appears behind me. He has to step closer and cough lightly before I register his presence. I look up, startled, and watch his face closely for a sign of recognition. I'm embarrassed he's caught me painting someone across the room. Does he think me weird? Creepy? Unimaginative?

'I like it,' he says, in my ear. 'Painting people is always tricky. I think you've really captured her essence.'

The phrase makes me wrinkle my nose—Becca can keep her essence.

'I'm not sure it looks much like the subject,' I say, in equally low tones, 'but, I don't know, I don't think it looks too bad.'

'No self-deprecating here,' Eamonn admonishes. 'It's good. You're really good at faces, not many people can do that.'

'I tried making a face geometrically, you know, when people say break it down into shapes, but it looked artificial.'

'It's a tricky technique to get right, to make it look smooth. But whatever you've done here is working. Good job.' He lays a hand on my forearm, bare skin. His fingers are cool.

He's looking at me now, not my painting, a lock of silver hair out of place over his eyes. He must be almost my age or thereabouts, but his skin is thick and firm where mine is thin and papery. He's smiling.

'Thank you.' I find myself suddenly stiff and awkward, not wanting to move in case he thinks I'm shrugging him off. What's going on here? His smile is easy, casual. He pats my arm—*pats?*—and moves away. I try to shake myself back to reality. I'm smiling, and suddenly it feels silly.

I look at my painting. It's not really Becca, but it's still something good. I like it.

We went to the Fitzwilliam Museum together, and he showed me around King's College Chapel, pointing up at the ceiling and telling me its history. We bought strawberries and went punting down the river. I lay back, eating berries and watching him attempt to look strong and manly as he propelled the boat.

'You're doing a good job,' I said, my tone just earnest enough to make him suspect I was teasing. I had a go too, and wobbled so much I thought I might fall in the river.

'I'll fish you out again,' Michael said. I couldn't get the hang of making the punt go forwards: every time I pushed, it went towards one bank or the other. Michael found it hilarious. He leant back with his hands behind his head. 'I'm in no rush,' he said, 'we can just zigzag the whole way.'

He showed me his rooms in King's. As a third-year scholar, he had a set—a bedroom with a separate study, and a kitchenette shared with another student.

'He's nice,' Michael said. 'Very quiet. Works hard, I don't really see him much.'

He cooked me dinner in his tiny kitchen, and we danced to the radio, and sat by the window to eat as darkness fell.

I checked my watch and groaned. 'It hardly seems worth it, going all the way back to college only to come in again for a nine a.m. lecture.'

Michael raised an eyebrow at me, and I realised what it had sounded like.

'I mean, I didn't mean, um,' I said.

'You could stay,' he said simply.

'Is that even allowed?'

'The porters don't have to know.' I twisted my fingers nervously. Michael shifted so he was sitting next to me. 'Hey,' he said. 'Hey, look at me.' I looked up. 'I'm not going to ask you to do anything you don't want to do.' I leaned over and kissed him. He smiled at me and twisted a strand of my hair around his finger.

'I want to,' I whispered. He tucked the strand of hair behind my ear, traced his fingers down my jawline, and drew my chin to his. He kissed me tenderly, sliding his hands slowly down my arms to the bottom of my jumper, and I raised my arms to let him take it off. He pulled me to my feet, and I followed him, eyes locked and trusting, over to the bed.

I only realised how much I needed a friend once I had Peter. And he was such a good friend. He was incredible with Robert, never fazed by him, and Robert very quickly fell in love. His face would break into a smile at the sight of him, and he'd run over with a cry of 'Peter!' and throw his arms around him. Peter would greet him with a 'hey, buddy!' and they'd high five: left, right, both hands.

I loved to see them together. It made it even more stark when Dad would come in from work and give Robert his cursory pat on the head.

Peter took the two of us to the zoo, and bought us ice cream. He made me laugh, he made me feel relaxed when normally I was a tightly-wound spring whenever I was out with Robert in public.

The biggest step was one day when I was at work. It was my day to pick Robert up from the childminder's he went to after school, but something had come up and I was entangled in meetings all afternoon. Five-thirty came around and I still hadn't left. I grabbed the phone and dialled Dad's work number, tucking the phone under my ear with my shoulder as I rifled through a folder for some papers that I needed.

'Hi Dad, it's me,' I said. 'Is there any way you can pick Robert up today? I just can't leave until I get this sorted.'

'I can't, Camille, I'm supervising this project and we have a meeting with the client at six I have to be in.'

I swore, and he told me to watch my language. 'What am I going to do?' I said, standing up and accidentally knocking the file off the desk. I attempted to catch it and pin it down with my knee.

'I don't know, maybe Edith can keep him an extra hour?'

'You know she won't do that, not after last time.' I ran out of limbs to keep control of things with. 'I'll figure something out, Dad, I have to go. See you later.' I let the phone drop, grabbed my folder and the wayward pages and put them on top of the filing cabinet. One of the other phones started to ring and I stared around the office in despair. There was only one thing I could do. Sticking my head out of the door and yelling in the general direction of the kitchenette that somebody had to come back and help me in the office, I grabbed my own phone again, and dialled Peter's number.

'Hello?'

'Peter it's me, Camille.'

'Hi Camille, good timing, I just got in from work.'

I took a deep breath. 'Can I ask the hugest favour ever?'

'Of course.' So steady, so sure. Unflappable.

'Can you pick Robbie up from the childminder's for me? He has to be picked up at six and my dad and I are both stuck at work, so—I'm really, really sorry to ask, I wouldn't ask at all, but I'm desperate.'

'Camille, it's fine,' he said. 'It's no problem at all. Tell me the address and I'll go right over.'

'Are you sure? I feel terrible.'

'Honestly, it's no bother, I'd like to see him.'

'You're a lifesaver. Thank you so much. I owe you big time.'

'I'll add it to your tab,' he said. I told him the address and promised I would be over as soon as I could, and then I rang Edith to tell her Peter would be picking up Robbie, relieved that for once I wasn't wheedling a favour from her.

It was raining as I ran from my car to Peter's front porch. Robert wasn't always good in new places, and I didn't want to put Peter to any more trouble than I already had. I was terrified I'd walk in on a scene of carnage, or find Robbie wedged into a small space and refusing to come out. If I was lucky, all I would find was Peter's crockery arranged perfectly by size or something.

No immediate signs of wreckage when Peter opened the door. In fact he looked as composed as ever.

'Hi, Camille,' he said, opening his arms for a hug. 'How was the work emergency?'

'Oh, nightmarish,' I said, stepping into his arms. He squeezed me, just for a second. 'I have a single mother with two children who applied for rehousing to escape an abusive husband, and now she's being threatened with eviction and there's almost nothing I can do.'

'Sounds like you need a glass of wine. A large one.'

I smiled. 'Very tempting,' I said, 'but I have to relieve you of Robbie before you completely lose your mind. Has he been awful?' I stepped inside.

'Not at all, he's been an angel. We're doing some colouring. Take your coat off, come in for some tea at least.' I hesitate. 'You're going to have to wait for Robbie to finish his picture anyway, you know he won't leave it half-done.'

'Fair enough. But let's go back to the idea of wine...'

He laughed, and led me into the kitchen.

Eamonn is standing behind Rosaline.

'I really like the way it draws the eye,' he says, gesturing over her shoulder at the canvas, 'as though there's something happening off-stage. Very nice.'

Rosaline nods seriously. 'I feel like it sort of lacks definition over here,' she says, 'I didn't want the colours to blend so much.'

Eamonn delicately plucks the paintbrush out of her hand, turns it, and puts it back the other way. 'Have you ever tried painting with the wrong end of your brush?' he says. 'Here.' He guides her hand. 'It's called sgraffito, you just—that's right—push the colour out of the way. You can use a colour shaper if you like, but to be honest a brush handle works just as well. And then of course if you don't like it, you can paint over and start again, as long as the top colour is still wet.' Rosaline nods again, concentrating. 'Very good. Really wonderful,' Eamonn says, releasing her hand.

Emmi is watching, somewhat sadly.

'She's so good at everything,' she says. 'Always has been.' Then she seems to realise that she's said it out loud, and is angry with herself. She crushes her brush too hard into the palette, furiously, not meeting my eye.

I say nothing, and I paint.

⟡

'Cam, we are not having this conversation.'

'We don't have to do this, Dad, we have a choice.'

'What choice?'

'We could give it up for adoption.'

'Who's going to adopt a disabled child?'

'So it spends its life in care, what does it matter to us?'

That moment was the only moment in my life when I thought my father was going to hit me.

'That child is all I have left of your mother, Camille, so it damn well matters to me!'

'That child *killed* my mother!'

'She wanted to raise him, and I am going to respect her wishes.'

'Well you're going to have to respect them without me. I'm not doing this.'

Dad's voice went limp.

'Don't leave me, Camille. I can't do this alone.'

⸻

'How's your art class going?' my husband asks. I look up, surprised. I'm making the bed.

'Well, actually, thank you. I'm really enjoying it.'

'That's good.' He comes over and kisses my cheek. He's buttoning up his coat.

'You taking the dog for a walk?'

'Aye. Just came in to dig out my scarf, it's getting chilly out. Evenings are drawing in, too.'

'Yes, won't be long and the Christmas lights will be out.'

'Halloween first.'

I plump up the pillows and arrange them carefully. 'I tried painting our honeymoon,' I say. 'Remember that waterfall we found, in the woods?'

He stops and smiles at me. 'I do,' he says. 'What a nice idea. Did it turn out well?'

'Not bad,' I say. 'I didn't finish it.'

'Why don't you?'

'I suppose I could. Eamonn said anytime he was in the studio, we could go in.'

'Well, there you go.' He winds his scarf around his neck and tucks the ends into his coat. He's not a tall man, my husband, and in his green puffy jacket he looks rather bulky. It's a very familiar outline to me, brings to mind wellies and walks in the countryside. Solid and safe. I go to him and put my arms around him.

'Hello, you,' he says, squeezing me back. 'I'm meeting Bill and the chaps for a game this afternoon. Why don't you take yourself off to the university and finish your painting? I love to see you doing something you enjoy.' I smile and lean my head against his cheek. He's not quite tall enough for me to use his shoulder.

'I might do. Have a good walk. Take enough doggy bags.' I kiss him and watch fondly as he leaves. I absentmindedly go to the bed and rearrange the pillows, and then I decide abruptly that I will go down to the studio. On my own. I will spend the day painting.

I spend the next half hour hunting through my handbags and my desk, looking for Eamonn's mobile phone number. I have to check that he is at work today. Eventually I find it, and with only a slight hesitation, call. He answers almost immediately.

'Hello?' His voice takes me aback. Almost brisk. Not like Eamonn at all. Wrong number?

'Hello, Eamonn? It's Camille Addison. From *Interpretative Art*. On Thursday nights.'

'Camille, hello, what a pleasure. How are you?' There's some warmth in his voice now. Feels better.

'I'm well, thank you, I was just wondering if I could

pop in and do some more work on my oil painting.'

'The waterfall, am I right?'

'That's the one.'

'Oh you should, that one has great potential. I'm actually just about to give a lecture, but how about I meet you outside the studio at twelve, just after, and I can let you in.'

'Yes, that sounds fine.'

'Ah, no, tell a lie, I've got a couple of second-years in there now. I'll just nip down and tell them you're coming, and you should be able to go straight in. Don't mind them, they're just doing the same as you. Except they're being graded on it. I'll come by and see how you're doing later this afternoon. OK? Do you know where everything is?'

'I'm sure I'll be able to find it,' I say, suddenly dreading having to paint under the gaze of two second-years. How old were they in second year? Nineteen, twenty?

'Wonderful. I'll see you later on, then. Happy creating!' And he's gone. I put the phone down and dither. I have to go now, he's expecting me, the second-years are expecting me. I go across to the bathroom to put some makeup on, running my thumb and forefinger up under my lower lip to get rid of smudges. I check the contents of my handbag and pick up the car keys. Then I remember my husband will need the car to get to his game with Bill, and I rifle through pockets for bus fare instead.

It's strange, walking through the university in the daytime. It's bigger, brighter, more alive. There are people around, walking between rooms and having discussions and buried in books. I prefer it in the evenings, I'm not so out of place then. I like being unnoticed, being there when everyone else has gone away and left only traces behind, flyers on the wall, scuffmarks on the floor, intellectual indignation in the air. It reminds me of being in school after hours, that feeling that you are doing something slightly illicit.

The door to the studio is ajar. I wonder if I should knock. I push it open hesitantly and stick my head through. Light is streaming in from the windows, highlighting the dust in the air. I can only see one figure in there, with a bandana around her head and headphones in her ears. She pays me no attention whatsoever. I creep in, trying to be unobtrusive, and go to the cupboard Eamonn keeps his evening class's work in. I glance over. Still nothing from the student. She bobs her head in time with the music. As I pass her on my way to an easel—the furthest one possible—I can hear the tinny beat. It must be aggressively loud with the headphones in.

On the floor at the far end, I see the other student, on her hands and knees on what appears to be a large collage of materials. She has a paintbrush in her mouth, and I can't for the life of me figure out what she's doing but she seems very preoccupied with it. She glances up as I pass and nods at me, in a friendly way, one artist to another.

I relax. I'm just going to disappear into my own little sphere and paint my own painting. I have all the time in the world.

To my surprise, I quite like having the other girls in the room with me. It's a nice atmosphere, of relaxed, productive creativity. At one point, a heavily pierced young man comes in, kisses the girl with headphones and admires her work for a while. They have a quick, low conversation—I think they're making plans for tonight—and he leaves again. At another point, I find myself tapping my foot in time with the girl's head bobbing.

My painting is going quite well, but by around twelve-thirty I've got to the stage where I need it to be fully dried before I can do the next bit, and the forced delay bothers me. I don't like leaving it unfinished, and I start to dab and fuss and pick at the canvas even though I know I need to leave it alone and come back next week. I'm only going to make it worse.

The door opens again and it's Eamonn. I like seeing him in here, instead of imagining him in a lecture theatre. This is where he belongs, among canvas and blobs of paint, not at a lectern in front of an audience. He passes the girl with headphones—'have you had lunch yet? Make sure you do'—and stands over the girl on the floor for a moment or two—'so where are you taking this in the next stages?'—and then he comes over to me.

'Camille, my dark little horse, how is it going?' He's positively exuberant—but in an Eamonn sort of way, sedately.

'I really should give up for the day,' I say, eyeing the damage I've done in the last ten minutes with a rueful eye. 'I need it to dry before I start messing around with the spray of the water and the light.'

'You're absolutely right,' he says, taking the brush out of my hand. I look up at him; he is very close to me. I like his colouring. The grey hair suits him, his skin tone.

I sigh. 'But I want to finish it. I can see in my head exactly how it should look.'

Eamonn takes my palette away. 'Art is not about *should*, it's not about perfection. And it most certainly can't be rushed.' I make a show of looking huffy. He smiles. 'I see I'm going to have to forcibly restrain you,' he says.

'How about over a cup of coffee?'

I'm taken aback for a moment. I can't quite gauge his intentions. Is he a well-meaning teacher taking an interest in his student, or is it more than that? Am I being vain even wondering if he's keen on me? Eamonn's smile is easy, his eyes creasing.

'Well it seems I don't have a choice,' I say.

'Excellent.' He helps me tidy away my area. We go to the little café outside the student library. I feel self-conscious being the oldest one there. The boy behind the till barely looks old enough to be out of school. I order a cappuccino and as I sit down, I panic. He's going to be expecting to discuss art, I realise, of course, that's the thing we have in common. How long does it take to drink a cup of coffee? Ten minutes? I can't talk intelligently about art for that long. I cast around desperately for the names of some artists I might know something about. I'm no expert or academic, I just quite like painting in my spare time.

'So how's it going?' Eamonn says, settling himself opposite me with an Earl Grey tea. 'Enjoying my class?' I'm surprised by the question. How am I meant to answer that? Eamonn laughs. 'Don't worry, you don't have to answer. I just like to scare my students when I get them on their own.' I'm feeling awkward.

'No, no, the class is great. I like that it's not too technical, more about just actually painting.'

Eamonn nodded. 'Sometimes if there isn't a time and a setting, people don't *make* the time for things like painting. Which is a shame. If I knew there were people with your talent not using it...' He places a hand dramatically across his heart.

'Now stop that. I'm just an old woman throwing paint

around.'

'In the most artful way possible.'

I smile in spite of myself. I'm feeling a warmth deep in my chest, and I don't think it's the coffee. *Don't be silly, Camille. Pull yourself together.*

───

It was one of his favourite things to say, that he stole me away from another man. I would laugh and say it wasn't true, I didn't have anybody to be stolen from. My favourite thing to say was that for the first two months I knew him, I called him East Asian Studies. He would reply that for the first two months he knew me, he called me Cheese Biscuits.

Week Six

Emmi doesn't come to class in week six. Rosaline shrugs when people ask where she is, and it's generally assumed that she's suffering from some illness or other. I notice Rosaline checking her phone quite frequently, though of course it could be something else. A boyfriend, most likely. Her hair is split into two long plaits that drape over her shoulders and down her chest. It looks nice.

I'm sitting next to Morris, and we're using stencils. Morris sits on the very edge of his stool, one foot out to the side, the other toe close, heel propped on a wooden leg. His boots are very dirty and flecked with paint. He's a joiner/decorator, I've learnt, so it's not unwarranted, but my mother would not have allowed boots like that in the house and certainly wouldn't have allowed him to go anywhere in them. I would have guessed, seeing them, that he was a bachelor, but there is definitely a ring on his left hand.

He's talking to Niall, on his other side, about football. I stretch uncomfortably. I'm too old to be sitting on stools.

'Jo, my partner, still sheds a tear over that match,' Niall is saying, laughing. He doesn't wear a ring. Rosaline is on her phone again, holding it down by her thigh like a naughty schoolchild trying to text under the desk. I shift my stencil. The effort we put into our relationships.

In my second year—Michael was studying for his MPhil by this point—I started leaving a toothbrush and some spare clothes in Michael's room because I spent so much time there. I preferred to do my work there, lying out on the floor to write an essay or curled up on the bed doing my reading, rather than in my tiny bedroom or in the library with its undertone of rustling pages and its aroma of intellectual panic. In the evenings we went to see speakers at the Union or watched Footlights shows or stayed in, snuggled up together on his bed.

'We never see you anymore,' Chloe complained on one of the rare occasions I was back in college. 'You've completely disappeared.'

'I know, I'm sorry,' I said, throwing my room apart looking for a book I needed to return to the library. 'There's just lots going on.'

Eloise and Patricia were living in a different building that year, so I barely saw them at all. I didn't mind. Michael was all I needed. Chloe became something of a lacrosse star and spent a lot of time with the other team members, and our smiles when we passed each other became emptier and more awkward as more and more time passed since we had thought of each other as friends.

I piggy-backed on Michael's friends. They were all

Michael's age, older than me, and I felt very sophisticated being part of their group. There was a philosophy Master's student, a fourth-year Physicist, a girl studying medicine and her boyfriend, a PhD mathematician. We had spirited discussions over dinner when we ate in Hall, or sat up late into the night in the Buttery. On the weekends the boys would play football on Parker's Piece, and once we cycled into Grantchester and drank cider by the river. I was proud to be part of it, proud to be Michael's Girlfriend.

In my final year at Cambridge—the third year of our relationship—Michael lived in London. He had his 1st class degree and his MPhil, and a promising job at the Foreign Office. It wasn't ideal spending my final year on the train back and forth, but there was a certain glamour to it, spending weekends in my boyfriend's tiny bedsit, cooking meals over the single gas ring and showering together amidst giggles and intermittently freezing water in the shared bathroom. He could afford a better place, especially after a few months of working, but he was saving; he had big plans.

I felt oh so grown-up. I was at the forefront of female independence, I waved the flag of emancipation with every T-shirt of Michael's I wore—sometimes it was all I wore all weekend—I shone the torch of liberty in every cigarette I smoked out of the tiny window. I wrote my essays at his cramped kitchen table, I read my reading list on the train.

Having allowed my bridges with the girls at Girton to smoulder thin, I carried on spending most of my time in Cambridge with people I knew through Michael—the Maths PhD had moved in with a new girlfriend, a girl doing a postgraduate Law degree. They rented the ground floor of a cosy house near the train station, and were friends with the second-year undergraduates on the floor above; we shared many a boozy weekday dinner, late-night essay revision, heated ethical debate.

'I think I would enjoy studying Law,' I said causally to Michael one Sunday morning, as he brought two mugs of tea and a newspaper back to the nest of duvet we had made.

'Oh yeah?' He climbed in next to me.

I shrugged, slightly embarrassed. 'It's about constructing arguments, right? It's the same basic principle behind writing a good essay. Except it would be about actually important things, instead of things that happened centuries ago.'

Michael carefully arranged crossed legs, duvet, tea and newspaper, and leaned back against the wall. 'You do know what legal precedent is, don't you?' he said with a slight smile, blowing on his tea.

I shook my head scathingly and sipped my own. 'I don't know, I just think it would suit me. I think I'd like it. Maybe enough to make a career out of it, which is more than I can say about History. The only thing I can do with a History degree is teach History, and I can't think of anything worse.'

'There are lots of things that are worse.'

'You know what I mean. It doesn't appeal to me.'

Michael was losing interest, absorbed in his paper. 'So go for it,' he said.

I shrugged again, pulling my knees up and huddling around the warmth of my mug. 'I don't know, it was just an idea. I don't know if I can see myself as a lawyer. But I can't really see myself as anything else, either.' I watched wisps of steam drift before my eyes and melt away. 'I don't know what I'm going to do after graduation.'

Michael turned a page of the newspaper and then reached out to squeeze my knee without looking up.

'Anything you like, Millie. The world's your oyster.'

But that's the problem, I thought as the first grey blobs of rain began to speckle the window. *I don't know what I'd like.*

In the weeks before my finals, I stayed in Cambridge to concentrate on revision and to use the library, and he rang me every night, even if he was still in the office and he was just checking in to say goodnight. My last exam was on a Thursday morning, and I was getting the train the following Friday afternoon to celebrate with him in London.

The exam exhausted me. I was sure I'd spent half the time writing irrelevant nonsense for one of the questions, and I was angry with myself because, until this exam, I'd thought things were going well. I was convinced that the last three hours had pushed my entire degree down the drain, and I left the exam hall kneading my forehead and wishing everyone around me would stop going over what they had written.

Michael was waiting for me outside the building, holding a huge bunch of red roses.

My heart melted at the sight of him. His face broke into the grin I loved so well, and he lifted me off the ground and squeezed me tight to him. I buried my face into his neck and breathed him in.

'What are you doing here?' I said delightedly, when he'd put me down and kissed me soundly. The roses were slightly squashed, but I pressed my face to them anyway. They were velvet sweet.

'I had to see you, and tell you I'm proud of you, and I love you, and I'm taking you out tonight to celebrate.'

'What about work?'

'I took a couple of days off. It isn't every day my girlfriend finishes a Cambridge degree.' I kissed him again, heartily. All the stress and the worry of the past few months evaporated, and I was just a girl free to spend my time being in love.

We went out to dinner, and toasted the end of my exams with champagne. Afterwards we walked hand-in-hand through Jesus Green, along a river speckled with stars.

'So I don't want to steal the thunder away from your special night,' he said, 'but I have some news of my own.'

'Do tell.'

He raised my hand and twirled me, making my skirt fly out, then pulled me close and linked his hands behind my back. 'I've been offered a job.'

I kissed his chin. 'You have a job.'

He bit my nose. 'I've been offered a job in Beijing.'

'Oh wow! That's amazing!'

He grinned, chuffed with himself. 'I know, it is amazing. It's just a twelve-month contract to start with, but it's such a great opportunity. I'm so excited.'

'When do you start?'

'In September.' I felt my happiness falter slightly. London/Cambridge was less than ideal, but we dealt with it because it was finite, we were working towards me moving to London to join him. But England/China—surely that was beyond even us. 'Come with me,' he said, his arms tightening around my waist and his breath hot in my ear.

'What?'

'Come with me.'

'To China?'

'Yes.'

'I can't go to China.'

'Why not?'

I gaped for the words. 'Because—I—my parents don't even know that I've spent the night with you. I can't just move across the world with you.'

'Yes you can.'

I searched his eyes, looking for a reason not to go. I couldn't see one. All I found in his face was love and eagerness and honest adventure. He wanted to do this with me. I felt possibility bubble up inside me.

'OK.'

'OK?'

'OK!'

He picked me up and spun me around and our laughter bounced off the water and he kissed and kissed and kissed me.

The world was pressing down on me, squeezing me, suffocating me. Doctors, nurses, specialists, therapists, taking notes, taking measurements, monitoring, telling me what to expect and how to deal with it and how to feel about it and so many leaflets. *It's normal to feel confused or scared*, they said, or, *it's important to take care of your own wellbeing.*

I wanted space, I wanted a chance to breathe. If people would just leave me alone for a second, if I could just press pause on the world, I could process everything. But the world carried on, whether I was ready or not.

The paediatrician was a stern, older man with a grey moustache, who shook his head a lot and spoke in the manner of someone who had already given up the case as hopeless.

'There are certain things we can expect, but the extent of how this affects his development can vary greatly,' he said. 'He may have difficulties with motor development, cognitive development, speech and language; they may be severely impaired, they may not be. We really just have to wait and see.'

The midwife who came for home visits was more positive.

'Well, congratulations on your little bundle of joy!' She announced, beaming, the first time she appeared on our doorstep. The impulse to punch her flashed before my eyes, and then subsided. I stood aside to let her in. 'Now I know a lot of this must seem overwhelming and scary, but there is really no reason to despair,' she said, seated on the sofa with the bundled baby in her arms. 'Robert is a beautiful, special, individual person just like any other child, and there's no reason he can't grow up to be happy, healthy and fulfilled.' The baby squirmed, unfocused eyes roving. The midwife rose to put him back in the cot, and came to sit next to me. 'This must be so difficult for your family,' she said, dropping the cheer. She took my hand in both of hers and squeezed it. 'But I promise you, you are not alone. We're a team, and we can do this.'

I had a team, I mumbled in my head. *This was not my*

team.

She gave me the number of a support group for parents and children with disabilities.

'Nobody knows what it's like to go through what you're going through,' she said. 'But other people do know what it's like to have nobody know, and that can help too. It's good to talk about how you're feeling and how you're coping, especially in a setting where you'll be listened to, and believed, and supported.' I said nothing. 'Just promise me you won't throw that away,' she said. 'That's all I'm asking for. Keep it somewhere, just in case, someday. Can you do that for me?'

I nodded, absently, already seeing it in the rubbish bin with the other leaflets. And then, for some reason, after she'd left, I hesitated. I shoved it to the back of the cutlery drawer instead.

I did end up fishing it out again a few weeks later, when I was going mad locked inside my own brain, unable to look at the baby, unable to find the words to talk to Dad, unable to face other people out in the real world, out of—shame? Anger? Envy?

I looked at the leaflet, and then I put it away again and shut the drawer.

Rosaline passes by Allie's easel as we're stretching our legs.

'Oh wow,' she says. 'That's awesome.' Becca glances over, a little mulishly, I think. 'Seriously, Allie, you're amazing.'

Allie blushes, and flicks the ends of her headscarf around her fingers.

'You should give it a name,' says Morris.

'Oh, I don't know, I'm really bad at names, I wouldn't know where to start.' She looks at Eamonn.

'Not worth agonising over,' he says lightly. 'I remember for my first show I spent ages worrying about names and nobody gives them a second thought. Certainly doesn't make a difference as to whether somebody's going to buy or not.'

'How many shows have you had?' Allie says girlishly, breathlessly, in awe. Eamonn mysteriously appears not to hear.

'You could be a professional, Allie,' Rosaline persists, and looks to Eamonn for approval.

'Anything's possible,' he says, and it's the closest I've ever heard him come to snapping.

Later, when we're painting again, I see him circling at a greater distance than usual. He casts an eye over Allie's canvas, and his expression seems almost wistful.

I dreaded the day Robert would ask about his mother. I knew it was coming—every book, every TV show, every kid at his school had a Mummy and a Daddy. Robert had always had a dad and a sister, and knew no different—but sooner or later he was going to realise that he *was* different.

He was sitting at the table, drawing, fist clasped around the pencil, head down, tongue out. I was loading clothes into the washing machine.

'Where's my mum?' he asked me. I paused, wondering if I'd misheard, knowing I hadn't. I raised myself slowly—*when did I start to have dodgy knees?*—and went over to the table. Robert loved to draw, but his creations were mostly abstract, he was more interested in the colours than in drawing actual objects. But this time it was a scene: a house, with a chimney, front door and window, a tree and a front path, a stick man and a stick woman.

I sat down and leaned my forearms on the table. Robert dragged the yellow crayon around and around in the top corner to make the sun. I reached out and pushed his fine hair back from his forehead.

'Do I have a mum?' he asked, not looking up.

I sighed. 'You did have a mum, sweetheart,' I said, 'but she's not around anymore.'

'Does everyone have a mum?'

'Yes, everyone has a mum. Remember we've seen ladies with babies in their tummies? Everyone comes from someone's tummy, in the beginning.' He put the yellow crayon down and picked up the green for the grass. I put my hand over his to still it, and ducked my head, trying to find his eyes. 'Robbie? Do you understand what I'm saying? Your mum isn't here anymore. She—died.' I didn't know if the word would land with him. We had spoken about death before, but it was a tough concept.

He pulled his hand away and bent his head closer to the page. Grass sprouted erratically underneath the house and up towards the sky.

'Robert! Are you listening to what I'm saying? Can you look at me please?' I could hear the volume of my voice rising. I tried to move the piece of paper away, but he grabbed it and pulled and it tore, and his face crumpled and he started wailing, and it was gone, she was gone, he didn't want to know about Mum, how could he not care what happened to my beautiful mother, what he did to her...

I clapped my hands to my mouth. I hadn't said anything out loud, but my heart was thudding. Of course I didn't want to tell him what had happened, of course I didn't want him to know, didn't want to tell him he killed her. He was such a sweet, caring person, and none of this was his fault. That was what broke my heart—none of this was his fault. He didn't ask for this any more than I did.

I tried to gather him in my arms and shush him, but he had worked himself up into a rage. One fist caught the side of my head and slammed my cheekbone into the corner of the hard wooden chair back, missing my eye socket by a millimetre. Pain exploded over my face and I couldn't tell which way was up.

Dad came running down from upstairs and took Robert away to calm him down. The door slammed behind them and the sudden silence reverberated around the kitchen. I realised I was on the floor. My face throbbed. I pushed myself backwards with my feet until I was nestled in the corner of the cabinets, drew my knees up and cradled my broken face in my arms.

I don't know how long I sat there. It sounded like Robert raged himself to exhaustion. After he had been quiet for a while, I heard Dad's footsteps on the stairs again. The kitchen door handle clicked. He walked to the sink and a moment later knelt down beside me, gently raised my head and pressed a cold dishcloth to my eye. I tried not to cry, because it hurt to crumple my face.

'I just wanted to tell him about Mum,' I whispered. 'I wanted him to know who she was.'

'I know, sweetheart,' Dad said. 'I know.'

Morris is enjoying himself with the stencils. He spent a long time bent over pieces of card with a Stanley knife, and now he perches, one stencil held against the canvas, another under his arm, one between his teeth. Cardboard shavings litter the floor around his feet.

Niall is doing less well. I can see him painting very delicately around his stencil, as though afraid to get any paint on it. He's getting frustrated, and Becca, on his other side, has noticed. She looks around. Eamonn has stepped outside to take a phone call.

'I don't think stencils are my thing,' Niall says. 'This isn't going well at all.'

'Try overlapping them,' Becca says, 'it doesn't have to be geometrically perfect.'

Niall shrugs. 'I don't know, I don't think it really fits with what I'm going for...' but his voice tails away unpersuasively.

'It'll be good, look,' Becca insists. And she gets up, goes over to him, and takes his stencil and brush from him. I'm surprised at her audacity, and that Niall lets her. Why doesn't he say anything? I would have told her to get her hands off my damn painting.

I try and lean inconspicuously to one side, to see around Morris. It seems Niall has gone for an underwater-type scene, a very delicate, precise pattern. Becca moves the stencil as she paints, blurring lines, making the shapes no longer uniform. Niall opens his mouth as though to say something—*why doesn't he say something?*—but nothing comes out, and he slumps down on his stool. I glance around. We're all sharing uneasy looks—Becca has crossed a line here. I wish Eamonn would come back in.

'Hey,' Morris says, not ungently. 'Why don't you let Niall have a go.'

Becca steps away from the painting. 'See? It looks good.'

It does look good, she's right. But it doesn't look like Niall. Niall still doesn't say anything. Becca shrugs, hands him back his tools, and goes back to her seat. We're all pretending to paint, all watching Niall for a reaction. He reaches for a jar of washing water and swirls his brush around and around in it, watching the colour blossom out in pale blue clouds. He doesn't look up.

I very quickly felt comfortable around Peter. He was easy to be comfortable around. We were sitting at my kitchen table one evening, after Robert was asleep. Dad was in his study. I'd known Peter for around eighteen months and had come to rely on him. Not just for help with Robert, for me, for keeping me sane.

'So how are you?' he said, placing two mugs of tea down on the table. He added sugar to his and stirred. I sat down, exhaling heavily. It had taken a long time to cajole Robert into bed. Sometimes he would just completely withdraw into himself, and it was as though you didn't exist anymore. He wrapped himself in his own little world and he wouldn't let anyone else in.

'I'm OK. I had to go into Robbie's school yesterday,

they're worried about his progress.'

'What did they say?'

'I think they want us to put him in a special school. He was OK for the first couple of years, but now he's in primary school he's really falling behind.'

'Is there no support they can offer him?'

'Well he has his teaching assistant three afternoons a week, and he spends a day a week in the "learning centre" with other kids who have difficulties. But he's just not making the kind of progress he needs to be. We can't afford to send him to a private school. I think he's just going to have to retake Year 3.'

'How do you feel about that?'

I shrugged. 'There's not really any other option. He's not really socially aware enough to be embarrassed about it—we just have to hope the other kids don't start being mean to him.'

'That's been a problem before, hasn't it?'

I nodded, and shrugged again. 'Children can be cruel. Robbie is obviously very different.'

'And how are you?' Peter said again. I looked up. 'Aside from Robbie.'

I smiled ruefully. 'I don't really exist aside from Robbie.'

'Of course you do.' I threw him a look, trying to keep it light-hearted. His eyes were deadly serious, and—I registered with alarm—affectionate. More than friendly affection? *Say something. Diffuse the situation.* 'My sister got engaged last night,' Peter said, offhandedly. I relaxed. There was nothing to worry about. Peter was just my friend, though I couldn't for the life of me figure out why— god knows there were thousands of friends out there with less baggage than me.

'That's wonderful,' I said. 'Is everyone pleased?'

'Over the moon. Mum was quite tearful last night when she heard the news.'

'Oh, I love weddings,' I said, wondering as I said it why the words were coming out. I'd never been to a wedding. 'How exciting.'

Peter was smiling at me. 'You need a break,' he said. 'Your dad's picking up Robbie from school tomorrow, right?'

'Yes.'

'Let's go to the pictures. Just you and me. I promise, nothing with rhymes.'

I leaned back in my chair. It was so tempting. 'I'm not sure when I'll be able to get out of work,' I said.

'I'm in no rush. Come on, you need some you time, and you won't do it unless I drag you.'

I smiled. 'You're right. Sounds good.'

'Well I should be off,' he said, draining his tea and standing up. 'I'll see what's on and give you a call tomorrow.'

'Tell your sister congratulations from me,' I said, giving him a hug. I stayed there for a moment or two, resting against him. He kissed my cheek.

'Get an early night, hey?' he said, and I smiled wearily and waved as he let himself out. I looked around the kitchen. If I stayed up, the only things I had to do were washing and ironing and cleaning. With two of us working full-time and taking care of Robert, household mainte-nance was barely kept above water. And if I was going to go out the following night, I should really make something for Dad and Robbie to eat while I was gone. But I just couldn't be bothered. I was tired.

I went upstairs. Robbie was sleeping with the door open. His cheeks were flushed, but he looked peaceful. He breathed heavily through his mouth. I went into my own bedroom, took off my clothes and left them where they lay. My room was a state, and god only knew what I was going to find to wear to work tomorrow, but I ignored it all and crawled under the covers and curled up into a ball.

I walked out of the cinema, and I was in a good mood. The wind was bracing, but I let my coat flap open and shook my hair out into the breeze. I had my arm through Peter's elbow, and we were laughing about the film. I can't remember what it was we saw, I'm not even sure I was paying attention at the time—I was just leaning back in my seat with my eyes half-shut, luxuriating in having nothing to do. I was so used to feeling heavy all the time, to everything being an effort, to forcing myself to get up and get going. I tried to imagine that I was weightless.

Peter suggested we stop for something to eat, and I glanced hesitantly at my watch.

'Come on, you told your dad you'd be out tonight, he won't be expecting you.'

'I know, but if Robbie's playing up—'

'Then your dad can deal with it. Act your age, for once. You're young, go out and enjoy yourself.'

'Where shall we go?'

'Anywhere you like. My treat. You can eat all the things you aren't allowed in your house.'

I squeezed his arm. 'I am fairly hungry.'

He steered me round a corner towards the centre of

town. 'Let's go then.'

And I let myself be steered.

I remember he was telling me a story about something that happened at work once, and I was laughing my head off. Which was surprising, because he was an accountant. The waitress had cleared our plates, and he reached over and took my hand.

'You're beautiful, Camille,' he said. I was caught mid-laugh, off guard, suddenly aware that my hair must be sticking out everywhere and that I was contorting myself into a double chin. He laughed at my reaction. 'It's a compliment, my love, the correct response is "thank you".'

I brushed my hair behind my ear and dropped my eyes. 'Thank you,' I said. 'I can't remember the last time I put my glad rags on.'

'You should do it more often,' Peter said with a smile.

I put my head on one side. 'You're so nice to me,' I said softly.

'You deserve it,' Peter whispered. I shook my head. 'You do. You're so selfless. You deserve your own happiness too.'

'I'm not selfless,' I said, 'a selfless person would do it graciously. I moan about it every day.' I looked at my watch. 'Ugh, I don't want to go home. How selfish is that?'

'Don't even think about it,' Peter said, and with a flourish he ordered dessert.

A silence fell across us as he drove me home, and it wasn't like our normal, comfortable silences. There was a fizzle of electricity through it, a suspense, an awkward-ness. As he pulled up outside my house, he reached out a hand to stop me undoing my seatbelt. I looked up at him.

'I—I'm very fond of you, Camille,' he said. Was he

nervous?

'I'm fond of you too, Peter.' False brightness.

'You know what I mean. Have you ever thought about us being—more than friends?'

I smiled sadly. 'I could never do that to you,' I said. 'I care about you too much to tie you down to me and my problems.'

And I got out of the car before he could say anything else.

I was sitting cross-legged on my childhood bed. I'd been home for about two months.

I'd almost expected things to be different. I wanted something to have changed, like I had, during my nine months away. I stared up at my wallpaper, my curtains, wondering if it looked smaller, more faded, but the truth was it was all exactly as it had been. It was like I never left.

I wrote to Michael every day, like he was my journal. At the end of the week, I'd put all the letters into an envelope and send them. Michael was busy with work himself, his letters were less detailed. He'd called once or twice, and I'd shut my eyes and tried to imagine him here with me.

I heard Mum's slow, heavy footsteps down the hall. I leaned back against my headboard and closed my eyes, remembering how lightly she had moved her stockinged feet when she used to dance around the kitchen with a spatula in her hand.

I thought about ignoring the doorbell. I didn't need whoever it was dumping their problems on me too—they could just go away and leave me be. But it rang again, insistently. If it was going to be answered, it would have to be me. I heaved myself off the bed and went slowly downstairs, as though it was me carrying around that extra weight.

When I opened the front door and saw him standing there, I thought for a moment that everything was going to be OK.

I had the sudden, bizarre idea that he'd read my last letter and he'd heard in my words how much I needed him and jumped on the next flight. But that was stupid—it was Tuesday, and I'd only sent the letter on Saturday. It wouldn't even have reached China yet.

But it didn't matter why he was here, all that mattered was that he *was* here, on my doorstep, folding me into his arms and holding me exactly where I needed to be.

'What are you doing here?' I asked, after he had kissed me, and come inside, and kissed me again. I led him automatically into the kitchen and picked up the kettle.

'I had to see you.' He sat down heavily at the table. His eyes were thick with jet lag. 'I'm exhausted.' I stood behind him and stroked the hair back off his forehead. I couldn't believe he was here. 'How are your parents?'

I inhaled deeply. 'Things are OK, I suppose. Mum's very tired, she's been quite ill. I think I said in my letter, she can't work at the moment, and money's becoming a real worry. I'm looking for something full-time, but no luck so far.' I was working in a pub a couple of days a week, but it yielded a paltry contribution. The kettle clicked, and I turned to make the tea.

'Full-time?'

'Well yeah, once the baby's here, there's an extra mouth to feed—we're going to need another income.' I sat down next to him at the table. He didn't pick up his tea.

'You're not—you're not coming back?'

'To China? No, I thought you knew that. How can I?'

'Millie, this isn't your problem. It's difficult, I understand that, but it's your parents' to deal with.'

I drew back. 'How can you say that? My parents' problem is my problem. We're a family.'

'You're going to give up your life for them?'

'Oh don't be so dramatic, it's not my life. It's a few years, until Mum can work again and the baby's in school. I'm just helping out. We can get our own place nearby so I can help with childcare. Team effort.'

Michael held my gaze. 'Millie, I've been offered a permanent contract out there.'

My head jerked slightly. 'What? No, you're coming back in August. China was only supposed to be for a year. I thought you wanted to come back and do a PhD.'

'Why sit over here and study it when I can be out there living it?'

My hands fell limply to my lap. 'You're not coming back?'

He leaned forward again, trying to catch my gaze but I wouldn't look at him. 'You can come with me, you can carry on teaching, it can be like it was.'

I shook my head, and tears I hadn't noticed gathering fell from my eyelashes. 'I can't do that,' I whispered. 'They need me.'

He took my hands. 'I need you, Millie.'

I shook my head more fiercely. 'You can't ask me to do this, Michael. You can't ask me to abandon my family.'

'Millie, I love you. Don't let this be the end of us.'

A sob escaped me when I heard those words, and I put

my head on my arms and cried. 'Stay here,' I mumbled into the table, 'stay here with me.'

He put his arms over me and rested his head on my back. 'I can't. I just can't, Millie. This is my career.'

'This is my family. I have to.'

'You don't have to do this, Millie, you have a choice. They can get through this without you.'

'I can't leave them.'

'I can't turn this down.'

We sat like that for a long time.

I've had to take the bus because my husband went to a garden centre this afternoon, and for some unknown reason he wasn't back by twenty to seven when I had to leave. After class, I pick my way back across the dark campus to the bus stop. Most of the buildings are empty, but there's a buzz of light and activity around the theatre. It's not a bad performing arts centre the university has, I've been to see plays there from time to time. There's a bar next to it, and there seems to be some event on tonight. It glows orange and I can hear the thumping beat of music, overlaid by loud chatter whenever the door opens to spill a few more bodies out amongst the talkers and smokers huddled in coats, speckled by firefly cigarettes.

One of the people coming out seems in a worse state than the others, worse than somebody should be at nine forty-five in the evening. I think it's a girl, and she's stumbling away from the bar, in my vague direction. Actually, she's going to fall right into the road if she keeps going.

I hurry forwards and put my arm out as she makes it to the pavement.

'Hey, you might want to watch out there,' I say, and it's Emmi. 'Hey,' I say again, 'woah there.' I take her gently by the arm and try to stop her wobbling. 'It's Camille. From the evening class. How much have you had?' I've heard about young people drinking too much, and I've seen things on TV, but I don't like seeing this close up. She's so vulnerable. Her eyes aren't focusing behind her glasses, and I don't think she wants them to. 'Why don't we sit down here for a minute?' I guide her to a low wall and we sit down. She leans against me, and I try to breathe through my mouth. Her cheeks are red and flushed but she is cold.

'I missed class,' Emmi murmurs.

'Yes. That's OK.'

'I was sad.'

'Why were you sad?' I'm glad of the darkness. I don't have to worry about where to look or facial expressions, I can just gaze out into the black. Emmi sighs, and I wonder if she's going to fall asleep or throw up.

'It's my own fault. I took the bastard back.'

'Ah. Boys.'

'Boys!' Emmi snorts. 'Found him screwing some other twat.' She starts to cry, softly. I say nothing. We just sit. After a while, and a few minutes' snuffling, she takes a shuddering breath, and the crying has stopped. I see the edge of a tattoo on the inside of her wrist as she raises a hand to wipe her face.

'Do you ever just wonder what the point is?' Ah. The philosophical drunk. Michael used to be one of those.

'I am the wrong person to have that conversation with,

I'm afraid. Massive cynic.'

'But, like, does anything make it worth it?'

'I think it's time you went home to bed.'

'Do you feel like your life is worth it? Have you achieved anything? Would it have even mattered if you'd never existed?'

'Alright, that's enough.' I heave her off my shoulder. 'Do you know how to get home? Is there someone you can call to come and get you?' She drops her head into her hands. 'Come on, Emmi, this is pathetic. Pull yourself together. I know it feels like the worst thing in the world ever, but I promise you there are worse.' She laughs, and gets to her feet, unsteadily.

'That's not comforting.'

'I know, I'm sorry. It's hard to have perspective at your age.'

She screws her face up. 'I hate it when people say that.'

'I know that, too. Can you get home?' Her hands go to her head again. She's going to have a mother of a hangover tomorrow.

'Yeah, yeah I can. I'm sorry. God, this is embarrassing.'

I shake my head. 'Don't worry about it.'

'Do things get better?'

'They might do.' I keep my voice neutral.

She nods. 'I'm this way,' she says, and off she goes, tottering. I hope she'll be alright. There's student accommodation not far from here, I know, perhaps that's where she lives. Has to cross a road to get there, but the night air seems to be sobering her up a little.

I try not to consider Emmi's questions on the bus ride home. The window is flecked with rain, fracturing the world outside. Have I achieved anything with my life? I read the adverts along the top of the bus. Who says I have to have achieved anything?

Neither of us could bear to hold the baby at the funeral. We gave it to one of Mum's colleagues, a nurse, who stood at the end of our row and jiggled the bundle ineffectually for most of the service.

I stood very straight as the coffin went past. I tried to imagine a rod running from the floor up through my spine and anchored to the ceiling. I thought my heart had broken when Michael went back to China, when I had watched him walk down my front path and willed him to turn around, willed myself to call out to him, to stop him. I said nothing, and he didn't look back.

I had thought that was the worst pain I could have experienced, but watching them bury my mother I felt myself shatter into pieces so jagged I knew they would never fit together again.

No Class

Eammon is away this week, at a conference in Glasgow.

'It works out quite well,' he'd said, 'it'll be like a little half-term break, and when we come back we can really get cracking on those projects. The course will run for an extra week at the end, if I hadn't mentioned,' he added. 'I'm not swindling you out of a week's worth of me.' A roguish grin.

I meet Allie for coffee again. She's breathy and distracted and I can see some sort of excitement beneath the surface. But I wait for her to bring it up, whatever it is. I stir my coffee slowly and deliberately and make conversation about a television show we both watch. Eventually, she can't keep it in any longer.

'Camille, I've just got to tell someone,' she says, leaning forward conspiratorially over the table. I raise my eyebrows as though I had no idea she had something to tell me.

'What is it?'

'Eamonn kissed me,' she whispers, and then she leans back and claps her hands over her mouth as though she can trap the words back in there.

My first reaction is unexpected. It's something like jealousy.

But that's absurd; Eamonn gives the same warm smile to everyone in the class. It would have been wildly misguided of me to think he had a special fondness for me. And Allie is so much more talented than me, any fool can see that. Her art spills out of her and it's good, it's really good. It isn't faltering and awkward and amateur like the rest of ours. Like mine. She's the right age for him, too, and she's pretty—why wouldn't he go for her?

I realise I've been silent a beat too long.

'Er,' I say, setting down my cup. It clinks a little too loudly on the saucer. 'What about your husband?' And then I worry I've misstepped.

Allie splays her fingers slightly and speaks through them. 'I know, I know,' she says, shaking her head. 'I'm a horrible person.' She lowers her hands and looks at me imploringly. 'But he's so talented and sensitive and amazing and he made me feel special and—I just went with it. It's so unlike me!'

I feel like I'm dealing with a giddy teenager. 'How did this happen?'

Allie rearranges things on the table, the salt and pepper, the cups, her teapot. 'Oh, I don't know. I've been spending a lot of time in the studio, working on my paintings. I mean, there was no reason not to, Jonathan's out at work all day and I just get bored in the house all by myself. And often Eamonn was there as well, and we—we talked a lot. We have a lot in common.' Is she starting to blush? 'Then one night he asked me out for a drink afterwards, and I couldn't see a reason not to. People go for drinks with their friends all the time. And we had a little too much wine, and he was walking me to the bus stop, and—he kissed me.'

I find myself completely incapable of having this conversation. What am I meant to say? 'Did you, um, kiss him back?' She nods, her eyes wide like a child's. I realise I'm not jealous, I'm envious—she's in the middle of that rush, that excitement, that heady thrill. It's a cliché to have an affair with your art teacher, but it's also romantic, alluring, flattering. I haven't felt anything like that in so long.

'And then I just ran onto the bus and went home, and I didn't even say anything! Oh, I'm so embarrassed.'

'When was this?'

'Last Friday.'

I cast around some more. 'That's it, I'm all out of questions. I don't know what to say. Isn't he married?' I'm sure I remember a ring on those broad fingers.

'Separated,' Allie says, delicately defensive.

'Are you going to tell Jonathan?'

'Of course not. Should I? I can't.'

'Are you going to... see Eamonn again? Outside of class?'

'Oh Camille, I've no idea.' The euphoria seems to be fading; worry is seeping in. She looks at me wide-eyed. 'What am I going to do?'

When the baby was about six weeks old, I found Dad at the kitchen table, crying. And that broke me all over again.

The pram was by the back door, emitting soft snuffling

sounds. Dad was defeated, back slumped, face crumpled, hands on the kitchen table in front of him. He didn't look up when I came in. I stopped in the doorway, taken aback, unsure what to do. Our conversations for the last six weeks had been perfunctory, functional. I did what needed to be done and retreated to sit on the floor by my bed and reread Michael's letters to me.

'You must hate me so much,' Dad said, then covered his face with his hands and sobbed. My insides shattered. Tears sprang from nowhere, filled my throat and burst from my eyes.

I sat next to him, put my head on his shoulder and my arms around him.

'I don't hate you,' I whispered, 'I could never hate you. I'm so sorry.'

'*I'm* sorry,' Dad said, sniffing and wiping his face. 'I don't know what I'm doing, Cam, I really don't. I'm so lost without her. I was on my way down one road, and I've ended up in a completely different place I never meant to come to. And I've dragged you with me.' He sat up straighter and turned to face me. 'I'm so sorry, Camille. This isn't your burden to bear. I shouldn't be putting this on you. You should go back to China.'

I was already shaking my head.

'It's not your burden, either,' I said. 'Neither of us asked for this. Hell, *Robert* didn't ask for this.' I took a deep breath. 'You're my dad, and I love you, and we're in this together.'

'You have your whole life ahead of you, Cam.'

'China was only ever meant to be for a year. I don't want to be teaching English forever. I can still finish my Law application, maybe in a couple of years.' I took a deep, shaking breath. 'I wish things had been different, I wish— if we had to do this—I wish we could have done it differently.' *I wish Michael had chosen me over China.* For the first time, there were words to the roaring pain in my head. *I wish he had loved me enough to do this with me, to stay with me.* 'But family comes first.' My voice wobbled dangerously again but I forced myself to keep going. 'Family comes first, and Michael and China and everything else can bloody well get in line behind, because... because I'm here, with you, and we do this together, and that's bloody that.'

I had thought about going back to China. I had thought about packing a bag and leaving in the night. I had wondered if he would apologise if I turned up on his doorstep. If I would be able to forgive him.

'Like it or lump it,' Dad whispered, reaching for my hand. It's what Mum used to say when I was being petulant.

'Like it or lump it.' I squeezed his hand.

The baby stirred in his pram, and then started to wail.

'Yes, very good,' I said thickly. 'We'll all just have a good old Addison family cry.'

'Do you have any ideas for your project yet?' I ask Allie.

'Actually yes. There's an idea I've been wanting to do something with. I think I might have a play with that.'

'What is it?'

'Oh, just a little idea of mine,' she replies mysteriously. 'What about you?'

'Absolutely not a clue.'

She smiles.

'Don't worry, something will come to you.'

I did end up going to the support group, when Robert started school. The group held parents-only meetings on a Wednesday evening in a Methodist church, and Sunday afternoon play sessions for parents and kids in the sports hall of a local comprehensive.

I didn't really enjoy meeting other parents of disabled kids, who often fell into one of two categories. There were the anxious analysers, who explained every detail of every development, what it could mean, what steps they were taking; and there were the positive deniers, who insisted their child's autism or cerebral palsy was a gift, and that they wouldn't change it even if they could.

It made me angry, at first. 'Who wouldn't choose to give their child a normal, healthy life if they could?' I said to Dad. 'Why would you make life more difficult if it doesn't need to be?'

But we agreed that it was important for Robert to socialise, and to meet other children like him. He wouldn't really speak a lot, but he would quite happily play with other children, if they let him.

When Robbie was nine, a new family appeared at the support group, a mother about my age and her young daughter. The mother appeared in the doorway and paused shyly. The daughter, dressed in jeans, a purple top, and matching purple bobbles on her two plaits, showed no such timidity. She strode into the hall, looked about with her hands on her hips, and came up to me.

'My name is Sarah,' she announced. 'My favourite colour is purple, and I think bread is better than toast.'

I gave this some thought. 'I like purple too, and it looks good on you. But don't you think toast has a bit more... structural integrity? You can hold it in one hand while you read the newspaper and it doesn't fall apart.'

Sarah frowned at me severely. 'Use both hands,' she said. 'Bread is yummier not toasted.'

'Well, you know Sarah, it's really important to know what you like and what you don't like. So, I applaud you for having such self-awareness. People spend their whole lives looking for clarity like that.'

She seemed satisfied with that, and stuck her hand out for me to shake.

Sarah had Down Syndrome. I recognised the wide-spaced eyes, the broad forehead, the shape of her mouth. She spoke thickly—it wasn't the clearest enunciation, but it was fluent. I was impressed, and a little sad.

'That's my brother, Robbie, over there,' I said, pointing. 'He'd love to make friends with you.' After she had scampered off, her mother approached me.

'Sorry,' she said sheepishly. 'She can be a bit forthright.'

'Not at all.' I shook my head. 'She's so articulate. How old is she?'

'Six,' the mother said. 'I'm Amy, by the way.'

'Camille,' I said, shaking her hand too. 'Robbie—' I pointed again, 'is nine and almost non-verbal. I mean, he can speak, but he doesn't do complex sentences.'

'That must be difficult,' Amy said.

'It's difficult for him, I think. He understands a lot and feels a lot but can't express himself, which is frustrating.'

Amy nodded sympathetically. Sarah was the third of four children, she told me. Her husband was a banker, which brought in good money but kept him away for long hours. Amy was a stay-at-home mum. I marvelled inwardly. Imagine bringing up Robbie and three other children at the same time. You may as well ask me to fly to the moon for all the feasibility I saw in it. A wave of inadequacy hit me. How could I find it so hard, when this tiny woman, with her slim frame and elfin haircut, single-handedly managed four times as much?

I lifted my Styrofoam teacup to my lips and watched the children over its rim. Sarah was small for her age, but if you didn't see her face, she could have been any young child with a speech impediment. She was bright, assertive, intelligent. I wondered if growing up with siblings had helped her, and then I turned back to Amy and asked if she'd just moved to the area, because I knew the comparison game was neither useful nor helpful.

Later I found out that Amy had a full-time nanny. Two adults to focus entirely on raising the kids. That made me feel better, slightly.

Girton organised a reunion on the tenth anniversary of matriculation. I had been receiving alumni newsletters and college magazines for all of those ten years, glossy pages and sleek requests for donations that went straight into the bin, unopened. I should have called someone to have my name taken off the mailing list, but I never got around to it.

The invitation came in a greetings card envelope, which I opened out of curiosity. Cream embossed lettering, and the Girton crest. I ran my finger down the crisp edge of the card. Ten years since I had first arrived there. Where had the time gone? I remembered that first day. I hadn't been nervous in the slightest, just excited, eager to dive in. I remembered my first-year bedroom, and meeting Chloe as she moved in next door. I hadn't thought about Chloe in a long time. I balanced the card on its corner, and spun it in circles. What was she doing now? Where did she live? What did she look like?

Of course I couldn't go to the reunion. I wasn't in touch with anyone I had spent time with at university, let alone the girls from my college. When I graduated, and we were all lining up ready to file into the Senate House in our gowns and hoods, and everyone was chattering in excited whispers, I realised that the people around me were strangers to me. Anna, two rows behind me, smiled politely and carried on her conversation. Some people looked at me like they hadn't ever seen me before. At the time, I didn't care. When I stepped forward to receive my degree, Michael was standing there next to my parents, beaming at me. I held my head high.

If I turned up, ten years later, I suspected nobody would even know who I was. *So good to see you again,* they'd say effusively, *what are you up to these days?* And then, as soon as I was out of earshot, they would turn to each other and whisper, *do you remember a Camille Addison? Was she even in our year?* And how would I answer that question—what am I up to these days? I'm single and living with my father, doing an unfulfilling job and raising my disabled half-brother?

I tossed the invitation onto the recycling pile. I didn't need to be reminded that everybody else had been leading successful and exciting lives. I didn't need to be reminded that I was nothing worth remembering.

We drive out to the National Park to give the dog a run-around. It's not a particularly cold day but the wind is up, ruffling her coat and lolling tongue, whipping my hair and teasing the colour out in my nose and cheeks. I keep my hands firmly in my pocket and bow my head slightly.

The dog is loving it. She runs off like a mad thing the moment we open the car door, and for a while she runs away from us and back, away from us and back, capering around like the world is going to end. Eventually she settles down, trotting along the path in front of us, sniffing points of interest and greeting other dogs with joyous glee.

My husband and I exchange terse nods with fellow walkers, the odd *afternoon*. We don't say much as we climb hills, trudge fields, open gates. The cold air feels good in my lungs. We stop for a pint at a pub nestled into a hillside, sitting outside and overlooking the valley. The sun isn't out but there's a brightness to the air. The scene before us doesn't look pretty, exactly, but rugged; the greens are fading and struggling against the bare browns, but it doesn't look dead. Ruggedly good-looking, I decide. And I find I want a sketchbook, some paints.

My husband comes out, sets a cider down in front of me and settles himself with his beer and a packet of pork scratchings.

'They had those wasabi peas you like,' he says. 'I didn't know if you wanted any.' I shake my head. He offers me his packet and I refuse again, lifting the bottle to my lips. 'Lovely out here, isn't it.'

It's not that high a hill or steep a valley, but it does for a moment feel as though we've been lifted out for a moment, out of our lives, away from things. The dog returns from the water bowl by the door and leans her head on my leg. *Away from what?* I think, dropping my eyes to the water rings on the wooden table.

'I'm going to buy some paints,' I say. 'It's silly spending so much on an art course and not even being able to paint at home.'

'That's a lovely idea,' he says mildly.

'I could set myself up in a corner of the dining room, maybe.'

He smiles at me. The dog pants gently. There isn't a bin outside, so when we leave, we leave behind water rings, and an empty packet of pork scratchings folded neatly into a bottle neck.

We were in the living room. An elegantly-coiffed news-reader was on the television, but I couldn't hear her over the noise of Robert banging wooden blocks on the coffee table. At two years and three months old, he could pull himself up to standing using its sturdy legs, and was delighted to be able to reach a new surface to acquaint his blocks with. I found myself smiling indulgently. I was darning tights, and didn't really mind the noise. I didn't like to watch the news anyway, didn't like to be confronted with the fact that there was a vast world beyond my little universe, countless people and immeasurable suffering, on a scale my brain could not engage with. The run in my tights, that was a problem I could address.

The red wooden block slipped from Robert's chubby fingers exactly as he drew his arm back for another bang. He brought his arm down anyway, surprise writ large over his face at the empty palm that arrived at the table. His brow furrowed and he squinted at the problem sideways, as he always did when puzzling something out. Even his breathing became heavy under the weight of trying to understand.

It was hard not to feel sorry for him. Everything was so much harder for him, from moving to thinking—and always would be. He would always have to work harder than everyone else. I wondered to what extent he would be able to recognise that, to what extent he would be able to see the unfairness of his situation and chafe at it. As I did mine.

He was behind other children his age, but he was also smaller than them. If you didn't know how old he was, if you didn't look too closely at how his eyes seemed too small and deep-set, at how his broad forehead looked outsized for his plump neck, he could almost be any normal kid. He had thin blond hair and tiny fingernails. He cried when something was wrong and laughed joyfully when he was happy. He was curious, watching everything, wanting to touch everything and put everything in his mouth. Just like any baby. I almost wished he could stay this age forever, and not have to grow up and watch everyone else outstrip him.

He was eyeing the red block now, lying innocently on the carpet a few feet away. His hand opened and closed a few times on empty air. Then, with his customary grim resolve, he raised one leg shakily and took a step away from the coffee table. I half-rose off the sofa, reflexively, ready to catch him if he fell. He wobbled, but stayed firm. A second step, and a third, and he was standing by the block. He thudded back down to his padded bottom and scooped up his treasure in both hands, holding it up for me to see, unmistakable triumph on his face.

I laughed delightedly, grabbing him up and swinging him through the air.

'Clever boy!' I said to him, kissing the top of his feathery head. 'Robbie, you walked! That's amazing!' We spun together in the middle of the carpet, and Robert clapped his hand with his block. 'Wait till we tell Dad,' I told him. 'He's going to be so proud of you.' I kissed him again and squeezed him to me. 'So, so proud of you.'

I thought about Michael all the time. I still do, sometimes. I wonder where he is, and what he's doing, and if he's happy. I think about our three years together, and I wonder what could have been. If I had gone back to China with him, would we still be together now? Where would I be, what would I be doing, would I be happy?

For the first few months, I wallowed. I cried in my room, I gazed listlessly for hours, I wrote him letters that I never sent. But then the baby was born and Mum was gone and there was no time for self-indulgence. So I put it away and let it rest heavily somewhere deep inside where it wouldn't get in the way. And I got used to it. That's how things were: this was my life now. Lonely was who I was.

I didn't want to think about the fact that I had never wanted to live in China long-term anyway. The fact that after the first two weeks I was bored of noodles, and buying bottled water, and how the vegetables tasted funny. After a few months, I had to admit that I disliked the smog and the traffic and the incessant shouting of rickshaws and taxi drivers and street sellers. I disliked being head and shoulders above everybody else, disliked the stark contrast between Michael's slick city life and the poverty at our feet. I disliked how I struggled with Mandarin, and I missed feeling at home. China was always foreign. I loved my work and my students, and I loved Michael and living with him and exploring with him, and spending Christmas with him and his cousin in Australia (where finally I was a reasonable height again). I loved being independent and I loved the idea of living abroad. It was fine for the moment. I just never wanted it to be permanent. Michael taking that contract was always going to have caused problems.

But I didn't think about that. It was easier for me to be aggrieved, to say this is why we're no longer together, this pregnancy and this baby, and to rage against that.

God, was it lonely. Even when I put missing Michael to the back of my mind, I missed being loved. I missed being told I was beautiful. Flirting was not something that happened, not since Robert came along. I didn't have time for hair curlers and lipstick, barely took any care over the way I dressed. I missed the butterflies of going on a date, I missed the buzz of excitement and pride walking down the road on a boy's arm and knowing that I was his girl, that this was my man. I missed the security of coming home to the same person every day, waking up next to the same person every day, having somebody to tell everything to and to kiss goodbye at night. I hated myself for it because I shouldn't need another person to be happy, but I did. I missed having someone to take care of—and Robbie didn't count because he couldn't appreciate it the way an adult could. He couldn't take care of me in return.

So when Peter confessed his feelings for me in the car that night, there was a part of me that really, really wanted to say yes. I wanted to be held again, loved again. But I didn't have the time for a relationship, nor did I want to burden anyone else with having to take care of a disabled child. It was kinder to say no.

And there was also the fact that, as much as I hated to admit it, as much as I wanted to feel the same way about him, I just didn't.

Week Seven

Allie offers to give me a lift to class.

'That doesn't make much sense,' I say to her over the phone. 'You live in completely the opposite direction from me. It will make your journey twice as long.'

'Please, Camille, I really don't want to turn up on my own.' She lowers her voice, and I wonder if her husband has come in. 'What if I get there first? What do I say to him?'

'Allie, you're acting like a teenager.'

'I know, I know. It will give us a chance to catch up,' she says brightly.

'It's been a week. I haven't done anything to catch you up on. I could meet you there, outside.'

'Please?'

'It's your car,' I say, giving in, and I tell her my address.

I realise fairly quickly that she needs someone else in the car to convince her to go to class. She keeps dithering and not wanting to go and threatening to turn around. My patience runs short.

'Allie, you can do whatever you like with your evening, but please drop me at the university first. I do want to go.' It's like dealing with a spooked horse. I keep my voice firm and steady and she does what I tell her.

'Oh, Camille, I can't go in there,' she says when she's parked. She switches the car off and wrings her hands.

'So don't.' I reach for my handbag and place it on my lap.

'But I want to.'

'Alberta. Stop getting into such a state. Go into that room, and paint whatever it is you're going to paint, and ignore Eamonn if you have to. Don't say a word to him. Or talk to him, as you normally would, and pretend it never happened. It was one silly kiss, and you're both adults.'

'That's not really the problem,' she says. 'I'm just worried that if I see him again... I won't be able to stop myself.'

Oh for heaven's sake. I take off my seatbelt and open the car door. 'Well you're not going to ravish him in the middle of the studio, not while I'm there,' I say briskly. 'Control yourself.' And I walk off towards the arts centre. After a moment, Allie follows me. I knew she would. It was the same with Robbie when he was stubborn.

Eamonn is checking his emails when we arrive. He smiles innocuously at us as we take our places and get settled, not really paying attention. Morris is already there, and greets us. Niall arrives, followed by Becca. Rosaline and Emmi are last.

I make polite small-talk with Morris, asking after his children. I keep half an eye on Allie. She is fussing around her workstation, getting brushes of different sizes and rummaging through her bag and doing anything she can so she doesn't have to look at Eamonn. Eamonn, as far as I am aware, is completely oblivious, not even glancing in her direction.

After a few minutes, he shuts his laptop and claps his hands together.

'Right!' he says. 'Sorry about that. Welcome back. I hope we all had a good two weeks. From now until forever we're going to be working on your projects, and you've pretty much got full rein. I have given each of you a canvas, and I want you to create a masterpiece. You can use any subject, any medium you can put onto canvas, do anything you like, but I want you to convey the idea of a *narrative*, of a *progression*. I want you to tell a *story*. At the end of the six weeks, we're going to put on a little showcase to share with each other what we've done. Now, I will be here to help, offer advice and constructive criticism, but I really want you to take control of this, I'm very much going to be taking a back seat.' We are all throwing furtive glances at each other to see who is looking confident, secretive, panicked. 'I've put some of all the materials we've used so far out on this table, you can help yourselves. Obviously if everyone wants to use the same thing, there's more of everything in the cupboard.' He spreads his hands. 'Begin.'

I slowly make my way to the paint table, trying to gauge everyone else's position and ignore the fact that I have no idea what to do. Allie is grabbing armfuls of oils; Becca is going for acrylics. Rosaline and Emmi are conferring.

'No ideas?' Eamonn says, behind me.

I make a gesture of surrender. 'You got me. Not a single one.'

'Well, why don't we think about the idea of narrative.

What does that mean to you?'

'A story?'

'It could be.'

'Something changing over time?' Niall suggests.

'Good. Now how can we start to think about representing that in art?'

Morris is listening too. 'Well there's a fundamental tension between the static nature of a picture,' he says, drawing a rectangle in the air with his hands, 'and the very concept of narrative or change. Maybe that could be exploited in some way.'

'Good.' I'm not finding this conversation helpful, and I think Eamonn can tell. 'Camille?'

I shrug. 'I get the whole spiel about narrative and concepts and what-have-you, but it doesn't really help me think of anything I can actually start to get down on canvas.'

Eamonn nods. 'You're a pragmatist, Camille. You want to get down to the nitty-gritty, the practical.' His tone is getting more mystical even as he's saying it.

I grab a couple of pencils in desperation. 'On that note,' I say, and walk firmly back to my easel. I stare at the white space in front of me. *What can I fill you with?*

Sarah became a permanent fixture in our lives. Robbie was infatuated with her, and she happily took him along on her adventures. She understood him, his facial expressions and gestures, his noises, his body language—somehow she always managed to hear him, even when he couldn't find the words to say. Eavesdropping on them playing together was hearing one half of a very much two-way conversation, a kind of connection I hadn't thought Robbie would be able to find with someone else. The relief it gave me made me quite emotional.

It was useful for us, too, to have an extra resource in the form of Amy, Sarah's mum. I was wary of imposing too much on her, but she seemed happy to pick Robbie up from school every now and then, to have him over to play. A warmth swelled in me when I saw the five of them together—Robbie, Sarah, her three siblings. They didn't treat Robbie any differently from anyone else. He fit in.

'I think it's really giving him some confidence,' I told Peter one Saturday afternoon. 'He loves to be sociable and join in, but he's shy.' Peter sipped his tea.

'Of course he is,' he said. 'He's just like any other kid.'

I raised my eyebrows. 'He's not,' I said flatly. 'And he never will be. Let's not delude ourselves.'

Peter frowned slightly. 'I think he's more *like* other children than not like them. He's curious, he's affectionate, he seeks connection.' At the table next to us was a raucous crowd of teenaged girls, looking impossibly young with braces and ponytails and acne, and yet at the same time, old. Adults, in miniature. Softer hearts, wider eyes, but adults-to-be. I shifted in my seat, uncrossing and recrossing my legs. There was no point ruminating on what would never be.

'Yes, he's *human*,' I said, trying to stop irritability rising in my voice. 'Of course he is, of course all of those basic human feelings are the same. But he is different, and his life will be different, and it will be more difficult for him. Those parents that say they wouldn't fix their children's chromosomes even if they could—that's blind, and misguided, and cruel.' My voice was louder than I intended, and Peter raised his hands in surrender. 'I'm sorry,' I said. 'I love Robbie, but if I could make his life easier for him, if I could make him like everyone else, I would, in a heartbeat. *Because* I love him, and he deserves happiness as much as anybody else. It's not fair that everything's harder for him.'

'I think you don't give him enough credit,' Peter said mildly. 'Robbie *is* happy. I don't think he thinks his life is difficult.'

'Well, we'll never know what he thinks about it,' I said. 'But you can't disagree that his life opportunities are limited.'

'He's not going to win a Nobel Prize, but so what?' Peter finished his tea and poured the leftover milk from the little jug into his mug, and drank that down too. 'I think you need to rethink your idea of success, Camille.'

To my surprise, Robbie started to make friends at school. He had just turned eleven, and was in a class with eight- and nine-year-olds, but it was working. Robbie was small for his age anyway. He was a very affectionate child, when you drew him out of his shell. He wasn't outgoing, wouldn't initiate a conversation. And he could tell, when people avoided him, or stared at him, or whispered about him, about how his eyes were far apart and gave the impression he was always looking sideways, how his tongue seemed too big for his mouth.

But sometimes kids surprise you. And this class—the third time Robbie had done Year 3—seemed to take to him.

They played with him in the playground. They let him work with them in group projects. Finally, the school let him move up through the years with everyone else. I'd never seen him so happy. All of a sudden he loved to put on his school uniform, and he'd let himself be taken to school with no fuss at all. He talked more at home, instead of sitting on his own. He was more cooperative, and threw fewer tantrums. Tensions hadn't been this low at home for a very long time; even Dad was more relaxed.

In February, Robbie was invited, for the first time, to a birthday party. Everyone in the class was going. He came out of school waving the invitation at me, and as soon as we got home he stuck it in pride of place on the fridge.

I felt a surge of something almost maternal. Robbie had friends, Robbie was happy, Robbie was doing well. And I would most likely have an easier evening with him in such a good mood.

I would still have to go with him to the party. I couldn't drop him off and leave like the other parents—like *the* parents, I wasn't a parent—just in case something happened, and something was more likely to happen if I wasn't there, if he was surrounded by strangers. I'd have take some food for him too—we had to be careful of his weight, and he was still wheat-free. It wasn't fair to ask the hosts to prepare a whole extra selection when they had enough to worry about catering for thirty children.

It was an exhausting day. For me, at least. I was more nervous than I thought I'd be, tightly wound all day in case something went wrong and I had to spring into action.

Robbie was bouncing around and singing loudly. I tried vainly to get him to calm down.

'Robbie,' I said, crouching down to his level, 'Robbie,

look at Cam for a second.' I grasped his arm to stop him jumping. He looked at me, a smile on his face, and I stroked his hair tenderly. 'Robbie, I need you to calm down for me. Can you do that?' I kept my voice and my face calm and composed, modelling for him.

'Excited, excited!' he shouted, clapping his hands. I took both of his arms and tried to hold them at his sides.

'I know you're excited, sweetheart, but we have to be quieter. Remember what we've been working on with Steph?' His behavioural therapist. 'We have to be nice and calm and quiet. Now, why don't we finish getting dressed, and then we can sit in the quiet zone for five minutes? The party's not for a few hours.'

'But the present, I give a present.'

'I've got the present, sweetie, it's all wrapped and downstairs on the hall table, and the card too. Remember, we wrapped it yesterday and put a lovely bow on it. Do you want to wear your special red top?' He nodded. I helped him put it on, trying to think of ways I could keep him busy until we left.

At least once we arrived, noise wasn't a problem. All the kids were squealing and running around. Robbie loved it. He couldn't get the hang of musical statues—I don't think he could hear the music properly, he just danced anyway, and didn't notice when the music was switched off—but he played *pass the parcel* beautifully. I hovered anxiously in the background and I think I got in the way of the host parents but I couldn't relax. There was a small kerfuffle over the food—he wanted to have the same sandwiches and cakes as all the other children, but with a paper plate and some swift icing-transference and the promise of ice cream I got him to eat his own food. He was an angel through the present-opening—in fact it was one of the other children who caused a fuss because she got jealous of the present she'd given and wanted to keep it for herself—and then to round it off there was a puppet show, and all he had to do was sit and laugh and clap, and I breathed a sigh of relief because it was almost over. One or two other parents had started to arrive in readiness for collection.

I went through to the kitchen, grabbed a few errant chocolate biscuits and ate them one after the other, leaning on the counter. I should have gone back out and tried to socialise with the parents, I knew. Everyone kept telling me it was important for me to make friends as well as Robbie, and if anything, I needed the parents on my side in case something were to happen at school. But I'd been *on* all day, I really didn't feel capable of being around people anymore. The bigger Robbie got, the more physically demanding it was to control him, and the more it exhausted me trying to do everything at his pace.

I thought I'd feel relaxed once the party was over and we'd made it through to the other side, but it didn't feel like relief. It felt like everything that had been tensed and poised in my muscles all day was being released into my bloodstream in an acid rush, and I could feel myself sinking into a bad mood.

Party bags were passed out and carefully choreographed *thank you for my lovely present*s and *thank you for having me*s all round, and finally, finally, I managed to get a hand on Robbie's shoulder and steer him back to the car.

'Did you have a good time?' I asked as we drove away. He pressed his face up to the window and waved vigorously until we had turned the corner.

'Yes,' he said decisively, and reached round to the backseat for his party bag. I tried to snatch it out of his hand.

'Not now, Robbie, you've had enough sugar. We'll save this for later, OK?'

'No, now!' he said, scrabbling for it. It was difficult to hold it out of his reach in a car.

'We'll go home and open it with Dad, and it will be a nice surprise to see what you've got. Then you can have the cake after dinner.' Robbie folded his arms, but he stopped reaching for the bag. I reached down and slipped it into my handbag.

'Did you like the puppets?' I asked, and I saw that Robbie wasn't really annoyed, he couldn't even keep a scowl on his face. He broke into his usual smile and started telling me about the puppet show, which eventually descended into him re-enacting it, loudly, using just his hands. 'That's nice,' I said, and longed for quiet.

At home, he got to launch into recounting the party all over again for Dad's benefit, and I smiled weakly at him and diverted myself into the kitchen. I could feel a headache coming on.

Dad came in.

'He's wanting his party bag,' he said. I waved vaguely at my bag, dumped on the kitchen table. 'Went well, then?'

I nodded. 'It was fine. He had a blast.'

'That's great. Going to be tricky to settle him down for bed. I was thinking we could—'

'Dad, I'm exhausted,' I interrupted. 'I need to not be around Robbie for a while, or my head's going to explode.'

'I thought you said it went well.'

'It did, but it's still stressful. Look, he's tired too, put the TV on and he'll calm down, and then you can put him to bed. Please just let me have a few hours for myself.'

'OK, sweetheart,' he said, putting one arm around me and kissing my cheek. 'Go out and unwind. Try and enjoy yourself.'

I drove over to Peter's and collapsed onto his sofa. He conjured up two glasses of wine.

'How did it go today?'

'I don't even want to talk about it. I mean, it was fine, but I need to have some Robbie-free time right now.'

'Good for you. I'll drink to that.'

We clinked glasses.

'What do normal people our age talk about?' I said, draining half my glass in one go.

'Oh, you know, sex, drugs and rock'n'roll. Live the high life, baby.'

I half-groaned, half-laughed. 'I'm in my thirties. When did that happen? I'm so old.'

'It just sneaks up on you like that. I'm even older, you know. I'm half-way to forty.'

'That's disgusting,' I said, and sighed. 'Thirty-two years old and what have I achieved? Boring office job and practically a mother.'

'What did you want to achieve?'

'I want a dog,' I said, starting on my second glass of wine. 'I always wanted to grow up and get a dog.'

'Why don't you?'

'Robbie's afraid of them. And there's no time to walk it.'

'What kind of dog would you get?'

I dropped my head back onto the back of the sofa. 'A

chocolate Labrador. Or a Collie.'

'I think I'm more of a cat person, myself.'

I threw a cushion at him. 'Blasphemy.'

After a while, I lost count of the glasses of wine. I think we moved on to another bottle but I might just have been seeing double. The wine sloshed around my stomach, unimpeded by anything except those chocolate biscuits. I drank to soften the world, to cushion myself against it, to remove myself from it. I drank until I was happy and silly and leaning against Peter, who had his arm around me.

'You're so nice to me,' I said.

Peter giggled. 'You've said that before.'

I looked up at him, still sprawled against him, my eyes unfocused. 'You are nice to me,' I insisted. 'You're so lovely.' I hiccupped. 'I think I'm too drunk to drive home.'

He kissed me.

He kissed me and I kissed him back. I leant forward to put my empty wine glass on the coffee table and we sank down onto the sofa. I pulled him to me and I kissed him like I was drowning and he was my oxygen.

He kissed me back just as passionately, running his hands through my hair and down my back and over my waist. I wanted them to keep going, wanted to remember what it felt like to be touched and to be held and to be alive. It didn't occur to me that this was *Peter*, that I should be feeling awkward and embarrassed, that I shouldn't be clutching him to me like this, that it shouldn't be his hands pressing into the soft bare skin under my t-shirt. I wanted them to be there, I wanted to feel something again, after so long numbing myself. But as I reached for the button on his jeans, he pulled away.

'Camille,' he said. He gently took my hands away. 'You're drunk.'

'And?'

'And this isn't how I want this to happen.'

'What about what I want?'

'This isn't what you want either.'

I propped myself up on my elbow. 'Don't tell me what I—' The room suddenly lurched. I must have turned green, because Peter leapt from the sofa, grabbed the bin from beside the fireplace, and stuffed it into my hands. I stared into it for a few minutes, wondering if I should wretch, but nothing came.

'Let's just leave this here,' Peter said, placing it next to the sofa, 'and you can sleep it off.' He pushed a cushion under my head and pulled a rug over me. I lay down, suddenly exhausted.

'Really sexy, huh,' I mumbled. The room was spinning slightly, but I didn't have the energy to open my eyes. I suddenly felt like the side of my head was glued to the sofa. Peter smoothed my hair off my face and kissed my forehead.

'You are to me,' he whispered, and retreated. I heard the click of the light switch and the soft whoosh and thud of the door closing. I felt the strong need to protest, to say something, but before I knew it the spinning darkness had pressed down in on me and sleep had dragged me into its depths.

'You know you asked us, in the first class, what the function of art was?' I say to Eamonn. 'What do you think the answer is?'

'Oh, I have no idea,' he says, looking shocked at the notion that he would know. 'I wouldn't dream of presuming to have the answer. I just like hearing what everyone else thinks.'

I woke up with a horrible taste in my mouth. The side of my face was squashed into the pillow and my eyes felt gummy. I opened them slowly, wincing at the light coming in. I considered the awkward position of my body and slowly tried to work out where I was. A sofa, certainly. My arm was stuck down between the cushions. Not my sofa. That wasn't my living room wall in front of me, so pale and clean. I flicked my eyes around. Coffee table. Empty wine glasses.

I shut my eyes again and pressed my face into the pillow, groaning inwardly. Peter's sofa. Peter's wine. Peter's kiss.

I tried to burrow my way back into sleep, but my head was starting to pound and my body was cramped and cold. I desperately needed to brush my teeth. Slowly, I sat up. The room took a moment to right itself. Needed the loo, too. My head wobbled dangerously, weightily. Maybe I'd just sit for a while first.

I heard a creak and the sound of feet upstairs. Oh god. Peter. I should have snuck out while I had the chance. I blearily considered how to get home without driving, but I didn't have the energy. I listened to him descend the stairs, pause outside the door, gently push it open and stick his head round. I gave him a weak smile.

'You're up,' he said. His expression was sympathetic. *Embarrassment just on my side then.* 'Oh, honey,' he laughed, 'are you suffering?' I nodded, giving him my best mournful eyes, and he sat on the sofa beside me and gave me a sideways hug. 'You want some breakfast?'

'Don't think I could cope with that,' I croaked, appalled at my breath and wondering if there was a mint or some gum anywhere.

'Coffee?'

I nodded. 'Strong. Then I really need to go home.'

He gave me a one-armed squeeze. 'I'll drive you.' And he left to make coffee.

He didn't bring up what happened the night before, and I sure as hell wasn't going to. We drove in silence, mostly, and I convinced myself it was by and large a comfortable silence.

'How do I look?' I asked as we pulled up outside my house. 'Can you tell we were up all night partying?'

'You look fine,' Peter said. 'Maybe get some make-up remover.' He indicated under my eyes. I scrubbed at them with my fingers and pulled my hair into a ponytail.

'Hopefully I can get into the shower before they see me,' I said. 'Wish me luck.'

'See you later,' Peter laughed, and I got out of the car. He didn't drive away straightaway like he normally did, giving me the disconcerting feeling as I walked up the drive and pulled out my keys that he was watching me.

I spent the next few weeks praying the subject wouldn't come up, and for once in my life my prayers were answered. Peter seemed more subdued than usual—or maybe that was wishful thinking from the vain side of me that liked being desired—and I was perhaps a shade more blustery, but we carried on like normal.

We were on a shopping trip, Peter, Robbie and I, for Dad's birthday present and some new clothes for Robbie. Robbie was galloping ahead in excitement and Peter and I were walking behind, laughing. The disapproving looks from the other shoppers were easier to deflect when there were two of us.

Robbie needed the toilet, so we took him to the disabled cubicle and waited outside in case he needed help. He sang loudly while he was inside, but instead of feeling embarrassed and self-conscious, I didn't care. And it was all because of Peter. He wasn't ashamed of Robbie so neither was I. I was so elated that I could do this, go shopping with my brother and my friend and feel fine about it, feel normal, that I leaned across a rack of shirts and kissed him. Not passionately, no tongue, but firmly and decisively.

He looked stunned as I pulled away.

'What was that for?'

I shrugged, happy. 'Just because.'

He put his hand next to mine on the clothes rack. I could see him wrestling, caught between taking it seriously and keeping it light-hearted. I didn't know which way I wanted him to go.

'At the risk of snapping you out of this glorious daze you seem to be in...,' he started, and then the toilet flushed and the door opened and Robbie appeared, and I had to catch him quickly and wash his hands with him before he ran back off into the shop.

Dad was away that weekend, visiting his mother, who was going in for an operation. I would have gone too, but Robbie wouldn't go into hospitals, and he wasn't great with long car journeys either. I invited Peter to stay for dinner, partly because it was easier on my blood pressure if Robbie was occupied while I was cooking, and afterwards we played *Snap* and *Snakes and Ladders* and *Guess Who*.

Eventually, when we had tricked Robbie into going to bed by waging his bedtime over a game of *Noughts and Crosses*, when I had read him a story and turned on his nightlight and gone downstairs, I turned the tap on to start the washing up.

'I'll do that,' Peter said, trying to take the gloves from me. 'You did the cooking.'

'And when has that ever changed who did the washing up?' I said wryly.

'Tonight, that's when.' He refused to let go. 'Go and put your feet up.'

'Stop trying to make me relax all the time and accept the fact that I am a working woman.'

'Stop resisting my efforts to help you.' There was that edge to his voice again, the tone that could go either way— it could be joking, good-natured banter, or we could get into a real argument. We stared at each other.

Carefully, I took the gloves from him and laid them on the counter, neatly folded. I turned off the tap, and took him by the hand and led him out of the kitchen. We went up the stairs, past Robbie's open door, and into my bedroom. I closed the door behind us, and looked at him.

Without breaking eye contact, I began to unbutton my

shirt.

'Camille,' Peter said, in a hoarse whisper.

'Sober as a rock,' I said, calmly. I was aware of my heartbeat, aware of my body and the space it took up, in a way I hadn't been for years. I slipped the shirt off my shoulders and tossed it lightly in the direction of a chair. I took a step towards Peter, and felt my heart beat harder as I did. Not faster, just harder.

I put my hands on his waist, and kissed him. He didn't break away.

'Are you sure this is what you want?' he said.

'I spend my life not being sure,' I said, kissing him again. 'I *never* know what I'm doing.' I slipped the free end of his belt through the buckle. 'For once, yes, I am sure.' I kissed him again, more firmly, and this time he stepped into me, his arms came around me, his hands slid up under my vest.

I thought I would have to block everything out from my mind—where I was, who else was in the house, who I was doing this with. But I didn't. It didn't feel wrong or awkward. It was fun. We giggled, we shushed each other, we tripped over jeans. In some moments, he was Peter, my friend, who cared about me, who I knew and I who I could relax around, and in other moments, he was a whole new person to explore, to experience. I gave myself up to it. Afterwards, when he had fallen asleep, I slipped out of bed, pulled on my dressing gown, and went downstairs to wash up. I scrubbed at the roasting pan, thinking how I should have left it to soak first. Before. I leaned my forearms against the edge of the sink and sighed.

Just after midnight, Peter came downstairs and found me sitting at the kitchen table drinking peppermint tea. He was dressed. Without saying anything, he sat down beside me. I took a breath.

'I'm sorry, about—that.'

He laughed. 'Trust me, Camille, that is not something you should be apologising for.'

'Is it OK if I ask you not to spend the night?'

'I thought you would. It would confuse Robbie if I was still here in the morning.' I nodded. He kissed me awkwardly on the cheek, and left. I heard him pick up his keys, and shut the front door softly. I stayed at the table in the kitchen, sipping my tea.

Rosaline and Emmi are arguing. The others are still milling, getting equipment, conferring, cracking knuckles. Preparing. The girls are close together, hissing, trying to be unnoticed.

'Just write the damn essay,' Rosaline says. 'It's what you're here for, isn't it?'

'Oh, leave it out.'

'Look, you want help, we try and help. Then you cry about being lonely when you're the one pushing everyone away.'

'I don't want *advice*, Rosy, I just need somebody to *talk* to, somebody to *listen*.'

Rosaline grabs her paints and straightens up. She's had enough. 'Bollocks do you. You just want to moan. And I'm sick of it, I'm sick of listening to it, the same stuff all the time.'

I expect Emmi to be angry, but suddenly I can see tears glinting in her eyes. She says nothing as Rosaline stalks to an easel and begins to set herself up. She walks to the easel on the opposite side of the room, staring at her feet. I see something in her that I recognise well—the feeling of being surrounded by people and so very, very alone.

Things didn't go back to normal after that. I was trying to avoid him, and he knew it. We worked within ten minutes of each other, in the town centre, and often used to take lunch breaks together by the canal. I started taking my break later, so we didn't coincide. When he called and invited me to a film, I said Robbie was going to a friend's house and I had to be there. When Dad suggested we invite him round for a walk or a kick around one Saturday when the three of us had nothing to do, I made up some excuse about Peter having plans.

When he sent flowers to my work, I knew I had to face him. I sat at my desk and stared at the colourful bouquet, but it didn't disappear. Ruth, who shared my office, *oohed* and *aahed* and said how sweet it was, but as I pointed out, it was only sweet if it was wanted. I drummed my fingers on the desk. Eventually, when Ruth was out of the room, and after many false starts, I picked up the phone.

'Hi Peter, it's me,' I said when he picked up.

'Hello. How are you?' His tone was cautious. He knew I was about to shoot him down. I closed my eyes and tried not to imagine him looking crestfallen.

'Fine thanks. I got your flowers.'

'Oh.'

'They're beautiful, thank you.'

'I'm glad you like them.' If he didn't know what was coming, he would be saying more, trying to make plans.

This felt brutal.

'Look, Peter.' On the other end of the phone, he sighed. 'I'm really sorry about what happened. I mean, I'm not sorry, it was great, but I'm not looking for a relationship right now. I meant what I said, I just don't have time with Dad and Robbie and everything. It wouldn't be fair.' Peter was quiet for a moment.

'I understand.'

'I just—I really needed somebody that night, and with you, I—I care a lot about you. You've no idea what you've done for me, and since I met you, things have just been so much easier.'

'And on the basis of that, you don't want to be with me?'

'I just don't think I feel that way about you.' My words faltered. It was like stabbing a bunny rabbit.

'OK. If you could have let me know that beforehand, I would have appreciated it.'

'I'm so sorry.'

'Right. Well, I have to go.'

'Thank you for the flowers,' I said again. I'm not sure he heard it before he hung up.

It was only later, as I was grudgingly putting the flowers in a vase (in the kitchenette, not in my office), when I noticed the note.

You are more than worth the wait. I know this is backwards, but might I have the honour of taking you out to dinner? Properly? Yours, Peter x

Shaking my head sadly, I threw the note in the bin.

'I haven't seen Peter around in a while,' Dad said innocently one night. I was sitting at the table, stretching my legs out. It had been a long day at work. I had to use the days Dad picked Robbie up from school to catch up on the things I let slide when it was my turn, and often, like today, it meant late nights in the office. Robbie was currently splayed out in front of the TV, in enraptured concentration. I shrugged in answer to Dad.

'I expect he's busy.'

'Has something happened between you two?'

'What makes you say that?'

Dad tried, and failed, to look nonchalant. 'Well, you're a girl, he's a boy, you know. I was sort of hoping the two of you might get together at some stage.'

I pulled a face. 'Dad, please. We're just friends.'

'I worry about you, that's all.' He dried his hands and sat down next to me. 'I know it's not fair on you to have to look after Robert all the time.'

'It's not all the time. We share it.'

'But you should have your own life, your own friends. You don't really know anyone your own age.'

'I have friends. There's Amy, and Fran. And—Debbie.'

'Amy and Fran are support group mothers, they barely count. Who's Debbie?'

'The woman who serves me at the bakery.' We laughed. The sort of breathy exhalation that isn't really mirth.

'I want you to be happy, Cam,' he said softly. 'I don't want you to give up everything for him.'

'I'm fine, Dad,' I said.

'Is there no young man that's caught your eye?'

'Dad, really. I don't need anyone.'

'Peter's a lovely chap.'

I looked at him warningly. He made a show of zipping his mouth shut. Then, he took my hand.

I squeezed it. We were both missing Mum, though neither of us said it.

I just start drawing, as though I'm not in a class, I'm just at home and doodling for no reason. I get quite into it, so much so that I don't even try and make conversation with the people either side of me. So much so, in fact, that I don't notice that at some point during the class, Eamonn and Allie have become involved in a conversation, in low murmurs, over Allie's shoulder as she sketches. About twenty minutes before the end of class, she comes over to my easel. I angle it away from her, self-conscious. She doesn't seem interested in sneaking a peak though, and my heart begins to sink.

'Hey, um,' she begins. *Positive start.* 'I'm really, really sorry Camille, but do you think you could get the bus back?' I look at her, none too pleased. 'I'm sorry, I'm really sorry, but,' she glances around and lowers her voice. 'Eamonn and I want to talk about what happened.'

'Why? What is there to say?'

She looks pained. 'I don't know, we just want to clear the air, I just—I'm so, so sorry, after I begged to drive you.'

'It's fine,' I said tersely, not meaning it. 'I can take the bus.'

'Are you sure? Are you absolutely sure?'

I give her a wide, fake, smile. 'Absolutely. You clear the air.'

She scurries off. I gaze dissatisfied at the fruits of the

last two hours of labour, and decide to call my husband to come and pick me up. I slip out into the corridor and pull out my phone.

'Hello?'

'Hi, Peter, it's me. I don't suppose you can come and collect me, can you?'

'Of course, what's happened?'

'Nothing, my ride just had a better offer.'

'I'll be there in fifteen minutes.'

'Thanks, darling. I just couldn't be bothered with the bus.'

'No problem. I love you.'

'Love you too.'

If it had happened now, if we had broken up now, in the age of emails and Facebook and god knows what else young people spend their lives glued to, we might have stayed in touch. We could have been friends.

Maybe he moved back to England after a few years. Maybe we could have met, caught up, for old times' sake. Maybe, when Robbie was older, and things were more stable, we could even have got together again.

But it didn't happen now. It happened then, when all we had were phones and letters. I sent him a letter once, sometime in the first year of Robbie's life. But he must have moved apartments, because I never heard back from him.

I haven't seen Michael since he left me for Beijing.

Week Eight

As it turns out, Allie's idea of "clearing the air" was closer to what I would call "dating the art teacher." But all due credit to her, she keeps it subtle.

It's the second week back, and while one or two people are mixing up paints, I haven't moved on from pencil. Allie's canvas is almost completely covered in a first layer of paint already; she's clearly been working on it during the week. Eamonn prowls as normal.

I think Rosaline must have a new boyfriend. She's barely put her phone down all class, and every time she checks it, she smiles the same way, quick and secret, a little duck of the chest and biting her bottom lip as she furiously taps out a reply. She's barely put three brush strokes on the canvas.

It doesn't occur to me to be bothered by the fact that she's so distracted, but it seems to be bothering Emmi, and it seems to be bothering Eamonn. Emmi keeps trying to lean over to start a conversation—despite Eamonn's best efforts to mix us up, the two of them always seem to end up next to each other—and never gets more than a vague murmur or a raised eyebrow in response. Eventually Emmi retreats into a sullen silence, glancing over at Rosaline every few minutes.

'Making progress, are we?' Eamonn says loudly, right behind Rosaline. She jumps, and grins guiltily.

'Slowly,' she says, shoving her phone out of sight under her thigh.

'Going to be ready for the show?' Eamonn says, in the same tone of voice. He doesn't seem to want to let it go. Is he upset over his wasted time, her wasted money, the lack of attention?

'Mhmm,' she says, bright and agreeable but not making any moves to carry on painting. She wants him to go away first. Emmi's eyes flick from Rosaline to Eamonn.

Eventually, Eamonn moves away to stand behind Niall, and Rosaline finally turns to Emmi, eyes shining with giggles. It's definitely a boy. Emmi is controlled and measured in her response, sitting upright and focusing on her painting. She doesn't give Rosaline what she wants. The studio settles into silence for a while. Eamonn stops circling and sits behind his desk, reading some papers, occasionally checking his laptop. There's a slight shuffling sound as Morris' leg jiggles.

Abruptly, Emmi stands up. The noise of her chair scraping is very loud.

'I need another canvas,' she says. 'I've messed this one up.' Eamonn gets up and comes over to her. He speaks softly—*nothing is beyond recovery, every mistake tells a story, let's see how we can work with this*—like he's trying to preserve the atmosphere or calm her down. 'I need a new one,' she says again. 'This is ruined.'

He places a hand on her shoulder and with the other gestures at her work, suggesting ways she can salvage it.

She reaches down for her bag, swings the strap over her shoulder, and leaves the studio. Eamonn glances round at us all—we're all watching—and follows her.

Rosaline seems to hesitate, wondering whether to follow, half off her stool. Her phone vibrates loudly on the wooden surface, and she snatches it up. She sinks back down to sitting as she replies, and again she loses herself to that secret, bashful smile.

The first thing I felt when I opened the door and saw him standing there was happiness. I was happy to see him.

Immediately following that, I felt embarrassment, awkwardness, and dread.

It was four or five weeks after we'd slept together. Not an unreasonable amount of time for friends not to see each other, but long enough for Robbie to ask where he was, why he hadn't been over in a while. Maybe that was why he was here. For Robbie.

'My sister's wedding,' he said, when he'd hugged me hello. 'You said you'd go with me, and I just wanted to see if you still do.'

'I'd completely forgotten,' I admitted.

'That's because you haven't had three different crazed women on the phone to you sobbing about wedding plans every night.'

'Three?'

'Mum, bride and, for some reason, bridesmaid. I don't really know how she got my number.' I laughed. I suddenly realised we were still hovering over the threshold and stood back to let him in. 'It's the weekend after next. Do you still want to come, or—?' He left the question hanging in the air. 'There's no open bar, but it's a pretty swanky setting, and I have it on good authority that the food will be amazing.'

Peter's sister's engagement had been a rather long, drawn-out affair, surviving one minor family feud, one potentially major almost-break-up, and months and months of saving for the dream event. It was being held in a very impressive country manor an hour's drive away, and for anyone not emotionally invested in it going perfectly, it did look set to be a good day. I had been surprised when Peter asked me to be his plus one, but it wouldn't be completely inappropriate for me to go—I had met Peter's sister Nancy, on several occasions, and we got on. It was a Saturday afternoon/evening do, and there was no reason Dad couldn't watch Robbie.

'I'd love to still come,' I said. 'If that's still OK.'

Peter beamed. 'Of course it is. I'm going to need someone to listen to me surreptitiously mock the whole affair.'

'Peter, I'm so sorry about what happened,' I said in a rush. 'I never meant to—I don't want to lose you as a friend.'

'No, I'm sorry I got so upset. I didn't mean to shut you out.'

'You had every right to be upset, I was completely in the wrong, I shouldn't have—'

'Forget it,' Peter said firmly. 'Forget it, and think only of dancing the night away in posh frocks and monocles. Monocles optional.'

I giggled in relief. 'OK, great. Oh, I'm excited,' I said, and I was. I wanted to get all dressed up for once, to look beautiful instead of tired and haggard all the time.

'It should be good,' Peter said, smiling.

'Do you want to come in and have some tea?' I asked.

'No, I should get going. Just dropped by to ask about the wedding. Is Robbie around to say hi to?'

'No, he's gone for a check-up. I would have gone with them, but I had to stay in and wait for the boiler man to come round, who still hasn't come, by the way.' I checked my watch. 'Typical, isn't it. I left work early for this.'

'Well, tell Robbie I said hello. And I hope the boiler man comes.'

'Me too!' I said, opening the door for him. 'Bye.'

I shut the door behind him and leant my forehead against it. Things would be OK. It wouldn't be the most comfortable, not right away, but we would be friends again. I hadn't ruined it. I pivoted my body so the back of my head was leaning against the door. I wondered if I could afford a new dress, and whether I should dig out my mother's pearls. I shimmied my way back to the kitchen.

Getting ready had always been my favourite part of going out. But this time, I didn't have anyone to get ready with. When I was younger, it had been my mum and Maria. At university, it had been the girls at Girton. In China, it had been Michael. Now, there was no one to giggle with or admire my dress, nobody to share the excitement.

Dad had taken Robbie to the park, so I was alone in the house. I turned the radio up and tried to make myself dance like my mother used to, but truthfully my heart just wasn't in it. I put my hair up in curlers and ran myself a hot bath, and lay there soaking for a while. I was glad of the loud music. I didn't want to be able to hear my thoughts.

I stepped into the dress I had bought (second-hand). It was a deep blue, off-the-shoulder with a ruched waist and a flared skirt, knee-length. I had to hold my breath to zip it up. I eyed my bare collarbone and raised my chin to stretch my neck. Was I getting too old to wear things like this? I spun around in a circle and watched my skirt fly out. At least I could still glean some joy from that.

By this point, Dad and Robbie were back from the park, and Robbie came bounding in to see what I was doing. It was about two o'clock—Peter was picking me up at half past to drive to the wedding. Robbie was excited at the sight of my dress, and I smiled at his childlike glee as he batted the material of the skirt up with his hands.

'Pretty, Cammy,' he said, as I finished my make-up and pressed my lips together.

'Thank you, darling,' I said, and he clung to my waist and swayed from side to side like we were dancing. I kissed the top of his head, lightly so as not to make his hair sticky. 'At least I have you to share this with.'

He started going through my cosmetics, fascinated by the bottles and tubes. I fiddled with the backs of my earrings, leaning in front of the mirror, and suddenly there was a snap and a rattle and Robbie burst into tears.

I spun around. Robbie was clutching the case I kept my mother's necklace in. A broken string was dangling from his hand and pearls were rolling all over the floor, bouncing off the table.

'Robbie!' I screamed in dismay, and he cried harder. I heard Dad thumping up the stairs.

'What's happened?' He stopped in my doorway. 'Oh.'

Ordinarily I'd have gone to Robbie and comforted him, drawn him onto my lap and shushed him and rocked him until he settled. But the sight of my mother's pearls, broken and scattered, made me burst into tears myself. I fell to my knees in my stockings and scrabbled for the pearls, reaching under the bed, trying to draw them all to me.

'Hey, hey,' Dad said ineffectually. He put his arm around Robbie's shoulders and led him from the room, stepping over my snatching hands, and after a while Robbie started to quieten. I knew that calming him down at that speed meant he'd been bribed with chocolate. Or maybe an ice cream.

When Dad came back for me, he found me sitting at the foot of my bed, legs crossed, a puddle of pearls resting in the lap of my dress. My face was tear-stained and mascara-streaked, and I felt like everything was ruined. He sat down next to me.

'Oh, Cam,' he said, putting his arm around me. I leaned my head on his shoulder and cried some more. He rocked me gently for a while. 'It can be fixed, you know,' he said. I sniffed, and ran my fingers through the pile of beads. Dad picked one up and inspected it. 'We can rethread them. It will be good as new.'

'It won't be Mum's,' I said.

He squeezed me. 'Hey now, don't let this ruin your evening,' he said. 'You can still have a nice time. You look beautiful, darling.'

I gave a teary laugh. 'I did, maybe. Not anymore.' I

wiped my eyes and my fingers came away smudged with black. 'I don't want to go, Dad, I can't face it today.'

'Yes you can. You get yourself cleaned up, and you and Michael can go off and have a lovely time.'

I paused. 'Peter,' I said.

Dad froze.

'Yes, Peter, obviously. Sorry.' I carefully scooped the pearls into my hands and stood up. 'Give these to me,' Dad said, 'and by the time you get back I'll have it good as new for you. You'll never know the difference.' I tipped them into his cupped palms.

'Do I have to go?' I said pitifully, sounding like a thirteen-year-old.

Dad kissed me on the cheek. 'You'll have a good time, I promise.'

There was a knock at the front door. I panicked. 'I can't let him see me like this, I'm a mess!' I wailed.

'I'll give him a cup of tea. Calm yourself down, sort yourself out, come down when you're ready. OK?' I nodded. Dad left to let Peter in, and I sat back down in front of my dressing table, taking deep breaths to steady myself. I wiped the make-up from my face, re-applied, and fished out another necklace—a silver pendant on a silver chain. I changed my earrings, too. The necklace looked a little small and plain against the bare expanse of skin, but there was nothing I could do about it. I fixed a few stray strands of hair and added some more hairspray. I considered the finished product in the mirror. I still didn't feel like going, but at least I looked the part. Shoes, bag, jacket. I descended the stairs.

Dad and Peter were chatting in the hall—sports, I think—and Peter looked up as I came down. The look on his face made me laugh. For a moment I was princess in a cheesy film.

'Wow,' he said, and I was pathetically grateful.

'Too much?' I said.

'Perfect.' He kissed my cheek. 'You look gorgeous.'

'Well you kids have fun,' Dad said. 'Don't worry about anything, pet.' He kissed me too. Peter offered me his arm. I tried to shake everything off, to be young and happy for this one evening. I tried to glide out the door with him. It almost worked.

I wasn't surprised when Robbie announced his intention to marry Sarah. He adored her, we all did. But my indulgent smile was tinged with sadness. Robbie would never be able to have that kind of relationship. Was it sad to lose something you couldn't fully comprehend?

Sarah handled it beautifully.

'You have to be boyfriend and girlfriend before you get married,' she said without missing a beat, barely looking up from her homework. Robbie nodded thoughtfully, chewing the end of his pencil. He graciously agreed that Sarah could be his girlfriend first.

Sarah finished her sentence, put the pen down, clasped her hands together on the table in front of her chest, and leaned towards Robbie. I gently pushed the pencil out of his mouth as I passed.

'Robbie, I'm flattered,' she said, 'But I have to concentrate on my schoolwork if I'm going to be a scientist. I don't have time for a boyfriend.'

Robbie nodded, disappointed but understanding. He asked if they could have ice cream, and I said absolutely, after dinner. He scowled at me playfully, and Sarah went back to her Chemistry book.

It's abnormally quiet in the studio after Emmi leaves. Eamonn slips quietly back in after a few minutes, alone. Eyes flick up and back down again. People are concentrating hard on their projects; we don't talk much. In fact, when people start to clear away, scraping easel legs and clattering boxes, it makes me jump. I hadn't realised so much time had passed.

I go to fetch some paper towels to wipe the pencil smudges off my hands. Becca is at the sink, and leans to the side slightly to let me reach for the paper, shaking her hands and rolling her gloves back down over her thumbs.

Allie packs away quickly and is one of the first out the door. But when I leave five or ten minutes later, she's still there, in the corridor, studying a display of third-year work.

'Were you waiting for me? Sorry, I thought you'd gone.' We walk towards the car park together.

'I think I'm having an affair,' Allie says abruptly.

I stop walking. 'Excuse me?'

'Eamonn,' she whispers, excitedly. She is plumper and her skin is thinner, but looking into her shining eyes is almost like looking at me at eighteen.

'Yes, I had rather assumed.' My tone is sterner than I'd intended. Moral rectitude, or jealousy? 'What happened? I thought you were going to clear the air.'

'We were going to. But the truth is, we're both attracted to each other, and it doesn't make sense to ignore that.'

I look at her pointedly. 'You do know you're married, don't you?' I expect a flicker of guilt here; all I see is defiance.

'Jonathan doesn't appreciate me the way Eamonn does. What I have with Eamonn is special, I can't turn it down.'

'What do you mean, "what you have with Eamonn"? You've barely seen him outside of class. Have you?'

'I saw him twice last week. We can talk for hours, about art and films and travel and everything. He makes me laugh. He makes me feel like I haven't felt in years.'

'Are you going to tell Jonathan?'

That's when her eyes drop for the first time. 'No. It wouldn't be good for the children.'

'I see.'

'Do you hate me?' she says anxiously.

'Of course I don't hate you. Look, if you're happy, I'm happy. But do you think you can cope with the stress of having an affair? Do you think it's fair on Jonathan?'

She sniffs. 'Jonathan hasn't paid me any attention for years. All he cares about is work and his stupid golf trophies, he won't even notice.'

'Well,' I say. 'How terribly saucy. My best friend is having it off with the art teacher.'

Allie blushes deeply and delightedly crimson.

Things got a little trickier once Robbie started high school.

It was a big school, and though they had some teaching assistants for special needs kids, they didn't have the staff or the time that Robbie really needed. Only about two-thirds of the children from his primary school went into the same comprehensive, and we lost several of his friends to the private school in town. The comprehensive was also fed by two other junior schools, and the new eleven-year-olds were much more aggressive than the accepting seven-year-olds he had met in primary school. These ones had burgeoning personalities, a growing awareness of popularity, a wariness of anyone that could cement their reputation as "uncool". And these were things that Robbie just didn't understand. The kids realised he had been held back for three years, they saw his distorted face and they asked if he had run into a wall. When the teachers saw the taunting, they stopped it, but the kids always regrouped.

Robbie became more and more withdrawn, spoke less and less, and it broke my heart because I didn't know how to make it better.

'I'm worried about Robbie at school,' I said to Dad one day after dinner.

'Kids can be cruel,' he said, peering at some bills through his reading glasses. 'All we can do is hope that he finds at least one person to be friends with. There'll be another one who's struggling to make friends, they can bond.'

'I'm worried about him academically, though. He's already falling behind, I don't know how he's going to last another five years. The school suggested we pay for a private teaching assistant two or three days a week.'

'We can't afford that.'

'I know.'

'Look, it's not like he needs to get the best marks, he's not going to be trying for university. He just needs to stick it out until...'

'Until what? What is he going to do after school? Is he going to get a job?'

Dad puts the bills down. 'What kind of job could he get?'

'I don't know,' I said defensively, 'but he's bright, he tries hard, he could do...something.'

'What *is* he going to do after school?' Dad said, as though he hadn't heard me, as though the thought was only just occurring to him. It probably was. He pushed his glasses to the top of his head.

'What do other people with Down Syndrome do?' It was unknown territory again, like they had just handed us the baby for the first time and we didn't know where to go or how to get there. 'What else can he do? Can we leave him here alone while we go to work?' And, unspoken: *am I going to have to look after him forever? Live here, forever?*

There was a long silence. Then Dad put his glasses back on his nose and picked up his papers again.

It was a beautiful setting for a wedding.

We drew up at almost four o'clock. The sun had begun to soften, and glowed gently on the stone. The building was very impressive, a sweeping drive encircling an ornate fountain at the front, circular turrets—*turrets? Is that the word?*—on each corner, scattered fairy lights just blinking into life. It had extensive grounds—I think they ran a riding school there, they certainly had stables—but nobody had wanted to risk an outdoor wedding.

Peter and I hurried in. The ceremony was due to start

at four. We were running late. As the brother of the bride (and guest), our seats were right at the front, and I felt horribly conspicuous hustling down the aisle, trying not to let my shoes clap too loudly.

We slipped into our seats, Peter kissed his mother on the cheek—how he avoided that monstrosity of a hat I'll never know—and squeezed my hand reassuringly. Almost immediately after that, the string quartet struck up, and bridesmaids began to float slowly down the aisle.

It was a long ceremony. Lovely, yes, but long. The bride and groom stood under a flower-strewn arch with the minister, flanked by bridesmaids and groomsmen. There were Bible passages and long speeches and emotional vows from both parties, and much sniffing and dabbing of damp eyes from family members. I ran a thumbnail over the cuticles of my other hand. There was a professional photographer, and everyone had to pause at length over rings and signings to get that perfect shot. But I had to admit, the couple looked happy as they went back down the aisle as man and wife. Maybe it was just relief.

Then there was a seemingly interminable amount of time spent milling, making tedious small talk with elderly relatives who looked eagerly from Peter to me and asked about another wedding. One of them even mentioned the pitter-patter of tiny feet. Peter steered me away from that aunt rather swiftly. People were taken in groups for photographs, according to the announcements of the rather harassed-looking photographer's assistant, a short, balding man with a crumpled piece of paper who shouted things like 'immediate family of the bride! *Immediate* family *only*, please!' Or 'bridesmaids and groomsmen! *With* bouquets, please!' The bride and groom seemed more grim than anything by this point, though they flashed winning smiles every time they were in front of the camera so that the frustration and irritation at family members and arrangements and logistics wouldn't be recorded for posterity. Peter wheedled me in front of the photographer for a shot of the two of us.

When that was over, we moved to a reception hall, circular tables dressed in linens with tall centrepieces, chairs with bows on the back and the ceiling draped in black studded with tiny lights. A dance floor, a DJ. The lighting was very dim, which made me giggle. I almost expected a disco ball.

We sat with some of Peter's sister's friends from childhood and university and one or two cousins. It was a rarity for me to spend time with people my age, and not to have any children involved. We didn't even talk about children (except one couple, but after the obligatory showing of photos they were thankfully silent on the subject of their offspring). I accepted a generous glass of wine and admired the lettering on my place card. Peter saw me smiling.

'Happy?'

'Very,' I said, leaning forwards and kissing his cheek. 'Everything's beautiful.'

'Isn't it just,' he said, looking around. 'Cost a fortune.'

'Did your dad pay for it all?'

'Some. Nancy and Greg chipped in, so did Greg's parents. Group effort, really.'

The food was indeed delicious. Over the starter, I had a critical conversation about the bride's dress with the girl next to me. We agreed that the bride looked beautiful, but for ourselves we would have made some changes.

'Fewer diamantes, more lace,' I said.

'Less train, more cleavage,' said my neighbour, and we laughed.

I had more wine with the main, and there was a spirited discussion about a book we had all read as children. Over dessert—and dessert wine—we turned to television stars, and film stars, and by the time we were drinking coffee, we were laughing over somebody's story about golfing with the father of a past girlfriend.

After dinner there were many, many speeches—father of the bride, bride, groom, best man, chief bridesmaid—and my neighbour and I got bored and started playing hangman on a napkin, sniggering like schoolchildren. Then Peter gave a toast to the bride and groom, and they took to the dance floor for their first dance together.

'So romantic,' sighed one of the cousins. When people started to get up to join them, Peter offered me his hand, but I shook my head.

'The next one, the next one,' I insisted, wary of all the slow-dancing couples.

We danced to something more upbeat. I couldn't remember the last time I had danced—properly, with a partner—and I'm sure we didn't look elegant stumbling around the floor, but I laughed so hard I thought I would burst my dress, so I didn't care. Afterwards, Peter asked his sister to dance, and I returned to the table to find somebody had bought a round of gin and tonics.

By eleven o'clock, it was just a good party. A great party. I and several of the other girls on my table had abandoned our high heels and were dancing together as a group. The gin had been flowing. The guys had loosened their ties and were trying to outdo each other in ridiculous dance moves. I felt happy and silly and when Peter grabbed my hand and spun me and pulled me close and kissed me, I kissed him back.

Then I stopped.

'Peter,' I said. 'We shouldn't, you know—I'm sorry.'

'Or,' he said, 'we could.'

My sodden brain paused. 'I mean, we *could*,' I agreed.

Peter still had his arms around me. 'Do you want to?'

'Well not *here*,' I said. And then, 'do you?' Peter laughed, and squeezed me closer to him. We were cheek to cheek. And then, lips to neck. He took my hand and led me out of the room and up the rather grand-looking staircase in the entrance hall.

'Where are we going?' I said.

'Did you know the second and third floors have been converted into a rather exclusive hotel?' he said.

'Really? When did that happen?' Then his words sunk in. 'Wait...'

'I can't drive home,' Peter said. 'I've drunk too much.' I opened my mouth, waiting for the protests to materialise, but nothing came out. I let myself be led up more stairs and into a room. When did he get the key?

'Oh wow, a four-poster bed,' I said. 'I've always wanted one of those.'

Peter's arms were around my waist.

'Peter...'

'Shh.' And I shushed. I was taken aback by his sudden assertiveness. I liked it. He kissed me, found the zip at the side of my dress, and pulled it down. When he pushed me gently over to the bed, I was happy to fall.

I woke up enveloped in cloud.

I'd never felt such a downy duvet before. I stretched luxuriously, like a cat, taking in the light streaming through the window, the drapes around the bed, the delicious pain in the arches of my feet from too much dancing.

I rolled over. Peter was lying next to me, his sandy hair falling over his forehead. He looked strange to me without his glasses, naked and vulnerable. His shoulder was dusted with freckles. I propped myself up on an elbow and looked at him for a moment or two. Eventually he stirred, his eyes flickering open. He made a noise halfway between a yawn and a stretch, and smiled up at me.

'Morning, gorgeous,' he said.

'Morning.' He sat up, scooting back to lean against the headboard. His bare chest was warm and pale. 'So,' I said.

'So,' he replied, and we laughed awkwardly, but only slightly awkwardly.

'Look, Peter, last night was great, and this—but, things haven't changed, I still don't want—'

'It's fine,' Peter said, 'I know. I'm not expecting anything.' I was dubious. He leaned over and kissed the side of my head.

'It was fun, Camille, that's all. I'm not expecting another wedding.'

'Are you sure?'

'Yes, so lie back down, relax, have breakfast with me, and then we can drive home again.'

'OK.' I snuggled up next to him, the duvet up under my arms to cover my chest. 'You're a good friend to me, Peter.'

'It was a great wedding, wasn't it?' he said.

'Best I've been to.'

'Have you been to any others?'

'No, but I can't imagine one better than that.'

'I've never seen Mum cry so hard.'

'I think it was stress, to be honest.'

'She's going to need to have a holiday to recover.' We reclined in companionable silence. 'Breakfast?' Peter asked. 'The bridal package includes room service.'

'How are you affording this?'

He shrugged. 'How often does your only sister get married?' he said. 'The whole family's staying over, so we can bid the happy couple bon voyage on their honeymoon.'

'How did I not know about these arrangements?'

'You're just oblivious, darling. The bride and groom leave at twelve, we should go down before then.'

We ate scrambled eggs and orange juice sitting up in bed, and then I slipped into the shower to take advantage of the tiny free toiletries, and got dressed in the bathroom for modesty's rather belated sake. It felt strange putting on the same dress as last night, very out of place in the brightness of the morning, and I discovered that at some point Peter had slipped back downstairs and retrieved my jacket and shoes.

Downstairs in the lobby, everybody looked tired and somewhat washed-out, but in a good way. The bride and groom were more relaxed than I'd seen them all weekend, and couldn't keep their hands off each other, holding hands or stroking a leg or looping an arm round shoulders, as though to say *this is mine, can you believe it*? The reception room from last night was being dismantled and cleared away. The ceiling had been revealed, boring blank tiles, the centrepieces had gone and the chairs were being stacked. It was sort of a sad sight to see. It was all over.

We said goodbye to Nancy and Greg as they climbed

into their taxi to go to the airport, and then everyone else was piling into their own cars and driving away too. I waited in the car while Peter hugged his mum and dad goodbye, and then the manor was receding in the rear-view mirror. I leaned back in my seat.

'That,' I said, 'was a perfectly lovely weekend.'

When Robbie was thirteen, Peter and I took him to a medieval-themed activity day for children about an hour away. It was in the direction of Nancy and Greg's house, so we arranged to meet up with them there for a picnic.

Nancy and Greg had heard about Robbie, from Peter and from me, but they had never met him before. I wondered how much Peter had told them about him. For a long time I didn't tell Peter the truth about Robbie and how he was born, other than that Mum had died in childbirth. If he thought it was a strange situation, such a large age gap between Robbie and me, or if he had worked out that, if Mum was around the same age as Dad, then she was over forty when she got pregnant again, he never commented. He accepted that we were a father and daughter raising a son/brother together, and I liked that he didn't pry. It wasn't his business, and it didn't affect his relationship with us in any way.

Eventually, of course, I told him, one afternoon when the world was feeling particularly bleak and heavy. I told him my mother had fallen pregnant by another man, and that it hadn't been consensual. Peter looked stricken.

'I kind of assumed it hadn't been planned,' he said softly. I nodded, pressing my back teeth together. I could speak about it calmly, but I couldn't stop my eyes from filling. I looked up and tried not to blink.

Peter was quiet for a while. I imagined him going through all the repercussions of what I had just told him, slowly, methodically. It was a relief to say it out loud for once, instead of just carrying it around with me unspoken. But that didn't mean I wanted everyone to know. My mother was nobody else's business.

Peter seemed to guess what I was thinking.

'I won't tell anyone,' he said. 'It's not mine to tell.' He gave me a long hug, stroking my back gently.

So Nancy and Greg knew Robbie was my brother, but didn't ask more. Maybe Peter had told them not to. Robbie spent the morning dressing up as a knight and having pretend jousting competitions with foam lances. The kids loved it. I watched an eight-year-old boy choosing a princess dress over chainmail from the selection of costumes, and smiled. Then he gave his sister a sword and she, alike resplendent in pink skirt, bustle and trailing hat, had a swordfight with an eleven-year-old squire.

I watched Robbie petting his imaginary horse. One of the youngest children, maybe five or six, came over and asked what he was doing. Robbie held out an imaginary apple for him to feed the horse, and he did. Robbie stroked the horse's nose and smiled and said something like *he likes that*.

Nancy and Greg arrived, and went with Peter to stake out a picnic spot. When the kids broke for lunch, Robbie came running over to me.

'Did you see me?' He flourished a pretend lance at me.

'I saw you, darling, you were great.' He was carrying a cut-out of a trophy. For the last half-hour he had been cutting them out of yellow paper and handing them to all the other children. 'Shall we have some lunch?' He took my hand.

I introduced him to Nancy and Greg, and he waved and said 'Hi.'

'How are the Middle Ages going, buddy?' Greg said, and Robbie smiled and blushed. We had a medieval-themed lunch—chicken drumsticks and crusty bread (gluten-free) and cheese and corn on the cob.

As we were licking our fingers clean, Nancy and Greg threw a glance at each other. Greg cleared his throat.

'Um, before we move on to dessert, Nancy and I have some news.' He reached behind him and pulled a bottle of Cava out of the plastic bag. He looked back at Nancy and she giggled. She took his hand.

'Greg and I are pregnant!' she said, and reached back into the bag to pull out a bottle of grape juice. 'So I can't drink champagne!' *I wonder how many times they rehearsed that little skit.*

'Oh my god!' Peter said. 'That's fantastic! Congratulations!' He leaned over and grabbed his sister in such a hug they toppled over onto the ground.

'Really, congratulations,' I said, kissing Greg on the cheek.

'Glasses, everyone,' Greg said, and poured bubbly into our paper cups. I kissed Nancy, and Peter clapped Greg vigorously on the back and ruffled his hair.

'There's going to be a baby,' I told Robbie, who was looking confused.

'Cheers!' we all said, even Robbie, who took a sip from his cup and pulled a face. We laughed.

'How long have you known? Have you told Mum and

Dad?' Peter asked. He reached for Nancy's stomach as though he'd already be able to feel his niece or nephew nestled there.

Soon after, Robbie went to join in a game of tag that some other kids had started. Peter and Greg were discussing baby names, and I laughed at Peter's enthusiasm and turned down a third glass of Cava.

'How old is he?' asked Nancy, looking over at Robbie.

'He's thirteen,' I said, 'but if you imagine he's about nine or ten, things will make a lot more sense. That's really where he's at developmentally. He'll get to the same stage as everyone else, just a few years later.' I paused. 'Except academically. He's never going to be a rocket scientist.'

'He's a great kid.'

'He is now. Try telling him he has to tidy his room or go to bed.'

'It must be hard for you, raising a sick child.'

I shrugged. 'He's not sick, he's just different.'

'He's still beautiful,' Nancy said.

'Of course he is. And he's affectionate and curious and he has the best sense of humour. He loves helping people out.' I said it with pride, but I think it came out sounding defensive. Nancy seemed to be a bit worried, and she reached out and took Greg's hand again. I looked at Robbie, who was doing roly-polies. Nancy and Greg would be lucky to have a child as sweet as Robbie, I thought.

Week Nine

Allie is being very secretive about her project.

This week she has actually pulled her easel further into the corner of the room so none of us can peek. It's also so that she can hide herself away with Eamonn and they can whisper together, I suspect. They're barely even subtle anymore.

It's week three of the project half of term, and I've finished sketching and almost the first layer of paint. I'm using oils, and I've been coming in an extra time or two every week to work on it. I've surprised myself with how hard I'm working on it, how much I've decided it matters to me.

So far it's the same image four times over, or it's supposed to look that way. I can't quite get it perfect but I don't have the time to agonise. I need them all to dry fully before I can start adding the next bits, that will differentiate them. I probably shouldn't try until next week's session, I should stay away for seven days.

I feel frustration at not being able to work on it, and

that makes me smile. It's nice to care about something again.

If anything, sleeping with Peter a second time made everything less awkward.

The tension was broken, we had acknowledged the situation, we both knew where we stood—*is he really OK with it or is he saying it to please me?*—we could be relaxed and comfortable around each other again, and I was more glad than I could say. I needed him as a friend in my life.

We saw each other maybe two or three times a fortnight—we'd have him over for dinner so he could play with Robbie, or Dad would watch Robbie and Peter and I would go to the pictures or play tennis together. Once or twice I went with Peter when he had lunch with friends, or to an open mic night or a barbecue.

Once, when I was taking time off work to take care of a cold-stricken Robbie, and I had finally convinced him to have a nap, I found myself wandering the silent house, room to room. It wasn't often I had the house to myself in the daytime. I surveyed the living room critically. I considered using my time to tidy the house, really properly tidy it, and then I went back into the hall and picked up the phone. I called Peter at work, tracing the wallpaper pattern with my finger.

'Hey,' I said when he answered. 'Do you fancy coming over tonight? We could have another board game extravaganza.'

'Are you bored of playing nurse?'

'Well after all these years, I'm kind of used to it.'

'That's not what I meant.'

'I know, I know. It is a bit on the lonely side. I could do with some company. Pull a sickie?' I stretched my voice into a wheedle.

Peter laughed. 'Sorry, I can't. These numbers aren't going to add themselves.'

'Isn't that exactly what calculators are for?'

'Calculators don't do it as flamboyantly as I do.'

'But tonight?'

'Negatori, I'm afraid. I have plans.'

That stumped me. I tried to recover. 'You mean you have friends other than me?' I said, pretending to be shocked. 'Scandalous.'

'Well, you know how it is, people see you having so much fun with me they just want some for themselves.'

'Greedy pigs.'

'Still on for tennis this Saturday though?'

'Sure. I'll see you then.'

'My best to Robbie.'

'Bye.'

I put the phone down. I was more disappointed than I expected to be. I went into the living room and started cleaning.

When Robbie was fifteen, the doctor started commenting on his weight. He would happily kick a football around with Dad in the garden, but as they each got older and less inclined to make the effort, the ball spent more and more time slowly deflating in the flowerbeds. I nudged it disapprovingly with a toe. Robbie was inside, glued to the television. I looked down at my own expanded figure. At school I had been quite the netball player, but now the only regular exercise I was doing involved either a supermarket or washing line. I decided Robbie and I would start running.

I presented the idea to him with sufficient enthusiasm that he went along with it. Dad said it was a great idea, and that he would happily cheer us on from the comfort of the sofa. Clad in old trainers and grim determination, we set out one day after school with the modest goal of making it around the block. We made a big show of stretching copiously before setting off, reaching down towards distant toes, bringing feet up to bums, stepping forwards into lunges, so that by the time we set off we were already out of breath from laughing.

I set a light, bouncy pace, but Robbie was soon panting in earnest. He clenched his fists and pumped his arms, and his face as we turned the last corner was bright red and shining.

'Come on, buddy, we can do this,' I said, skipping sideways next to him. 'Another lap, what do you say?' After having to drag myself out the door, I found myself not wanting to go inside just yet. It had been so long since I had done something just for the sake of doing it, moved for the sake of movement and not for the sake of fetching, carrying, sorting, surviving. I felt more energised than I had in years, felt like I was moving blood that had lain sluggish for an age.

Robbie shook his head firmly. 'No... more,' he gasped, holding onto the garden wall with one hand and bending forwards, other hand on his hip, panting. 'No... run.'

I tried to impress upon him the importance of getting exercise, and then Sarah came up with the idea of a dodgeball game on Sundays. The school that hosted the

Sunday sessions agreed to give us access to the equipment cupboard, including a large bin of foam balls and some coloured bibs. The result was chaotic, but successful, and we made a regular thing of it.

Robbie never went back to running, but I carried on with it, on Saturday mornings. I perfected a route that took me to the far side of the park without hitting too many traffic lights that could break my rhythm, through the park, and then a gentle decline home. I wasn't breaking any speed records, but I arrived home sweating and, underneath the pounding heart, feeling accomplished. Powerful.

At first, I felt self-conscious in my grubby trainers, my baggy t-shirt and my tracksuit bottoms, certain that I looked like I didn't know what I was doing and that everyone was laughing at me, but soon I stopped caring. Settling into a rhythm, I could quieten my thoughts. I could feel the cool air on my face.

There were other people around in the park on a Saturday morning, dog-walkers and mums with prams, other joggers. I started to notice that if I left before about eight-thirty in the morning, somewhere in my route across the park I would pass a man running in the opposite direction. He wore Lycra shorts and a fluorescent yellow lightweight jacket, so he was quite noticeable. A good idea if he went running at night, I supposed. Always better to be visible.

I was musing this to myself without realising I had been gazing at him the whole time he was approaching. He nodded to me as he passed, one runner to another, with a small smile, almost a smirk. I dropped my eyes in sudden embarrassment, mortified to have been caught staring. If my face hadn't already been bright red, it would have flooded with colour. I was still shaking my head and cringing inwardly by the time I slowed to a breathless walk at my front drive.

I hadn't noticed before—don't think I had even looked at his face until he nodded at me—that he was quite attractive. Longish hair held back by a sweatband. Not the kind of look I would have thought would appeal to me, but it suited him, opened up his light-blue eyes. I gave myself a small shake as I let myself in. *Don't be silly, Camille.*

He was there the next Saturday, too. This time I kept my eyes down, watching the rhythmic pounding of my feet on the ground, until he was just passing. I looked up and caught his eye. He smiled at me again, and then he was gone. I couldn't work out if I had returned the smile in time for him to see it, and cursed myself. Then I wondered if I was running embarrassingly slow, and sped up, and cursed myself again because of course he wasn't watching.

It gave me a little rush, this wordless exchange. I was disappointed on the days I didn't see him, or something got in the way of my Saturday run. Not real disappointment, nothing I dwelt on for long, but a twinge, a passing *oh well*. On the days we did coincide, we exchanged a nod, a casual lifting of the chin in acknowledgement, and a smile. Sometimes he would raise a hand.

Once, when I was up and running unusually early, I saw him warming up by the entrance to the park, the one I usually exited. I recognised the fluorescent jacket reaching down to upturned toes. He leant against the back of a park bench to do press-ups, and then came around the front of the bench to do some kind of lunging step-up exercise. I forced myself not to change my pace, and he didn't look up or see me before I had slipped through the gate.

I wondered if I should start doing some strength exercises. It would only help my running, surely. The next time I ran was a weekday evening, to make up for a missed Saturday, and I veered off the path into a patch of grass with the vague intention of doing some squats. But there were too many people around, a group of hoodies sharing a joint, an older couple sitting quietly on a bench. Overcome with self-consciousness, I pretended I was taking a shortcut across the grass to another path, and carried on without breaking pace. I kept my head low and hoped nobody had been watching me.

I come back from the loo and Rosaline, next to me, is talking to Niall, on her other side.

'How am I supposed to know what I want to do for the rest of my life?' she's saying, brushing hair off her face with her wrist. She has a small birthmark high on her cheek, between ear and eye. 'Everyone seems to have this passion and this ambition and know exactly what they want to be doing. I just feel aimless. I feel like—I feel like I don't even want to be planning for my future, and apparently that makes me abnormal. I've no idea how I want to spend my life. It's such a long *time*. I don't know what I want for dinner tomorrow, how am I meant to know what I want to do for fifty years? *Fifty years*. It's so *long*. I can't think of anything I'd want to do for that long.'

I hold my breath to stifle myself. It does sound like a long time, and yet it seems only yesterday I was Rosaline's age. As far I remember, back then I didn't look on my future as an effort. I was excited about it.

'You don't have to have everything planned,' Niall says. 'Nobody really knows what they're doing, you just try different things until you find the right one.'

'What if I never find the right one?' Rosaline says, but she doesn't sound maudlin. Just curious.

Niall shrugs. 'Keep looking, I suppose.'

'Sometimes I wish I'd had really pushy parents, I feel like that would have taken the pressure off. I wouldn't have to make a decision.'

'They don't have any advice?'

Rosaline sits back from her painting, resting her wrists on her thighs. 'No, my parents—my mum and my step-dad—they've never told me what to do. They say I can do whatever I want to do. I think they think that's comforting. They're very supportive.' She wrinkled her nose playfully. 'Damn them.'

'Ah, don't knock it. I spent years working in finance because my parents wanted me to have a "good career". Couldn't stand it, bored me to death.'

'Were they proud, though?'

'Actually, my parents don't speak to me anymore.'

On either side of him, I can feel Rosaline and myself pausing, identically, waiting. Niall doesn't look left or right from his canvas.

'They don't approve of my partner,' he says. 'They disowned me, I guess you'd say.' A beat. 'So then, I thought, why am I wasting my life in a job I hate to please people who won't even look at me? And I quit, and I trained as a teacher, and I now teach a lovely class of nine-year-olds.'

I'm surprised at hearing this much from Niall. And touched.

'That's awful,' Rosaline says. Niall shrugs. 'Are you happy?'

I wonder what could be so offensive about this Jo that would make parents abandon their child. Perhaps they're racist. Or religious. Perhaps Jo is. At last, Niall glances at Rosaline. He smiles.

'Yes,' he says. 'Jo makes me very happy.'

I feel a swell of admiration for Niall. Good for him. I wonder briefly if his parents are terribly unhappy. I wonder if they gave him an ultimatum. I wonder how long Niall deliberated, or if he ever wavered from Jo. I wonder if he's ever wistful, or if he ever regrets.

One day, the phone rang, and an excitable Sarah told me her cat had had kittens, and that Robbie and I had to come and meet them immediately.

'I'm not sure Robbie's that keen on animals, honey,' I said hesitantly. 'I don't want anyone to get scared or hurt.'

'Robbie loves my cat,' Sarah declared, undeterred, 'and he'll love the kittens. Please come and see them, Cam, they're so cute and tiny.'

The new mother cat was in a box under the kitchen radiator, with a cluster of five mewling kittens. Robbie's eyes grew very wide, but he hung back.

'It's OK,' Sarah said, taking his hand. 'You can stroke one.' They knelt down together by the box, and Sarah showed him, carefully stroking one of the tiny kittens with a finger. Robbie copied her, his tongue between his teeth with concentration. He looked up at me to check he had done it right, and I couldn't help but melt at the honest joy on his face. He stroked each kitten in turn with great tenderness, and then sat back on his heels and watched them crawl blindly over each other.

'So little,' he murmured. 'So pretty.'

'We have to find them homes when they're big enough,' Sarah's brother said. 'Do you want one?' Robbie's eyes swelled with hope.

'I don't think so,' I said hurriedly. 'Pets are a big responsibility. And they can be quite expensive.' He deflated again. His disappointment was as honest and unabashed as every other emotion of his. I twisted my lips—it felt wrong to deprive someone like Robbie, with so much love to give, of something to love. I wished he wasn't so afraid of dogs.

'Do you know if there's a petting zoo around here?' I asked Peter that night, after Robbie was in bed. 'I think Robbie would really like it.' Peter was finishing off the washing up.

'Isn't he afraid of animals?' he said.

'It's just because he's never really been around them,' I said. 'I think it would be good for him.' I wiped the table down. 'Might be crowded though, might be a bit much for him, with lots of excitable kids.' I reached around Peter to squeeze the dishcloth into the sink, and he adorned my nose with a blob of Fairy bubbles.

'Maybe we can arrange something special for Robbie,' he said. 'After hours.'

'Hm,' I said, unconvinced. 'Sounds pricey.'

I asked around at work and started making phone calls. I located a petting zoo, asked a few of the parents at the support group if their children would like to come, and made enquiries about the possibility of accommodating a group of differently-abled children who would love the chance to meet some animals. In the end, it didn't cost that much, between us all.

We went one Sunday in late September. The sun was bright but the air was crisp, and the children's faces were soon rosy. There were eight kids, five parents and two members of staff. The petting zoo had some rabbits, some guinea pigs, some pygmy goats, as well as chickens strutting in the pen next door, and ducks on the duck pond.

We sat the kids down and bestowed a guinea pig on each of them. One girl couldn't face it and squealed whenever the animals got too close, but did manage to reach out and stroke a guinea pig who sat placidly on a staff members' arm, chewing a blade of grass.

Robbie sat as still as a stone, one arm curled protectively around the animal in his lap, the other stroking it rhythmically from top to tail. It had a chunk of carrot with it to keep it occupied, and every so often it tossed its nose in the air before going back to nibbling. Robbie's face was pure, concentrated bliss. He didn't want to let anyone take the guinea pig away from him, but we convinced him that the little animal needed a rest and that we could come back and see him later. There was a scuffle involving the rabbits, who thrashed their back legs if not held correctly, and frightened Robbie.

'Wanted hug,' he mumbled into my middle. He liked to hug everyone.

'I know,' I said, stroking his hair. 'Hugs are important.'

There were a few tears, a few scratches, a lot of mud and a messy picnic lunch, and everyone went home very happy.

Robbie fell asleep in the car on the way back. I leaned my head back too and closed my eyes. Peter reached one hand over from the steering wheel and squeezed my leg.

'You did so well, Cam,' he said. 'Everyone had a blast. I don't think Robbie's ever been so happy.'

I smiled, keeping my eyes closed.

'I'm glad,' I murmured. 'He deserves to be happy.'

Peter rang me when Nancy went into labour. Dad was stuck in traffic and Robbie was in a bad mood and I had dinner on the stove and the last thing I wanted was to answer the phone, but I went out into the hall with the wooden spoon in my hand, and as I listened I stretched the cord as far as it would go to try and keep an eye on Robbie, who was stomping around knocking things over with a scowl that could freeze lava.

'That's great,' I said to Peter. 'How long has it been?'

'About three hours I think. Still a long way to go.'

'Are you at the hospital?'

'No! I really want to be there, but there are parents and best friends and Greg's brother's family's dog's aunt, or something. The doctors are getting stressed, Nancy's getting stressed, it's just better if I don't join in right now.'

'Mhmm,' I said, holding the phone between ear and shoulder and trying to catch Robbie's attention with the spoon to get him away from the stove.

'I'm going to take tomorrow morning off work and hopefully go and meet my niece!' He sounded so excited.

'That's great, Peter. I have to go now, but keep me updated,' I said, hoping he wouldn't.

'OK. You'll have to come and meet her too at some point.'

'I'm sure I will, at some point,' I said. 'Bye now.' I put the phone down and snapped more harshly than I meant to at Robbie that he had to do his homework. I stirred the sauce angrily, scrubbing at burnt onions at the bottom of the pan.

It was a rage of envy. This is what people should be doing at my age, starting a family, at the beginning, with years of independence and adventure and relationships and careers behind them. They should be dealing with pregnancies and babies and new mortgages, not teenagers.

I began savagely chopping vegetables, and told Robbie that no he may not watch television until he had finished his homework. He tried to go into the living room anyway, and I had to go over to the kitchen door and close it, and stand in front of it with my arms folded until he sat back down at the kitchen table and picked up his pencil, his face screwed up with anger and his head heavily in his hand and his feet kicking in frustration. I ran a hand through my hair and sighed. I felt like huffing and shouting too, and folding my arms and stamping my feet, but the washing machine started beeping at me and the dinner needed attention, and as much as I hadn't wanted this life thrust on me there was nothing I could do about it.

Robbie slammed his textbook shut and pushed it away from him.

'Stupid,' he said, and folded his arms and sat back in his chair and stared at me like he was daring me to argue.

'It's a boy,' Peter said the next day. He called me at about three-thirty in the afternoon, when I'd just had a whole load of paperwork delivered that had to be dealt with. I'd been waiting for it all day, and I only had an hour before I had to leave to pick up Robbie for his physiotherapy appointment. I was struggling to remain interested in Nancy's baby.

'Is it?' I murmured, reaching for the stapler.

'Yeah, everyone was surprised. But he's beautiful, he's beautiful and he's healthy and he's called Gabriel.'

'That's wonderful,' I said, putting my pen between my teeth while I held the papers together.

'Yeah, it is, I still can't believe it. She's a mother! I'm an uncle!'

'OK, Peter, that's great, but I have to get back to work,' I said, trying to keep the irritation out of my voice.

'Can I come over later? I've got some polaroid photos.'

'Um, sure, we have to go to the physiotherapist, should be back by seven, seven-thirty.'

'Great, why don't I bring round some dessert?'

'Sure. Fine. I have to go.' I put the phone down and it began to ring again, and I banged my head on the papers on my desk.

Robbie showed a teenaged lack of interest in the photos of the baby, and I had to admit I felt the same. It was a nondescript bundle in blue cloth, however much Peter insisted he was beautiful. I made interested noises while I scrubbed at the dishes in the sink. It was a while before I realised I was still making them and Peter had stopped talking.

'Are you OK?' he said. 'Am I talking about Gabriel too much?'

'Just a tad,' I said, my teeth gritting ever so slightly.

'Are you jealous?' Peter said teasingly, coming over. 'Is that biological clock ticking? The maternal instinct kicking in?' He hugged me round my waist from behind. I wriggled away and turned around to face him.

'No,' I said truthfully. 'I don't want a baby.' Peter was looking at me tenderly. I wished he wouldn't.

'Then what is it?'

I gave a half-shrug. 'They're doing it right. They have their lives ahead of them, and I'm only a few years older and I'm already done. I'm closer to forty than thirty, and what do I have to show for it?'

'A beautiful, healthy brother,' Peter said.

To my shame, I could feel tears pricking in my eyes. 'This isn't how it was meant to happen,' I said, hating the crack in my voice. 'I'm not in the job I want, I'm not in the relationship I want, I don't even exist outside of caring for Robbie.' The tears started to spill. Suddenly Peter was very close, he had his hands on my face and he was wiping away my tears.

'You do exist. You exist to me,' he whispered. 'I want to give you all the things you want, you know I do.' He only made me cry harder, and he wrapped his arms around me and held me tight, stroking my hair. 'Why won't you let me love you?' he murmured into the side of my head. I buried my eyes in his shoulder and squeezed him as hard as I could.

There had been times, in the years since Nancy's wedding. Once, on what would have been my mother's birthday, when I was feeling vulnerable and emotional, we had kissed. That's all, just kissed, just for comfort and closeness and intimacy. Twice we had slept together. But I never let him be my boyfriend—that was a term for teenagers, not for adults—I never let him tell me he loved me or hold my hand or say we were together.

He pulled away from me and looked into my eyes.

'Camille, you are the biggest part of my life, you know that. I'm always going to be here, I'm always going to be tied to you. Why won't you let us be together?'

My eyelashes were wet and stuck together and my breath was catching in my throat. I looked into his eyes, his beautifully kind, caring eyes, and I decided that for once, I wanted to be taken care of.

'OK,' I whispered, and I don't know if he heard me or understood me, but he pulled me close again and rocked me there in the kitchen.

When Dad tells the story of how Peter and I ended up together, he makes out that Peter pined after me for ten years. It wasn't like that.

He had girlfriends for the first few years I knew him—in fact when I met him, that first time in the supermarket, he was seeing a girl called Angela who worked in a shoe shop, though he said they only went out two or three times.

'Annoying girl,' he would say. 'Such a whiny voice, it *pierced*. I did end up buying a pair of shoes from her though, just out of sheer awkwardness.'

'Why did you talk to me,' I asked once, 'that day in the supermarket?'

He seemed surprised by the question. 'Because you looked like you could do with someone being nice to you, for a change,' he said.

'You pitied me?' I was taking up a pair of trousers for Robbie at the time, pins in my mouth.

'Not at all. You looked tired and stressed, and I thought how hard it must be for you, raising a child like Robbie, and you had your ID card around your neck, so I knew you worked as well, and I had a lot of respect for how you handled the situation. I thought, if there's anybody who would be cheered up by a random person showing some basic kindness, it would be you. So I tried to be kind.'

'And in the café? Why did you ask for my number?'

'Because, my darling,' Peter said, 'you looked extremely beautiful, and extremely bored.' I held the needle up, trying to re-thread it.

'You wanted to show me a good time?'

'I wanted to see that smile again. Besides, I'd already finished with Angela by that point.'

'Philanderer.'

He kissed my shoulder. 'You cured me of my womanising ways,' he said, and went back to reading.

He'd had a reasonably serious relationship for almost two years, after he'd expressed 'fondness' for me but before we'd shared the kiss. Her name was Claire; I had met her a few times and they seemed to make a good couple. I never discussed Peter's relationships with him.

He wouldn't gush about how amazing and wonderful his girlfriend was, he wouldn't come to me to moan about her when they had fights. Sometimes he wouldn't even tell me he was seeing somebody new. We'd just see him slightly less, maybe have an extra person join us for coffee every now and then.

I know at least one of them broke it off with him because of me, because of his closeness to Robbie and me.

I don't really know how I felt about Peter's girlfriends. Whenever I did get him in a conversation about one of them, I'd be supportive, in a teasing way, trying to nudge him towards making it serious or thinking about it long-term. I wanted him to find somebody to be happy with, who wasn't me, who could be for him everything he needed that I couldn't give him. But also I was terrified I'd lose him as a friend. He was my support system, more than all the groups and parents and professionals ever had been.

Claire had actually been a client of his, the owner of an events company who needed an accountant.

'Was she wooed by your mathematical genius?' I said, popping a slice of cucumber into my mouth and grinning. 'Wowed by your powers of addition, bowled over by your multiplication?' Peter rolled his eyes and looked uncomfortable. We were having lunch, one workday, by the canal next to my building. I knew he'd been on a few dates with a woman, and had been pestering him to tell me who it was.

'I invited her to lunch,' he said. 'She said, "Is that how you break it to people that they're bankrupt?" and I said, "No, that's how I break it to people that I'd like to take them on a date." She laughed, we went to lunch, that's it.'

'Do you like her?'

He shrugged. 'She's nice. Why don't I ever get to tease you about your dates?'

'I don't have dates to be teased about,' I said, and added, 'I'm far too busy and important for frivolities.' I steered the conversation back to safer ground. 'Are you seeing her again?'

'Pictures on Saturday night.'

'Saturday night, ooh la la,' I said, nudging him. He shrugged me off, and I laughed.

After a couple of months, he brought up the idea of meeting her. I tried to keep my face neutral.

'Why would you want me to meet her?' I said.

'You're both important people in my life,' he said patiently, 'and I'd like you to meet her.'

I imagined some kind of interview situation. 'When?'

'We're going to a jazz evening this Sunday. You could come.'

'Ooh, a school night, don't know about that,' I said. I fervently did not want to meet her.

'It won't be late, we've both got work in the morning.' I wondered if I could use Robbie as an excuse somehow. 'Please? I think you'd really like her.'

I sighed, and stabbed my fork into my salad. 'OK. Let's jazz.'

The club was dark and smoky, and loud. I thought it would be best to turn up fashionably late, but by then the band had already started and it was difficult to make conversation.

Peter and Claire were sitting on stools by the bar, watching the band. Claire's legs were crossed, one foot resting on the bar across the bottom of her stool, bouncing in time to the beat. Peter had a hand on her thigh, with the other resting a pint of beer on his leg. I took a deep breath, and went to join them.

I clapped a hand on Peter's shoulder. *You're going for jovial? Really?* He looked up, and his face broke into a beam when he saw me. He'd thought I wasn't coming. He reached around to put his beer on the bar and gave me a hug, then, with one arm still around me, gestured at Claire and, presumably, said something along the lines of 'Camille, meet Claire.' I reached out a hand, and shook hers. She was pretty, dark hair in tight curls, a rounded nose, wide eyes, slim calves. Weak handshake. She leaned in.

'I've heard so much about you,' she said. I would have replied, but the drums started up a solo, so I just smiled and nodded in a *lovely-to-meet-you-I've-heard-so-much-about-you-too* sort of way. I hoped she understood. I caught the bartender's attention and ordered a gin and tonic.

When the band took a break, we could talk more. Claire seemed very nice, very outgoing and friendly, a loud laugh that contrasted deeply with Peter's softly-spoken demeanour. I stayed until the end of the band's set, and then I made my excuses. Peter walked me out.

'She's lovely,' I said, kissing his cheek goodbye. 'Really, she is.'

Peter smiled, but not as broadly as he usually did. 'Say

hello to Robbie for me,' he said.

I nodded, and walked away towards the bus stop.

———

'Pub?' Morris asks as we're all gathering our coats and bags. He's looking mostly at Becca and Allie and Niall. Emmi mumbles about deadlines and being tired.

'I'd love to come,' Rosaline says unexpectedly.

'Me too,' I say before I can stop myself. I'm feeling exhausted, just from concentrating so hard. But productive too, and proud. I deserve a drink. 'I'd love to come,' I say, and Morris is surprised, but pleasantly, I think.

'Sorry, folks, I've got to get off,' Eamonn says, and Niall says his partner is waiting for him. So Morris, Allie, Becca, Rosaline and I go off together. A strange motley crew, I think, and the thought gives me a sort of glee.

The pub isn't crowded, isn't empty. Morris has a beer, Becca a cider, Allie a house white, Rosaline a Southern Comfort and lemonade, and after a moment's hesitation I order a whiskey. We sit at a table by the slot machine and playfully refuse to give out any details of our projects. I swirl the whiskey in my glass, wondering how long it's been since I've felt this comfortable in a social setting.

One of the bartenders, a girl barely old enough to drink herself, nudges a wine glass off a table as she clears the empties, and it breaks. Two lads at the bar jeer and clap, and she blushes furiously. She takes the full tray behind the counter. I follow her with my eyes, my hand still gently circling my glass. The girl's manager slams a broom into her hands, more forcefully than necessary in my opinion, and tells her to get back out on the floor and sweep it up.

I drop my eyes again.

'So, apparently, I've been using it wrong all my life,' Allie is saying, elbow on table, holding her wine glass by her ear. 'Stoic doesn't mean ignoring pain, it just means reason over emotion. Of course the way he says it sounds terribly complicated, but I'm sure that was the gist. My little philosopher.'

'That doesn't sound like much fun,' Morris says mildly.

'I don't know,' Becca says. 'Life might be a lot easier without emotions.'

I smile and shake my head, and sip my whiskey.

I didn't ask him why he and Claire broke up. When he told me, I hugged him, gave him a beer, and curled up on the sofa with him while Robbie sat on the floor, and we watched a video.

He didn't pine for me for ten years. That's an exaggeration.

Week Ten

Emmi has stopped coming to class.

'She's having problems at uni,' Rosaline tells me, after I sidle innocently up to her for information. 'She's missed a load of deadlines and they're threatening to kick her out. I think something went on at home, I'm not really sure. She's pretty messed up. I don't see her around that much.'

I think about when the two of them first came in, that first lesson ten weeks ago. They'd come in together, they'd sat together, they'd whispered together. They seemed like the best of friends. I'd assumed they were close, but here was Rosaline having apparently let Emmi fall completely off her radar without a second thought.

'Is this about that chap? The ex-boyfriend?' I was remembering the night a drunken Emmi had stumbled into me on my way to the bus stop. Rosaline shrugs— shrugs! As though she couldn't care one way or the other.

'Could be,' she says. She doesn't seem keen on continuing the conversation.

It was difficult, at first, to register any difference in our situation. We were officially "together", an "item"—boyfriend was still too strange a term for me—and I think I was expecting a paradigm shift in my life, but the truth was very little changed, at least right away. He was already a big part of my life.

It made me a bit nervous, unsure what to do with myself, how to negotiate our changed status. That night, we had cups of tea at the kitchen table, as we had many times before, and he held my hand across the table.

Dad came in, in a foul mood over something that happened at work, or maybe the football score, and stamped upstairs for a shower.

'I should go,' said Peter, giving my hand a squeeze and standing up. He took the mugs over to the sink, and I stood, suddenly awkward, not knowing how to say goodbye. I followed him to the hall. Why was I following him? *It's my house, I should walk him out.*

He opened the door.

'I'll call you?' he said. I nodded. He leaned forwards and kissed me, briefly, on the lips. He smiled, and left.

He did call, the next day, and asked if he could take me out on a proper first date. That made me smile.

'Let me treat you right, doll,' he said in an American accent.

'OK,' I said, relenting. 'That sounds nice. I can't do this week, there's too much on and Dad's working long hours.'

'How about Saturday night?'

'Actually Sunday night works better for me. Is that a

strange night for a date?'

'No problem, we can make it work,' Peter said. 'Now, I think it's been a while since you did this, so I'm going to talk you through it.' I swivelled on my chair, my smile growing. 'I'm going to pick you up, meet your father, and walk you to my car. If I open the car door for you, you'll be impressed by my courtesy. We'll go to a restaurant and enjoy good food and good wine, and partake of witty banter. Afterwards, we might adjourn to the bar, or if the dessert menu hasn't taken our fancy, I'll take you to a little spot I know of that does the best tiramisu in town. We might take a little evening stroll, and I'll drive you back home in plenty of time for you to get all the sleep you need for work on Monday. How does that sound?'

I gave an exaggerated sigh. 'I don't think that's going work,' I said.

'Why not?'

'I'm not a huge fan of tiramisu.'

He sucked his breath in through his teeth. 'Right. Well. Shall we call the whole thing off?'

'Yeah, probably best.'

'Alright. Six o'clock?'

'See you then.' I put the phone down, grinning like a bashful teenager. Ruth came back into the office from a coffee break.

'What are you so happy about?' she said.

'Oh nothing,' I said, turning back to my desk. 'It's just that I have a date this weekend.' My tone was flushed with pride.

'Really? How exciting,' she said, approvingly. I tried to turn my mind back to work, but I couldn't wipe the smile off my face and I was already thinking about clothes. I fiddled with a strand of hair. *He likes me.*

'It is exciting, isn't it?'

Staying the night proved to be a bit of an issue.

We'd been together for a while. I'd told my dad in an exceedingly awkward conversation that Peter and I were "in a relationship", and he'd seemed surprised that it had taken us so long. We didn't go to bed together for the first couple of months. It wasn't a conscious decision, we just both wanted to give ourselves time to get used to each other in this new context. Holding hands, like school-children. Sitting with his arm around my shoulders. Kissing.

But, inevitably, eventually, we took things further. And every time, I had to get up, get dressed, and drive back home so I'd be able to get Robbie ready for school the next morning. We considered, briefly, him staying over at my house, but I couldn't cope with the idea of my dad next door and Robbie across the hall.

It was a tricky conversation to have with Dad. On the one hand, he wanted me to have my own life. I could see the guilt he felt for relying so heavily on me weighing on him every day. But on the other hand, he did rely on me. And I wasn't entirely sure he was keen on me spending the night with Peter—a relic of Mum's Catholicism? Either way, I could have sworn I detected a blush beneath his glasses. But he seemed to make a conscious effort to shake it off.

'No, you're right, of course,' he said. 'You're an adult, you need your own life, your own relationships. I'm sorry you've been stuck here with your old dad so long!' I could have said something at this point but I didn't know what. There had been no choice, and we both knew it. 'I'm sure I'll be able to cope with Robbie on my own a couple of days a week.'

'He is getting so much better now,' I said. 'He doesn't need help getting dressed and he can get his own breakfast, and he likes to pack his bag the night before. He can make his own lunches, but sometimes he's a bit slow so you might have to help him. Really the only thing is making sure he gets up on time, he likes to sleep in. Sometimes he'll have a bad day, he'll throw a tantrum— but you know all of that.'

'That I do,' Dad said. 'It's fine, I can get him off to school no problem. It'll just be tricky getting into work on time.'

'I wonder if he could go to school on public transport,' I said.

'Do you think he'd cope?'

I sighed. 'Probably not yet. In a few years, maybe. He's just not quite there yet.' Dad nodded. 'Maybe I could stay over at Peter's on weekends.' Dad nodded again, this time more slowly. I knew why he was hesitant—on a weekday, he'd have an evening and a morning alone with Robbie. On a weekend, I could be gone for all of both days. It was a long time with a child like Robbie, and with nobody else there, it could be extremely isolating. 'I wouldn't be gone the whole time,' I said. 'I could even come back for breakfast.'

'Don't be silly,' said Dad, sounding like he wanted that very much.

'Well, let's start with this weekend and see how we go,'

I said. 'How does that sound?'

'That sounds wonderful,' Dad said, getting up and squeezing me on the shoulder as he went to get a glass.

'I can pick Robbie up from school, we can have dinner and I'll go over to Peter's after. Then I'll be back Saturday after lunch.'

Dad poured himself some water. 'That's fine. Don't worry about me, Camille, I have raised a child before. And you were much more difficult than Robbie.'

'Hey!'

'Strong-willed,' he said, smiling.

Robbie went to a children's session at the tennis centre on a Saturday morning. Dad would have to get him up and ready and take him, and wait while he was there, bring him back and sort out lunch. Then hopefully Robbie would play by himself in the afternoon, giving Dad some time to do his own things, and then I'd be back. On Sunday, Sarah was coming round and then they would both go to the support group playtime. It would be fine. I kept running through plans in my mind.

'Relax, sweetheart,' Dad said. 'I'm happy for you and Peter. He's a lovely man.'

'He is, isn't he,' I said, biting the skin at the edge of my thumbnail. Dad batted my hand away.

'You're getting like your mother.'

I ignored him. 'He treats me really well,' I said.

'Good. You deserve someone to treat you nicely.' He peered at me. 'Are you nervous?'

'A little. Isn't that crazy?' The talk was veering too near the too-personal now, so we cut it short. I went to call Peter. And thus, we began our weird little split-personality relationship, half quasi-married couple in their own house, half teenaged drop-you-back-at-your-parents' arrangement.

Strangely, it worked. I loved my weekends at Peter's, finally being on my own again, having space and time and quiet and somebody to love me. And it made the weeks easier too, long hours at the office, the doctors' appointments and sitting in traffic, the cooking and the to-ing and fro-ing and the calming Robbie down when he had one of his moods. I had something to look forward to at the end of it.

I wondered if I should explain to Robbie about Peter and me, but it didn't seem necessary. He didn't seem to register any change, even when he saw Peter greet me with a kiss. I realised it wasn't that he thought we were still "just friends", it was that he'd always thought we were together.

Sometimes, if I could wangle it, I'd get Dad to pick Robbie up from school and I'd go straight to Peter's, and we'd go out for dinner just the two of us, or with his friends, and for twenty-four hours it was just how I'd imagined my life would be fifteen years ago.

A weekday evening dash to the supermarket.

I got out of the car and walked around it to see if I'd parked well enough. Robbie hopped down, carefully shutting the door behind him. A young woman was wheeling a full shopping trolley towards a minivan. She had an infant strapped to her chest, and two more kids running around her feet. Watching her trying to push the trolley, stop her children getting caught under the wheels, find the car keys and keep her hair out of her eyes, I felt some kind of harassed solidarity with her, and offered her a weak smile as she passed, which she returned distractedly. As she was loading bags into the boot of her car, the two older kids got into a spat, which ended with the little boy in tears and his sister running off to crouch behind a red car in terrified glee.

The boy stood in the middle of the roadway, threw his head back and bawled. Robbie, naturally, went over to him to give him a hug. The mother, glancing up wearily, came to life at once.

'Hey!' she shouted, abandoning the shopping trolley and running forwards awkwardly, one hand clamped to the baby. 'Hey, get away from him!' She grabbed her son by the upper arm and dragged him out of Robbie's reach. She glared at me, and back to Robbie, and marched the boy back to the car, calling for her daughter in a tone that brooked no messing around. The girl came running. The woman strapped both children into the car before stalking off to retrieve her errant shopping trolley. She was muttering to herself, but the only word I caught was "Mongol". She had the grace to flush darkly.

Robbie stayed exactly where he was. I could see him struggling to stop the corners of his mouth pulling down. My heart ripped away from my chest. It was true we attracted stares, mostly curious, sometimes hostile, though these days I barely noticed them. Rarely had anyone been so vicious.

I reached for Robbie, wanting to shield him, but of course it was too late. The damage was done. I ushered him back to the car, and he let himself be shepherded. He climbed in, shut the door, and carefully clicked his seatbelt in. His chin was buried into his chest, and tears started to fall.

In desperation, my agony for him turned to anger against her. *How dare she.* I swung angrily out of the car park and had to pull over after we rounded the corner because I was shaking too much to see straight. I reached over to Robbie and let him cry into me.

'Darling, there are horrible people in this world, and they believe horrible things, and they do horrible things, and they deserve nothing but horribleness.' Robbie mumbled wordlessly. 'I know you just wanted to help,' I said, rocking him. 'I know everyone deserves a hug. You're the sweetest, kindest person I've ever known, and that woman doesn't know the first thing about you.'

Robbie stayed in his room for the whole of that evening.

The next day, finding myself with nothing to take to work for lunch, I grudgingly joined the queue in the cafeteria. It was normally an easily-avoidable expense. As I was fumbling with my purse, someone reached across me to take an apple from the bowl beside the till. I glanced up distractedly, and saw a man was smiling at me. Nonplussed, I took my change, made what I hoped was a polite face, and manoeuvred my tray away.

I had sat down and unwrapped my sandwich before I realised I recognised those blue eyes. Today the hair was falling forwards into them, when normally it was held back by a length of while towelling, but they were the same eyes.

I swivelled in my seat, scanning the cafeteria. Endless

grey suits. I couldn't see anybody's eyes. I turned back to my tray and told myself no one was staring at me, but my cheeks burned anyway. I crammed my sandwich, crisps and drink into my handbag and got up, returned my tray and left, trying to shake the feeling that I was walking under a hot spotlight.

I ate my crushed lunch outside, on the wall by the canal, keeping my back to the building. I didn't go running that Saturday. I told myself I was tired and needed a rest.

My eyes took on a life of their own, scrutinising everyone swiping in through the turnstiles, everyone in every lift, everyone who passed by my office. Ruth laughed and asked if I was expecting someone. On the Friday, Ruth had the day off, and I sat alone, drumming my fingers on the desk and staring at the empty doorway and eventually stood up, abruptly, dislodging a stack of manila folders, grabbed my bag and went down to the cafeteria.

I sat in a corner so nobody could sneak up on me and ate my jacket potato without really noticing it, hoping to catch a glance of blue eyes. I didn't see him. Telling myself to stop being so silly, I returned my tray and headed back towards the lift—and he passed me, deep in conversation with another man, who was gesturing emphatically.

I stopped still and watched them go, marvelling.

He worked here. My smiling runner, working in the very same building. I almost pinched myself. I scurried back to my office like a child smuggling a secret.

In the afternoon, I was jolted out of doodling by a phone call. It was Peter, calling to invite me to the cinema.

I sat up as though electrocuted when I heard his voice, shoved the piece of paper under my keyboard and brushed my hair out of my face.

'I could pick you up from work if you wanted to catch the early showing?'

'Um, yeah.' I cleared my throat and nudged the mouse to get rid of the screensaver. The revived screen glared at me brightly. 'Yes. Sounds good.' I stared at the cursor as it blinked gently at me and tried to remember what film it was Peter wanted to take me to.

Of course, then I started seeing him everywhere. Had something changed, or had I always crossed paths with him so many times at work and had just been too wrapped up in myself to notice him?

When he saw me seeing him, when I walked past a meeting room doorway where he was being delayed by someone talkative, or when our eyes met across an expanse of lobby too wide to bridge with words, we shared a secret, knowing smile. *I know you,* the smile said. *I've seen you, outside, in the real world, and I don't even know your name.*

Of course, eventually we saw each other and there was no loquacious colleague, no intervening hallway, nothing to stop us speaking. So we spoke.

I was waiting for a lift, and he came to stand beside me, also waiting. He was smiling that smile.

'It's you,' he said, carefully keeping his gaze up at the floor numbers illuminating as the lift slid towards us.

'It's me,' I agreed.

'You run,' he commented, sagely.

'I do. So you do.'

The smile tugged us both out of the charade.

'Tim,' he said, turning fully to me and holding out a hand courteously.

'Camille.' His handshake was firm, dry, and lingering.

'Nice to finally meet you.'

'What are the chances?' I said. 'What do you do here?'

'I'm an urban planner, I just started in Transport.' Urban planner sounded so... sophisticated, I thought.

'I'm in Housing,' I said, indicating the ID card on my lanyard, though I don't know why.

'Amazing. Everyone needs housing.'

I pulled a face. I wouldn't have called my job amazing.

The lift arrived with a loud ding. He graciously gestured me in before him.

'So, just started as in new to the area?' I asked, making conversation.

'How about we do a proper conversation, instead of the usual fly-by?' Tim asked, laughing. The doors opened— my floor. Three floors below Transport, I knew.

'If the stars align,' I trilled, walking out of the lift without looking back. I widened my eyes, cringing at myself. Was I—*flirting*? Was *that* what that was?

My face was still red by the time I sank back into my desk chair, and Ruth raised her eyebrows at me.

The following week, Peter called and asked if I wanted to meet for lunch.

'I don't think I'm going to manage a lunch break today,' I said regretfully, 'I'm a bit snowed under.'

'OK. You can get through it all, I'm sure,' he said, tenderly. 'Try to take a bit of a break if you can, it's good for you.' I put the phone back in the cradle and kept my hand on it, scanning the desk in front of me. He was right, I told myself, I needed a break. Even if it was just ten minutes. I grabbed my lunch from the fridge and headed so determinedly out of the building I didn't notice Tim, and he had to put out a hand to stop me.

'Can I join you?' he asked.

'Of course,' I said, taken aback, and suddenly panicking over what I had brought for lunch. Was it embarrassing? Would I make a mess?

'Let me grab a sandwich,' he said, indicating the cafeteria. 'Two minutes.'

I stood with one leg crossed over the other, clutching my packed lunch like a schoolgirl, imagining that all the people who walked past were staring at me as I waited in the corridor. No one paid me any attention.

We sat on the low wall by the canal. The sun flickered weakly through wind-tousled clouds and I tried to keep my hair out of my forkfuls. Tim ate his sandwich, one foot propped on the wall he was sitting on to make his knee into an armrest. We talked about work, the woman in HR you had to avoid at all costs, the facilities manager who would go above and beyond to help, the promise of a brand-new civic centre that had been dangled before us for years.

'So how long have you been here for?' he asked me, crushing his empty sandwich packet between two hands.

'Oh, forever,' I said breezily. 'I'm a true veteran.'

'I don't think anyone under thirty can call themselves a veteran of anything,' he said. 'Unless you've literally been in the army.'

'Maybe I have,' I said. Then, 'Wait, how old do you

think I am?'

'Mid-to-late twenties?'

'Oh bless you.' I laid one hand on his shoulder and another dramatically over my heart. 'I don't believe you for a second, but it was lovely of you to say.'

He laughed, opening a packet of crisps and offering them to me. 'No, really,' he said. 'How old?'

'You're off by about a decade,' I said, helping myself. 'And in the interests of my dignity, that's all I'm saying.'

'Oh, a woman of mystery, I like it,' he said, raising an eyebrow at me. My laugh faltered in my throat, and I looked down, embarrassed.

My painting has rather suddenly become very difficult. I'm starting to move on to the finer detail and I'm struggling. My jaw is beginning to ache from clenching it in concentration.

'Breathe, Camille,' Rosaline says, laughing. I give her a tight smile back, but the frustration is getting to me. I'm trying to paint a youthful, healthy shine, and it looks like a schoolchild has just learnt that shadow goes opposite to light and is drawing a picture with the sun in the top left corner. It looks laborious. It looks amateur.

'I just can't get it right,' I say. Allie, across the room, looks up and smiles serenely. Serene is the word to describe her these days, like she's suddenly found the key to happiness and has settled into permanent contentment. If there is any guilt, any turmoil or emotional struggles going on beneath the surface, she hides it, completely and absolutely. I'm not sure if I admire her steadfastness and determination—dedication, almost, to her affair—or if I find it slightly disquieting. Does she really have no qualms? Even if Jonathan does ignore her, and he must if he is oblivious to what's going on—do marriage vows mean nothing?

I eye Emmi's empty seat. Perhaps my attitude is just old-fashioned. Out of date, now.

'What is it you're trying to do?' Morris, on my left. He doesn't look up. I slump back on my stool.

'Just make it look halfway decent,' I say.

'Try something different.'

That irritates me. 'What, try and make it look terrible?'

Morris shrugs, selecting a different brush. 'You know what they say, doing the same thing and expecting different results.'

'What?'

'Einstein, wasn't it? Definition of insanity.' Him and his wretched quotes.

'So apparently I'm insane?' I'm cross now. His tone is too blasé. I want some artistic sympathy—if I can't get any here, where can I?

Morris surprises me. He snaps right back. 'Well what do you want me to say? You want me to do it for you?' I try to reply but find I'm grasping for words in the empty air. I can see Eamonn has noticed, from the corner of my eye. He doesn't come over. He prowls behind Allie and Becca, keeping his distance. *Coward*, I think desperately. Morris regards me, his chin high, his eyes challenging, and turns back to his paint pots.

My heart hammers like a child chastised. I can feel my cheeks burning, though I don't think anyone else has heard. Eamonn is determinedly looking the other way. I'm feeling scolded and embarrassed and exposed like I haven't been in years.

Calmly, I lay down my brush, stand up, smooth my trousers and walk over to the sink. I run cold water over and over my hands even though they're spotless, until I feel still. Then I walk back to my station and resume my painting and I don't look at Morris and he doesn't look at me.

Robbie left school at nineteen, when his classmates were sixteen. His speech therapist put us in touch with an organisation that helped to place people with Down Syndrome in full-time work, and they found Robbie a job in a café. He had a series of training sessions after closing time so he felt comfortable in the setting, and we had a trial run one Sunday when the café was normally closed, with Sarah and some members of our support group.

Even so, the weekend before he started working for real was a nightmare. On Friday night at dinner he was silent, and barely ate. He wouldn't look up from his lap, he wouldn't talk, he wouldn't register either of us, not even when I pulled his chair away from the table so I could crouch in front of him. He took himself off to bed without wanting to read with me, and as I stood outside his closed door, I heard him crying.

On Saturday morning he came bounding downstairs, cheerful as anything, saying that he'd changed his mind and he wasn't going to work, he was just going to stay at home from now on. Dad buttered his toast and replied carefully that Robbie couldn't stay at home all day every day on his own. Robbie shrugged.

'OK. I go to school. Stay there forever.'

'You can't do that either, buddy,' Dad said. 'You're a grown-up now. Grown-ups have to go to work.'

Robbie's face darkened. I could see his mouth working furiously as he tried to think of a response. But he knew Dad was right. As Dad set Robbie's plate in front of him, he flipped it up into the air, sending toast and jam flying and the plate clattering upside-down. Then he swept his arm across the table so the plate crashed to the floor and shattered into pieces.

I froze. It had been a while since we'd seen a fully-fledged rage. Robbie's anger terrified me. When he was happy, his joy was simple and pure and complete, but it was the same at the other end of the spectrum—all-consuming, boundless. I knew he was only angry because he was scared, but there was nothing I could do to make it better.

Dad caught Robbie by the wrists as he spun around and held him so he had to look at him.

'Robert Addison. Listen to me. You do not throw things. You do not smash plates. You are an adult, and you are perfectly capable of acting like one.' Robbie glowered. Dad lowered his voice, with an obvious effort. 'I know you're nervous, and I know you're scared, but you are more than capable of doing this job. You just need to keep calm and focus, remember what we used to work on?'

Robbie wasn't having any of it. He stamped his feet and yanked his arms out of Dad's grasp. Robbie was young and stocky, and Dad was sixty-six and weary—he went careering backwards and knocked into the corner of the counter-top, hard. I saw him bend in pain.

'Robert!' I moved forwards, but he was frenzied,

crying and shouting and struggling to breathe, arms and legs thrashing. 'Robert, stop that behaviour right now!' With difficulty, and sustaining a blow to the face, I managed to get Robbie upstairs and in his room. I shut the door and leant my weight back, holding it shut. 'And you will stay there until you can learn to calm down!' I shouted through the door. He pounded on it for a while, but eventually he subsided. He knew what being shut in his room meant. Soon I heard nothing but choking, hiccupping sobs.

I went downstairs to see Dad. He was sitting awkwardly in a kitchen chair, one leg straight out.

'Are you OK? What did you hit?'

'My lower back,' he grunted. 'On this side,' he indicated his stretched leg. He looked at me.

'He give you another shiner?' I nodded, going to the fridge for some frozen peas. I leant against the counter, holding them to my face, just under my eye.

'He just doesn't know how to cope with feelings of anxiety,' I said. 'He tries to fight it out of him.'

After twenty minutes, when the peas were back in the freezer—it wouldn't leave much of a mark, it hadn't been intentional—I went back upstairs. Robbie was sitting on his bed, waiting for me.

I sat down next to him and held my arms out. He lay against me, and I rubbed his arm and started humming softly, the same tune my mum would hum to me when I had a nightmare.

'I'm sorry, Cammy,' he said.

'I know, darling. But we can't go around behaving like that, can we? We have to recognise the feelings, and stop, and count to ten, remember?' He said nothing. 'The feelings aren't going to hurt us, we just have to know that they're there and that they will go away eventually. Are you going to apologise to Dad?' He nodded into my chest. 'The job will be good, I promise. You can wear the special apron, and use the coffee machine, and the squirty bottle to clean the tables. It's everything you like.'

'People,' he said.

'I know, baby, I know. Some people will be nice. Some of them will be very nice, and some of them will be only a little bit nice, and one or two might be not nice at all. But we're going to smile at all of them, and be polite to all of them, and the ones that aren't nice, we're going to let them walk right out of the door and forget all about them.'

I left very soon. I knew Robbie would want to cuddle for a long time, but he was still in trouble. I had to make sure he understood that.

He did apologise to Dad, but for the rest of the day he was very mopey and quiet. He didn't seem to want to do anything, just looked forlorn.

'Leave him to it,' said Dad. 'I don't think anything's going to help him.'

On Monday morning Robbie dragged his feet like he was six again. He slumped against the door in the car as I drove him to work. We were hoping he would be able to get into the routine of catching a bus, but on the first day I took a half-day from work so I could drop him off.

'Come on, Robbie,' I said, after we had been sitting in the parked car for ten minutes. 'You can do this, I know it, Dad knows it, you know it. Show us how big and brave and clever you are. And this evening we'll all have dinner at home together just like we always do. It's like school, only you get paid. Can you do this for me? Pretty pretty please?'

Eventually he did manage to go into work. The manager—who had had all kinds of employees before and was truly fantastic with Robbie—greeted him cheerfully, ignored the fact that Robbie was mumbling into his shirt, and got him straight into it, stacking up some mugs. I sat and ordered a coffee, just to keep an eye on him for the first half hour. He seemed to be doing OK, though he kept his eyes down and seemed to be permanently blushing.

Eventually, I had to leave him to it. I waited until he was stacking the dishwasher in the back room, and I slipped out. I would worry about him all day.

I grab Allie by the arm as we stretch our legs and invite her out to the water fountain with me. Morris is still ignoring me, and I don't want to stay in the room with his childishness. Allie can tell my mood is a bit off but I don't think she knows why. She laughs uncertainly.

'Everything OK?'

'Just fancied some fresh air. It feels stale in that studio. How's your painting going?'

'Oh, well, I think. I'm really enjoying myself. Not sure anyone will appreciate it apart from me, but that's OK. I'm having fun.'

I pour myself a plastic glass of water. I keep my tone level. 'How's Jonathan?'

Allie's smile drops a notch or two, and she clenches her left hand. I can see her middle finger moving up and down against the ring.

'He's fine.'

'You don't seem too bothered by him. His being married to you.'

229

'Why should I let him get in the way of what Eamonn and I have?'

'*Because* he's married to you?'

'We might have had a wedding but any kind of marriage is long gone. He does his own thing, I do mine.'

We begin to walk back to class.

'Would he be upset if you told him?' I ask, trying to be gentle.

'I don't know. Probably.' She stops and turns to face me. 'Am I doing the wrong thing?'

'I don't know how I can answer that.'

'Should I tell Jonathan? Should I end it with Eamonn? Tell me what to do.'

'I'm not going to do that, Allie. You're a grown woman, you can make your own decisions.' I wonder what I had intended to achieve with this conversation. I was never going to tell Allie what to do, that isn't my way. It's her life, her choice to make. I'm happy for her happiness, I really am. I just didn't realise I'd be so disappointed in her.

Peter proposed on my forty-first birthday.

We went out to dinner, the four of us—Dad, Robbie, Peter and me. It was a lovely evening. Robbie was happy and talkative. He'd wrapped everyone's presents to me and tied his own tie and was proud of himself. We ate Italian food, and afterwards the waiter brought me a slice of cake with a candle on it, and they all sang to me, and I blushed, pretending I thought all this fuss silly and unnecessary.

We shared the cake, leaning forwards on our elbows and fighting with our forks. Robbie licked the excess chocolate sauce off his fingers.

We walked out to the cars together.

'Happy birthday, pet,' Dad said, giving me a kiss. I'd walked arm-in-arm with him and he'd leant heavily on me, though he tried not to. He was having problems with his hip.

'Thanks Dad,' I said, and gave Robbie a hug.

'We'll see you on Friday for dinner, yes?' I said. I noticed Dad wince as he lowered himself into the car.

'I think Dad should go back to the doctor about his hip,' I said as Peter and I drove home. 'I don't think the exercises the physio gave him are working.'

'It takes time to resolve these things,' Peter said.

'I still think he should have painkillers.'

Peter nodded. 'Maybe.'

I reached out and squeezed the hand that Peter was resting on the gearstick. 'Thank you for tonight, darling, it was lovely.'

He smiled at me. 'You're welcome. Happy birthday.'

'Forty-one,' I mused, looking at my reflection in the wing mirror. 'When did that happen?'

At home, Peter tossed the keys to me and told me to let myself in while he put the bins out.

'They don't go out tonight, do they?' I said, fiddling with the keys. 'Peter?' I opened the door. Peter didn't respond. 'Silly man,' I said, putting down my bag, taking off my coat and going towards the kitchen for a cup of tea.

On the kitchen table was a huge bunch of flowers, and rose petals were scattered around it. I stopped dead. I turned around.

'Peter?'

He came in behind me, smiling that crooked smile of

his. He took me by the hand and led me into the kitchen.

'Camille,' he said, 'I love you. I can't imagine my life without you.' He reached into his pocket and went down on one knee. 'Will you marry me?'

I recognised the ring instantly. It was Mum's. It was a beautiful antique, gold with a sapphire stone surrounded by tiny diamonds. Dad had kept her engagement ring and her wedding ring in a box by his bed, next to her photo, since she died. I felt tears spring to my eyes. *Stop being so emotional.*

'I didn't want to ask you at the restaurant,' Peter said. 'I didn't want to make a scene or make you feel like you had to say yes.'

I realised I still hadn't said anything. I was standing with my hands pressed to my stomach, staring at him. *Words, I need words.* A hand went to my mouth as though to pluck some out.

Did I want to marry Peter?

All I could think of was the question. I couldn't think of how to reach an answer.

I liked things how they were, the situation worked. We were more stable than we had been since Robbie was in primary school. Would marriage change that?

'Yes,' I said, calmly. 'This is beautiful, thank you darling.' I watched him get to his feet and slide the ring onto my finger. He hugged me close.

I stared at the ring on my finger the whole time he was making tea. It fit me perfectly. Marriage needn't change anything. I'd always wanted a wedding, even though I'd never envisioned myself being quite so old when it happened. Would I still make a beautiful bride?

Peter set the tea down and sat beside me. 'What are you thinking?' he said.

I stroked one of the petals. 'Nothing, sweetie,' I smiled. 'Just imagining wedding dresses.' He leaned forwards and kissed me lightly on my lips.

Darling Peter. My faithful companion, my saviour from the lonely abyss. He was so nice to me. There were worse ways to live out your life than being loved.

After class I walk past the performing arts centre and the theatre and the bar, hoping to catch a glimpse of Emmi. But no sign. I worry about her. Then I remember that there's no reason for me to worry about this girl I barely know—she could have just not liked the class, she could have found some other use for her Thursday nights. She could be in trouble, yes, but there was little I could do about it, and little reason for me to shoulder it anyway.

I walk back to the car park and drive home.

'Does anyone ever call you Mike?' I asked Michael. We were in bed, after that first time, facing each other with the duvet pulled right up to our ears. I could feel the warm skin of his stomach against mine, the muscles of his legs intertwined through mine. I basked in the delight of being so close to him. He had a hand over my waist, stroking his thumb up and down the bare skin of my back. He wrinkled his nose.

'No, not really. My grandpa used to. I don't really like

it.'

'Why not?'

'Mike sounds like a guy you'd find in the local garage with grease all over his hands tinkering with a truck. Or a bodybuilder. Michael sounds intellectual. You can trust a Michael.'

I laughed. 'You're silly.'

'What about you? Do you prefer Cam, or Millie, or Camille?'

'I don't really mind,' I said. 'People call me all three. My dad calls me Cam. My mum calls me Millie.'

'I like Millie,' Michael said, giving me a small kiss. 'It's pretty and feminine and sophisticated, just like you.'

I nibbled his nose. 'Then I shall be your Millie. I shall be Millie, and I shall be yours.'

'Does anyone ever call you Millie?' Peter asked once.

It was sometime during our first year of marriage, when I was still baffled by the title 'Mrs' and kept catching sight of the ring on my finger in surprise.

I was looking over some papers for work, and Peter was trying to fix one of the cupboard doors—I remember because it was such an un-Peter thing to do. DIY wasn't his strong point. The question came out of nowhere, and suddenly there were tears in my eyes. I was mortified. I must have been hormonal or something. *Don't let Peter see.*

'Er, where did that come from?' I said, trying valiantly to stop my voice from shaking.

'I don't know. My sister knows a Camilla who gets

called Millie. I think it's pretty.' He was peering closely at the door hinges, and I tried to discreetly turn my head to the side and scrub away the tears.

'No, nobody calls me Millie,' I said. 'I, um. I don't really like it.'

Week Eleven

I drive into town with Peter. I have some jobs to do—banks to visit, birthday present to buy for Lucy, Nancy's second child—and Peter is going to browse the market for seedlings and then meet me for lunch.

'Not that there's much to be planted at this time of year,' he says. 'But I like to have a gander.'

I'm fumbling with the receipt as I walk towards the fountain where we always meet in town. I have to keep it safe because the chances are that Lucy will want to exchange whatever I buy. I'd rather just give them money and let them buy themselves something they want, but Nancy made a remark years ago about how impersonal a gift money is, so four times a year—two birthdays and a Christmas present each—I have to do this rigmarole. *They're Peter's relatives*, I think, every time I'm faced with a shelf of potential gifts, *why doesn't he do this slog*? They're too old for presents, really, anyway.

My bag slips through my fingers and I stop in the middle of the pavement to sort myself out. As I clip my purse shut and put it back in my bag, I look up to see Eamonn sitting in the window of a Costa Coffee, not ten metres away. I start, and look around, wondering bizarrely for a moment if I should hide. But he doesn't seem to see me.

He's sitting across from a teenaged girl, maybe fourteen, maybe as old as sixteen or seventeen. A woman brings a tray with drinks over from the counter and sets it down on the table. His wife and daughter.

It jars, seeing him out of context. His face isn't relaxed and jovial, it's set hard, and it looks like they're having a stern discussion, the parents and the girl.

I don't want Allie to know I've seen him like this. I imagine, briefly, Eamonn and his wife running into Allie and her husband, in the supermarket maybe, or at the cinema. Would they introduce their other halves, cordially, or ignore each other? Would it give them a secret thrill, or would it just lay their guilt bare?

I shoulder my bag again, and walk on to meet Peter.

Robbie did reasonably well at the café.

He loved working the till, but customers could be tricky. Most of them just stared a bit too much, some of them spoke extra slowly and loudly, and a few extremely rude ones refused to touch him. They'd slide their money across the counter instead of putting it in his hand, and make him do the same with their change. He was becoming quite skilled at using the coffee machine, which he liked, and he could stack and unstack the dishwasher forever without getting bored, though he had a habit of singing while he did so. His least favourite job was being sent out to clear tables, bring back dirty plates and cups, wipe tables, squeeze past people and feel their eyes and whispers following him.

The other employees of the café also seemed to give him a wide berth. They didn't say or do anything, and as far as I could tell they weren't even talking about him behind his back. They just ignored him. I don't think they meant it maliciously, they just had him mentally categorised as "not like everyone else" and therefore weren't interested in him. It was easier for them not to try to interact.

So Robbie wasn't the happiest he could have been, but the arrangement worked. He would get the bus into town, walk to his café, do his shift, get the bus back. They were even very obliging with his shifts, trying to get him as close to a Monday-Friday 9-5 routine as possible, to minimise the amount of time he would be at home on his own, which he tended not to like. Dad and I didn't have to take it in turns to rush from work or arrive late, and with Robbie earning his own money, Dad could start to think about retirement, which a few years before, with child-minders and teaching assistants to pay, had seemed like an impossibility.

Then one day, someone with a dog came into the café.

It was fine while Robbie was behind the counter, popping muffins in to warm and plating up paninis. The dog was very docile, well trained, and lay quietly under her owner's chair, head sticking out and resting on paws.

It was lunchtime, when more people sat down to eat than came in for takeaway coffees, and the number of tables with empty plates and cups was stacking up. The shift supervisor asked Robbie to clear them away.

He got as far as the door between the back-of-house and the café floor, and then he could see the dog and he stopped. It wasn't sleeping, otherwise he probably could have managed it. I imagined it gazing up at him, lazily curious, blinking. He didn't move.

'Excuse me,' one of the girls said huffily, trying to squeeze past him with a plate of freshly toasted sandwiches. He was blocking the door. The supervisor heard the tone and came over.

'Robert, get out on the floor, it's a mess, clean it up.' Robbie didn't want to. I knew the look that would have been on his face, his eyes wide and scared as he turned to the supervisor and shook his head. The shift supervisor did not have the patience of the manager, nor the understanding. Perhaps he'd been having a bad day. Perhaps he had problems at home. Perhaps he was just an unpleasant man. He raised his voice. 'Robert, are you deaf? Move it!'

The waitress who had delivered the sandwiches now wanted to get back into the kitchen. She shoved past Robbie, who took a few steps backwards, and just happened to collide with an elderly lady who was making her way to the toilet.

The lady fell, and put her weight on one arm, which broke. In the ensuing chaos, with everyone clustering around her and clamouring and calling for an ambulance, Robbie slunk into the kitchen and hid under a counter. When they called me at work to come and collect him, he was still there. The old lady had been taken to the hospital, and the café was almost empty. The supervisor told me that Robbie was on no uncertain terms absolutely and completely fired, and if the café suffered legal action, he would be held accountable.

Robbie said nothing on the way home. At dinner, he cried.

There were times, in my job, where I had to deal with people from the Transport department, but I never seemed to cross paths with Tim professionally. It didn't stop him from emailing me. Little one-line conversations flicked between us. I deleted every message of his after I'd replied, and then kept going back to refresh my inbox, wanting more.

- *Saw you come in late today, tut tut.*
- *Stop staring out the window and get some work done.*
- *Nice blouse though.*
- *What do they even pay you for?*
- *Canal lunch today?*
- *I'm far too busy and important.*
- *I've been summoned up to 9th this afternoon. You may never see me again.*
- *The realm from whence they never return.*
- *See you Saturday morning?*

I leant back in my chair, swinging it from side to side. Now that I knew him, had spoken to him—was friends with him?—it felt weird to run past him on a Saturday morning jog. It was suddenly more embarrassing that he would see me red-faced and sweating in my old, oversized t-shirt. Every part of the interaction took on a new awkwardness in my head—when we saw each other but were too far away to speak, should I wave? Look down? Keep staring at him? Should I stop to pass the time of day, or would that interrupt his run? Maybe he was aiming to beat a personal best. What if he suggested that we run together? I didn't want him to follow me home and see that I still lived with my father, but I couldn't run in his direction and be late getting back to Robbie.

I hadn't told Tim about Robbie. There hadn't been an opportunity—we hadn't discussed family, or anything into which I could slip a casual mention.

I glanced around to make sure nobody was behind me who could see my screen, then turned back, opened our email thread, and quickly typed,

— *Sorry, my Saturday mornings have been monopolised.*

Should I make up some kind of injury to avoid him suggesting another time? I decided it would be too much hassle trying to keep track of a complex lie.

— *Sorry, my Saturday mornings have been monopolised. Struggling to find the time to fit in a run these days, really.*

I hoped he wouldn't ask any more questions about it. If he pressed the idea of running together, I'd say *yes, sounds like a great idea, I'll let you know when I next manage to squeeze one in.* I stopped running through the park on Saturday mornings. I tried to run on a weekday evening, but it was often difficult with dinner and next-day preparations and getting Robbie to bed. When I did manage it, I ran around the entire circumference of the park, on the outside, and I kept my head down and hoped I wouldn't see Tim.

'He definitely has a crush on you,' Ruth said knowingly, one day after Tim had popped by our office for no real reason. I scowled, hoping it would hide my blush. She held her hands up in surrender. 'I'm just saying. Blue eyes, tousled hair, cheekbones that could cut glass. Not to be sniffed at, my friend.' I rolled my eyes and brushed her off.

A few weeks later, we were in a pub down the road for a colleague's birthday drinks. I found myself considering Tim from across the room, where he was engaged in what seemed to be an animated conversation. Ruth was right; he was good-looking. Hair slightly too long, perhaps. Although, I remember, I used to tell Michael he'd look good if he let his hair grow a little. Ruth was probably also right that he had a crush on me.

I frowned down into my drink. Robbie was with Peter, but I would need to go soon to get dinner on for the two of them. Next to me, Ruth raised her eyebrows and indicated the far corner, where she'd seen me staring at him. I shook my head, downed the rest of my glass, and stood up.

'I'm going to have to go,' I said, hugging Ruth and shouldering my bag. 'Before you put any ideas in my head.'

I squeezed my way through knots of people to say happy birthday and goodbye to my colleague, and then made my way towards the door. A hand caught my elbow before I got there, and I glanced around. Blue eyes.

'Leaving so soon?' Tim said.

'I'm a busy woman,' I said, my voice faltering slightly. 'Things to do, people to see, you know how it is...'

'One more,' he said. 'Stay for one more.'

For some reason, I said yes.

Perhaps I was drinking very slowly. Perhaps the one more turned into two more. Somehow, Tim and I were seated next to each other on a squashy pub sofa, in an emptying room. We both had one arm draped over the back of the sofa and one knee bent up on the cushions, facing each other. I was out of breath from laughing.

'I really should—' I began to say, leaning forwards to put my empty glass on the table—*were all of those empties ours?*—when Tim put a hand on my knee. My startled eyes flicked up to his calm, blue ones. My skirt had ridden up and I could feel the heat of his hand through my flimsy tights. My face was suddenly slack with seriousness.

'Another one?' Tim asked. He glanced around. 'Maybe somewhere else?'

I tried to swallow, but my throat was dry. *Even after drinking so much?* He was very good-looking. He knew that he was, but still. He was good-looking, and he seemed to think the same of me. He sought me out.

I dropped my eyes. 'I have to go,' I said quietly, over the pounding in my chest. He leaned forwards, ever so slightly.

'Do you?' he whispered.

I stood up. 'I have a boyfriend,' I said, at normal volume. 'I should have said, I'm sorry.'

243

Tim's face hardened, just slightly. 'Right,' he said.

'Sorry. Thanks for the drinks. I—' I grabbed my bag and coat. 'I'll see you later.'

'Sure.' His voice was wooden. I left the pub without looking back.

On the bus home, I leant my forehead against the window, trying to cool my burning face, desperate to get home.

Peter was making chili and rice, with a kitchen towel draped over his shoulder, and Robbie splayed out in front of the television.

'Sorry I'm late,' I said, dumping my things on a kitchen chair and hugging Peter from behind as he stirred the pot. 'Had one too many birthday drinks.' He turned around inside my arms and gave me a kiss.

'A few too many, it smells like,' he said, with that crooked smile. 'Did you have fun?'

I nodded, not releasing him. 'I love you,' I said.

He tapped me on the nose with the handle of the wooden spoon. 'Is somebody drunk?'

I kissed him again. 'I do, so there.'

'I love you too, pet. You have room for dinner?'

'Copious room,' I said. 'It smells delicious. I'll round up the troops.'

Two weeks to go until show-time. I'm sitting next to Becca.

I think when we first started, I thought she was quite a dark person, very angry and, as she said, full of pain. I feel like she has become brighter over the weeks, and if it's not exactly a smile on her face as she paints, it's at least fervour. She paints with passion, like it's a necessity, almost. Maybe it's true, what she said. Maybe she does paint her pain away. I like the idea of her coming to class and leaving happier. She's too young to be so jaded.

Morris says hello like he always does. He doesn't seem embarrassed or self-conscious or annoyed after his outburst. He's perfectly cheerful. He's that kind of person, I've realised—when he's angry it comes out, but when it's gone, it's gone. I tend to hold on to things, I bear grudges. It's an effort for me—I'm still affronted—but I try to act like everything's normal. Perhaps I had been whingeing.

My painting is finally beginning to look how it's supposed to. It's almost the finished product I had en-visaged. It's not perfect, by any means, but I've given it a good shot.

Becca is mixing up various dark concoctions, and adds a vivid line of red to the edge of her palette. I think about what Allie said, way back in our first class. "Pretty" is not a word you could ascribe to Becca's art, I muse. But maybe that's OK. Maybe she likes raging at the world.

Robbie didn't take well to unemployment.

He was entirely capable of taking care of himself alone in the house, though I liked to be around if he was cooking or doing something potentially dangerous—he could be clumsy at times—he hated being cooped up on his own. He hated the silence.

He wouldn't really go out on his own. He was more likely to get anxious and upset if we weren't there, to panic at dogs or traffic or certain people, and without us, there was no safety net.

Dad and I didn't know what to do. We couldn't have Robbie being unemployed, alone in the house with nothing to do all day, all week. Some kind of nanny? I didn't know where to start with that one. I asked around at several volunteer places, charity shops, a soup kitchen, but they all said they didn't need any help, or had a long application process. We needed something for Robbie to do right away. It was the stress of school holidays all over again—which we had managed in the past with holiday clubs, Sarah's house, child-minders, and taking annual leave in turns—except this could go on indefinitely.

Dad took Robbie for long walks around the park, and tried to talk him through what had happened, tried to make him understand that he couldn't let it knock his confidence because it had been an accident. But he refused to contemplate another job. We couldn't even get him to go to an interview the Down Syndrome organisation set up for him.

At first, we tried helping Robbie to be OK with unemployment. In the morning, Dad left food for him, telephone numbers in case of emergency, and a list of jobs for him to do—little chores to keep him busy, always including two or three that were outside the house—going to the shops, washing the car, walking round the block.

But he couldn't do it. He tried, he tried really hard, but the third time Dad came home to find him huddled behind the sofa, having not left that spot to eat or even to go to the toilet, we knew this wasn't going to work.

Dad decided to retire. His company had been putting pressure on him for years by this point—they didn't want to keep paying an old man like Dad when they could get in young, fresh blood. When Dad told them he was finally agreeing to go, they let him shorten his notice period to two weeks. I took some annual leave to watch Robbie for that fortnight, and then, with Dad's pension and Robbie's jobseeker's and disabilities benefits, we hoped we'd be able to make things work.

Surprisingly, Peter wasn't happy about this.

'I wish you wouldn't use all your holiday leave for Robbie,' he said. 'I was hoping we'd be able to go away somewhere.'

I snorted, rather inelegantly. 'Honey, I haven't been away anywhere in years. I don't think I've been on holiday since I got back from Beijing, apart from a week at the seaside. It just doesn't work in our situation. We've always had to use time off to watch Robbie.'

'But things will be different when we're married.'

'Well yes, but only because Dad will be retired, not because we'll be married.' I kept deflecting when Peter brought up the wedding, couldn't think about it when everything with Robbie was so stressful and uncertain. Peter didn't seem happy with my answer. 'You know Robbie always comes first, Peter. There isn't any other way. Either he comes first or he doesn't come at all, and we ruled out that option when we decided to raise him. You know that. I can't change it.'

Peter pressed his lips together, and said nothing.

It was over six months before Robbie found the job at the supermarket. It wasn't our local supermarket, but after weeks of asking if they were hiring, eventually they said the superstore in town had vacancies. I marched straight there. I was on a mission, and I had done my research. Under the Disability Discrimination Act, they couldn't refuse to hire him—for a job he was capable of doing—on the grounds that he had Down Syndrome. I knew what Robbie was capable of doing, and I was going to get him hired.

As it turned out, I didn't actually need to go in there all guns blazing. They were very friendly and helpful, and keen to improve their stats on disabled employees. I went with Robbie to the interview, and sat at the back of the room keeping my mouth shut. The interviewer was the speaking-loudly-and-slowly type, but only a little bit, and Robbie shone. He glanced back at me a few times for reassurance, but not once did I have to step in, explain, prompt. I was so proud of him. He was calm and polite and at one point even made the interviewer laugh.

And so Robbie got his job as a shelf-stacker.

He loved it. It was perfect for him—he got to arrange things just so, all facing the same way, all tessellating, and he never got bored of tidying a shelf customers had left in a mess. He was around people all the time, so he didn't get lonely, but he didn't actively have to interact with them, so if someone seemed off with him, he could walk away. Two of the checkout ladies took a shine to him, were always kind and asked how he was, and he would sit with them if they had their lunch breaks at the same time. He even began to be recognised by some of the regulars, like the mum with her small son who did the shopping every Thursday morning, or the man who permanently had five o'clock stubble and often came in of an evening for beer and crisps.

Now Dad could be at home anytime, it didn't matter that Robbie worked shifts. Dad had some time alone to enjoy his retirement, but he could still be around to do things with Robbie when he wasn't at work.

Things seemed to be going fine. More than fine, they were as close to normal as they had been since Robbie was born. I was no longer rushing into work or rushing from it, Robbie as an adult was much less worrisome than as a child or teenager, visits to his doctor and his specialists were much easier to fit in around shifts, and I had a fiancé who treated me like a queen. Things were stable. Things were good.

So one day, when I was out shopping, and I happened to stumble across a wedding planner, I stopped and picked it up. It was beautiful, with a glossy cover that looked like a scrapbook and lace effects and sections for everything. So pretty and so organised.

And I had a wedding to plan.

I bought it, feeling a kind of illicit thrill—I never spent frivolously like this—and as I drove home I kept stealing glances at the corner of it peeking out of the bag on the passenger seat. When I parked, I pulled it out and ran my hand over the smooth cover. *Really, Camille. You're too old to be acting this silly.*

That night I sat up in bed, the planner propped up on my knees. Peter was ambling around the bedroom getting ready for bed.

'I'm so excited to start planning,' I said, flipping through all the sections. 'Venue, catering, flowers, bridal party.'

'Who will you have as bridesmaids?' Peter asked, in the tone of one humouring a child reciting their Christmas list. I paused.

'I don't think I'll have any bridesmaids,' I said eventually. At school, Maria and I always said we'd be each other's chief bridesmaid. Main responsibility: the hen night.

'Are you sure?' Peter said.

'Maybe Lucy can be a flower girl,' I said. 'That would be cute.'

'I'm sure she'd love that.' He disappeared into the bathroom and came back with his toothbrush in his mouth. I flicked back to the beginning.

'Guest list,' I said. 'Let's start with that. Who shall we have?' I forced the excitement back into my voice and poised my pen. 'Dad and Robbie,' I said, 'your parents, Nancy and co. What about extended family?'

'Um, Dad has two brothers and a sister, they're all married with kids. Mum has a sister, married with kids. Seven cousins in total, one of them lives in South Africa. We can send them an invite to be polite but they won't come.'

'OK,' I said slowly, scribbling. 'Friends?'

'Well I'm going to ask George to be my best man. Then there's Freddie, Will, John one and John two from the office. Plus wives. Bill, Robert, Neil, Jessica and Graham from Uni, Callum, Maggie and Rebecca from the tennis club...' I stopped writing. The list went on and on. 'It's looking like a big wedding,' Peter laughed. Then he realised I wasn't smiling. 'Cam?'

I shut the book and put it on my bedside table.

'I don't want to do this right now,' I said, shuffling down in the bed and pulling the duvet up. 'I'm tired.' I shifted so I was positioned for sleep, facing away from him. My eyes stayed open.

'Cam?' he said again, moving up the bed and resting a hand on my side. 'Are you OK?'

'I'm fine,' I mumbled. After a moment, Peter got up, and I heard him rinse his toothbrush and turn the bathroom light out. When he slipped under the covers and switched off the light, I said, 'I don't have any friends to invite to the wedding.' Peter said nothing. He rolled over and spooned me, an arm over my side and holding my hand. I let myself be held.

'You should take up a hobby,' Peter said a few days later. He was coming back from a Saturday afternoon tennis match, looking quite the part in shorts and a sweatband. I raised my eyebrow at him, coming down the stairs with an armful of cleaning supplies.

'What kind of a hobby?'

Peter slung his racquet bag over the bannister and went to the kitchen for a glass of water.

'Line dancing. Woodturning. A book club. Anything.' I followed him into the kitchen, put my load down on the counter and folded my arms.

'Line dancing. Really. Have we met?'

'I just think you should make the time to do something you enjoy, that's all,' he said, draining the glass and refilling it.

'Do I enjoy line dancing?'

'You might do, you'll never know until you try.' He leaned over for a kiss and I swatted him away.

'You're sweaty. And I really don't think I'm going to be trying line dancing anytime soon. Or wood carving, or anything.'

'But why?' Peter said, refusing to drop it. 'You might meet some nice people.' I turned away and started putting things in cupboards.

'I'm not going to turn up to some book club and ask a group of strangers to be my middle-aged bridesmaids,' I said curtly.

'I'm not suggesting you do,' he said, and there was a note of pleading in his voice. 'But you could make some friends.'

'I don't need friends. I have you, and Dad, and Robbie, and you all keep me quite busy enough,' I said briskly. I glanced back at him over my shoulder, and I hated the pity in his eyes.

'Robbie doesn't take up so much time now,' he said gently. 'He doesn't live with you, and he's going to work independently, and you deserve to focus on yourself for a bit.'

'*Deserve*,' I scoffed, 'what's with all this *deserving*. Things are what they are.'

'Don't be a martyr, Cam. I know your life took an unexpected turn, but you can't be bitter about it forever. Why not find something to enjoy? You used to run quite a bit, why don't you look for a running club?' I kept my face turned away. 'Or you could play tennis with us. Or take a cooking class.'

I turned back around to face him, leaning my back against the hard edge of the work surface and putting both hands down on it behind me. 'And what exactly are you saying about my cooking skills?'

He came over to me and threaded his arms through mine, and this time I didn't bat him away. 'I want you to be happy, Cam, and I think some friends would do you good. I know you think interest groups are artificial, but you might meet someone you really connect with.'

'If you want to call the wedding off, all you have to do is say the word,' I said.

'Just think about it, will you?'

'How do you always manage to see the world so differently from me?' I said.

He kissed me lightly and pulled me away from the counter for a proper hug. 'That's why we're so good together, my dear. It'd be boring if we always thought the same.'

I rested my head on his shoulder.

'You need a shower,' I said. 'You stink.'

Nancy and Greg decided to take a holiday for their fifteenth wedding anniversary, and the kids stayed with us. Gabriel was twelve and Lucy was nine. Anyone looking at us—man, woman, kids, wedding rings—would have thought us a normal family.

On the weekend, we picked Robbie up from Dad's and we all went to the zoo. Robbie was twenty-seven, had taken to wearing baseball caps, and loved seeing Gabriel and Lucy. He liked to walk along with one on each hand, and he got as excited as they did at the sight of the monkeys. Peter and I walked along behind them.

'What time does the plane get in on Monday?'

'Mid-morning, I think,' Peter said. 'They'll pick the kids up from school, and I'll drop their stuff off with them at some point.'

'Good, good.'

'Can't wait to get rid of them?'

'Not at all.' I was enjoying the pace, a slow amble, almost a wedding march, which kept us within distance of the kids as they zig-zagged from one exhibit to another and gazed in wonder at each cage. 'The week has been a lot less stressful than I thought it would be. They're good kids.'

Peter shrugged. 'They're normal.'

'Excuse me?'

'No, I didn't mean that,' Peter backtracked hurriedly. 'Just—they're kids. Good kids.'

I watched as Gabriel pointed out for Robbie some mountain goats perched in a shady corner of their tower of rocks. Robbie had been working at the supermarket for over seven years now. I was proud of him—I never thought he could do it. I spent the first few months just waiting to be told that something had gone terribly wrong, that he had broken down or somebody had kicked up a fuss, or he just couldn't cope. But he had done well—the staff loved him, he had regulars, he was happy. It was a huge achievement for him, but I couldn't express to anyone else why this made me swell with pride so much. Nancy would tell anyone who stood still long enough that Gabriel was the star of the swimming team, and that Lucy was a budding chess prodigy. But pride over a shelf-stacker? For anyone else, it was a basic job, an embarrassing job. For Robbie, it was as though he'd discovered relativity.

We had lunch on a picnic bench by the adventure playground, and afterwards the children went to play. Robbie told us about a Lamborghini that he had seen in the supermarket car park one day, and how he and Dad were working on a thousand-piece jigsaw at home.

Gabriel ran up and asked Robbie if he'd like to play a game with them. Robbie smiled—really, he had a beautiful smile—and got up to join them. Peter got a call about something at work, and while he wandered around with the phone to his ear—he couldn't stay still on the phone—I started packing up the plastic boxes and cups. After a moment or two, I realised the movement of the kids and Robbie struck me as odd. They weren't running like they were playing or chasing, it was more—sinister. My senses were heightened to this kind of thing. I could smell young maliciousness a mile off.

I got up and innocently circled them, trying to work out what they were doing. Robbie seemed to be trying to catch something on the ground—a leaf?—and Gabriel was trotting in front of him, backwards, facing him. Lucy was following, laughing and mimicking Robbie's stumbling steps as he reached for whatever it was. Mocking him. I realised Gabriel had something on a string and was pulling it to keep it just out of reach.

I ground my teeth. *Cruel.*

I marched up to them before they could realise I was on to what they were doing, and stamped down on Gabriel's string. Robbie was panting, and I could see he was getting upset, part frustration and part humiliation. Lucy stopped short a few feet away and Gabriel looked up from my shoe to my face. The laughter was draining out of his face, replaced by guilt.

'What's going on?' Peter said, coming over and clearly recognising the thunder in my face.

'Yes, Gabriel,' I said dangerously. 'What's going on here?' He looked from me to Peter.

'We were just playing a game,' he said.

'You were teasing Robbie,' I said. 'And he only wanted to play.'

Peter noticed my tone. 'Why don't you take Robbie for an ice cream,' he said, taking a half-step between Gabriel and me, 'and we can have a little chat.' He placed a hand on Gabriel's shoulder. Lucy crept up, behind Peter. I couldn't help but feel they were ganging up on me, the three of them against Robbie and me. Robbie took my hand, and I squeezed.

'Come on,' I said, struggling not to shout at Peter. 'Let's get a Mr. Whippy.' I led him away. He was downcast, not saying anything. Only twenty minutes ago he'd been happy and talkative, and now he'd completely withdrawn. He wasn't stupid. He knew what was going on.

I squeezed his hand again.

'Hey buddy,' I said softly. 'What's going on up there?' I didn't like it when he shut himself off. It led him to bad places.

'Laughing at me,' he mumbled.

'They were being stupid and mean,' I said, 'and they shouldn't have done that.' I stopped, and gave him a hug, holding on until he relaxed against me. I kissed his head. I wished I could protect him from things like this, from people who couldn't see past the squinted eyes and the clumsy gait. I'd been wishing it for years. It broke my heart that I'd never succeed.

Peter went off to the pub with a whole crowd of friends for his stag do. He offered to ask Nancy to organise something for me, but I said no. I didn't want a pity hen party.

I ran myself a bath and lit some candles and put on some music, and smeared on one of those face masks. I'd never had one before, but I'd heard so much about the need to "pamper yourself" from endless magazines in doctors' waiting rooms, and I thought I'd give it a try. I lay back in the bath, hair in rollers, face covered in gunk, and wondered if we had any cucumber in the house for eye-slices. I'd never really been sure what they were for but they went with the whole image. I lay and stared at the ceiling and found myself thinking about Michael, of all things. I wondered what his life looked like now. Had he stayed in China? Did he have a Chinese wife? Did he have children? He didn't have the genetics for a receding hairline, but maybe he was going grey. I tried to picture him, to age my memories of him, but the images swam out of focus. I wondered what would have happened if that phone had never rung, if we had gone to that event in our ball gown and tux, if we had talked about what to do with his job offer together, as a couple.

I got out of the bath, blew out the candles and scrubbed the muck off my face. I put on my pyjamas and dressing gown and went downstairs. Robbie and I watched a film and painted our toenails.

We had a small wedding, around forty people, in the function room of a moderately up-market hotel. Robbie was ring bearer, and Dad gave me away. I wore a dress with a lace boat-neck for modesty (too old for cleavage) and carried a bouquet of blush pink roses.

Week Twelve

I visit Dad every Saturday. He's been in sheltered accommodation for two years, since we sold the house. It's mainly for his hip, he's not very mobile these days, and sometimes he needs help in the bathroom or getting out of bed. Secretly I think since he moved in, he's been letting his mental state unravel. I think it's just easier for him. It's being taken care of, for a change, instead of worrying and agonising and organising, the sudden relief has made him swing too far in the other direction. Only occasionally is he really confused, not knowing who I am or where he is. Most often he just likes to sit on his own and drift off into his own little world. It's funny, when he does that, he reminds me of Robbie.

His eyesight isn't great these days, but he gets a lot of audiobooks from the library and sits in his chair with his hands clasped across his stomach and his eyes closed, listening. Or not listening, who knows. He plays games of whist with some of the other residents. He goes to bed early. I think he's happy. At the very least he isn't unhappy.

'Hello, Dad,' I say, going into his room. He looks up.

'Hello, love,' and raises his face for a kiss. He's an old man now, I can't avoid it. It makes me sad, but it doesn't seem to bother him too much. I remember when I was a child and my grandmother, my mother's mother, always seemed to be moaning about how she couldn't do this or couldn't do that and she was falling apart and in general seemed to hate the whole process of ageing, watching her body decay. Dad took it peacefully. For him it was respite.

'How are you?' I sit down opposite him.

'I'm well, I'm well,' he says. 'They've started an aerobics class on a Wednesday afternoon, I join in a bit.' He rotates his shoulders and pats his stomach. 'It's all that delicious chocolate cake Elsie whips up. I'm getting fuzzy round the edges.'

'You look great to me, Dad.'

'How are you and Peter?'

'Good, we're both good. Peter told me to tell you his... somethings have taken root, or taken leaf, or... something. I'm sorry, I wasn't really listening.'

Dad laughs. 'How's the painting going?'

'It's good, it's really good. I'm really enjoying it.' I'm surprised by the enthusiasm in my voice, and even more surprised that I mean it.

'I remember you drawing a lot as a girl. Could never get you to pay attention in lessons, you were always scribbling.' I nodded fondly. 'We've had school children here this week, doing some community project. I've been telling them all about your mother.' He looks up at the photo on his bedside table. It's their wedding photo. I look at it too. I love that photo. She looks so young and smooth and so very, very happy. But it makes me remember how she died, older than her years and lined and weary with troubles. She didn't deserve that.

I picked up the picture and stared at it. I wasn't tearful. I was just sad for what hadn't been.

'What were you telling them about her for?'

'Oh, I don't know, they were supposed to be keeping us company or entertaining us or something, and they didn't have a clue what to do. I thought they might be interested.'

'Were they?'

'I think they enjoyed it. Not as much as I enjoyed telling them.' He smiled, and closed his eyes.

'How about a game of rummy?' I suggest. He nods, still smiling, eyes still closed. I pulled the card table over, fetched a deck and began shuffling. 'Why don't Peter and I take you out to lunch next week?' I said. 'There's a new Greek place opened not far away. I know you like Greek.' Dad opened his eyes and smiled at me.

'I'd love that.'

I dealt out the cards.

It was June.

The sun was out but the wind was up, and only the optimistic had their jackets off. Robbie had the Saturday off work, and Peter suggested we drive down to see Nancy and the kids, as they had just finished exams.

We took a picnic, and a Frisbee and a pack of cards. Greg was away on business, but Nancy came, a tartan rug over her arm. Lucy was in the teenage throes of sullenly not wanting to be seen with her family, but as she had finished her GCSEs and most of her friends still had a French exam to go, there wasn't much else for her to do. Gabriel, who had finished his A levels over a week ago and was thus in the stage between drunken revelry and extended boredom, was in surprisingly accommodating spirits, and he enthusiastically set to work trying to tease his sister out of her sulk.

I'd never really learnt to be completely comfortable around Nancy's children. They were strange to me—I was used to Robbie. As tiny children, they had wide, shining eyes and delicate necks and agile fingers. As toddlers, they were like an eight-year-old Robbie, and to see them so small and so advanced was alien to me.

I misjudged gifts wildly. While I was still playing Snap with Robbie, they were playing Monopoly and Scrabble. I couldn't pitch conversations, especially not with Lucy, who was fiercely bright and would fix you with a piercing, patronising stare. *Duh.* Gabriel tended to glue himself to video games and would grunt at you whatever you said.

I felt uneasy around Nancy, too. Her with her picture-perfect kids—pigtails and football boots, matching lunch-boxes in pink and blue—I felt like she pitied me and my broken child, felt smugly proud of their school reports and party invitations. I knew most of it must be in my head. It wasn't like that anymore, it wasn't as bad as when Robbie was born, when nobody had heard of Down Syndrome and people recoiled in horror and called him deformed. This was a new age of acceptance, where differences were celebrated, and not wishing it on your own children didn't mean you hated others for it.

I told myself I was being ridiculous, and my defensiveness was unjustified, and then sometimes I'd catch Nancy looking at Robbie a certain way, or smoothing Lucy's hair in a superior manner, and I'd feel the urge to draw Robbie to me protectively. Certainly after the fifteenth anniversary incident—and I was never sure that Peter had spoken to Nancy about that like he said he would—I was even more guarded, but Peter loved them and loved being part of their lives, and after condemning him to childlessness, I couldn't kick up too much of a fuss. I had to be a supportive wife, an involved member of his little family unit.

It was easier now the kids were approaching adulthood. Gabriel was a laid-back sort of chap, and he'd chat to Robbie like he was anyone else, even if Robbie wouldn't always follow his slang. Lucy still had some growing up to do. She oscillated wildly between a wide-eyed little girl and a supercilious cynic.

There were lots of dog-walkers in the park, so we had to hunt for a while before we found a spot where we could spread out the picnic things and avoid any unwanted canine attention.

'How'd the exams go, Gabe?' Peter asked, as Nancy and I began unpacking our respective bags. Well, mine was a plastic supermarket bag; hers was a wicker basket. Hers was more picturesque, definitely, but they both did the same job of carrying the food.

Gabriel shrugged. 'Dunno, really. Probably screwed some of them up.' He didn't seem too bothered. 'Have to wait and see. I'm just glad they're over.'

'Your offer's an A and two Bs, right?' Gabriel nodded, grabbing a piece of chicken from one of his mother's salads as she set it out, and popping it into his mouth. She slapped at him ineffectually. I distributed paper plates and plastic cups.

Lucy lounged out on her side and stuck a headphone in one ear, pretending not to be paying any attention to us and reaching for food with one hand. Gabriel sat with his legs splayed and ate more than I could have believed fit inside his gangly frame. Nancy slipped her shoes off and curled her legs demurely beneath her.

'So, what are you going to do with your big summer?' I asked. Lucy looked at me with bored eyes, and said nothing. Gabriel was busy loading his plate.

'Couple of mates of mine are going to Spain in August,' he mumbled through a mouthful. 'Gonna go if I can afford it. Need a job.'

'How's the business going?' Nancy asked Peter, and I wondered if I'd be able to eat with my gloves on.

Later on, the clouds cleared, so there was a consistent if feeble heat from the sun.

I don't know what snapped Lucy out of her mood—some mention of a favourite actor or band or maybe just Gabriel's incessant needling—but Gabriel, Peter and Robbie were throwing a Frisbee around and Lucy was joining in, acting like it was stupid and tossing her hair and flapping her hands, but running after it all the same. I was lying back, resting on my elbows, feeling surprisingly relaxed. Most of the food had gone. Nancy was watching the kids, picking at leftovers.

'I can't believe Gabe is leaving school already. Where does the time go?' I said. I didn't mean it—it had been almost eighteen years, I could very much believe he was leaving school—but it was the kind of thing I'd heard mothers say, and Nancy had that vaguely emotional look on her face so I thought it would be appropriate. It seemed to go down well. Her eyes became slightly mistier, she sighed and said something like *they grow up so fast* or *what happened to my little boy*—maybe I'm making up the sigh, that sounds a bit too much—and I rolled my eyes and ate another cherry tomato.

'How's your work going?' Nancy said. It was a slightly stiff question—we both knew she wasn't interested—but I appreciated her making the effort to make conversation.

'Ah, boring, same old, same old. We've got no money, the public hates us, they have problems and they expect that we'll fix them if they shout at us. The joys of local government,' I said. I gestured at the game. 'Want to join in?'

'Oh, no, I'm not wearing the right kind of shoes,' Nancy demurred.

If I had been a different kind of woman, I might have grabbed her hand and pulled her up and insisted, but I didn't, I just got up and went to join them myself. I was fifty-two years old, but I decided you're never too old for Frisbee. There was lots of running to collect the fallen disc and ridiculous diving from Gabriel and Peter. I tried throwing gently to Robbie but it floated to the ground barely three feet from me. Peter deliberately threw way over my head, making me run backwards, staggering, giggling. Robbie threw to Lucy, but the wind caught it and Gabe took a few steps and snatched it out of the air above Lucy's outstretched hand. Lucy squealed and jumped for it, and somehow we ended up in a game of chase, each of us trying to grab the Frisbee.

I'm not sure Robbie knew entirely what we were doing, but he joined in enthusiastically, whooping and running as fast as he could. Peter and I ground to a halt after a few laps around the trees, and we stood and watched the children chase each other.

'Too old for this,' Peter huffed, putting an arm around my shoulders. I laughed, and poked his stomach.

'Out of shape, old man,' I said. Eventually, the kids ran back over. I think Lucy had got hold of the disc at one point, but Gabe had grabbed it back, and Lucy gave up and came over to us. Gabe followed, grinning with victory. Robbie could barely breathe for laughing. Gabe grabbed a bottle of water, took a swig and passed it to his sister. Robbie bent over and grabbed his thighs.

Nancy had packed up the picnic things, and stood up, slowly, stretched her legs and grimacing.

'Pins and needles, pins and needles,' she said, taking a few hopping steps. She leant on Lucy, who pulled a face and wriggled away. Gabe hefted the picnic basket, I rolled up the rug, and we began checking around for litter and forgotten spoons and jackets and getting ready to leave. Robbie was still wheezing.

'You OK, buddy?' I said, putting a hand on his shoulder. The group started to walk off, but Robbie clutched at my arm. I bent down, suddenly worried. 'Do you want to sit down?'

He nodded but he couldn't seem to find words. He looked pained, but he wouldn't tell me what was bothering him. Had he sprained an ankle? Headache? He was shifting his shoulders. Chest pain?

I guided him to a bench and sat with him. I made an *it's fine* gesture to Peter, not wanting everyone to come and crowd around Robbie.

'Are you OK?' I said again. 'Have some water.' He took a sip, and slowly, his breathing began to calm. He nodded, and took my hand like he was scared. 'You want to tell me what's wrong? Legs? Head? Are you dizzy?' He still wouldn't say anything. The clouds had come back again, and there was the promise of tea at Nancy's house, so when Robbie seemed better we set off to join the others, and he let go of my hand.

It was strange to me whenever I accidentally caught sight of Robert as someone other than my Robbie. When I saw him how anyone else might see him. He was an adult— thirty years old—and he had crows' feet from laughing all the time and grey hairs scattered through his head. He wasn't a child anymore. He was old. And, of course, I was even older.

I still had to look after him. That wasn't ever going to change. He lived with Dad but he was as much my responsibility as ever, even though he had a job and was doing really well and he even cooked for himself with Dad's supervision. People didn't automatically assume I was his mother when they saw me out with him—I could be his sister, his carer, a nurse, a friend, anybody—which was great. I didn't miss the days of judgemental looks, of people assuming I was at fault because I'd given birth to a faulty child. *He's not mine*, I'd want to scream, *I didn't make him this way*. And then I'd feel guilty, because it wasn't my mum's fault either. It was his fault, that bastard who'd surprised her and attacked her and held her and forced her and made her have this child when she shouldn't have had to.

I didn't think about him as much as you might expect. Robbie's father.

He had been leaving, moving away. A farewell party thrown by the nurses. She had known him for years, always been kind to him, always smiled, the same way she did with everyone. Had he always so badly misinterpreted her kindness, her smiles? Was it just the drink that had distorted things? Had the impulse always been there, the idea, the urge, always held back until it wasn't anymore?

I thought about it a lot in the months after I came home and had to see her lumber around the house, cumbersome and in pain, hand on lower back or swollen belly. A hand grabbing her arm, maybe, or around her waist, leading her into an empty room. Or maybe he came to her when she was alone, a hand on the thigh. Against the wall, or forced to the floor. Rough carpet, or concrete. Screams, or muffled. Heavy weight, pinning her. Tears. Torn clothes.

There were too many unknowns. It tortured me. I couldn't ask her, I couldn't think about it. But I couldn't stop thinking about it. It made me choke because it was awful and it terrified me, and it made me wretch because it was my mum. I should have hated him more than I did, but he was as nameless and faceless as a phantom to me, and how can you hate something that doesn't exist? I needed something concrete I could focus my hate on, and I just didn't have it.

I told her to go to the police. She refused. Tearfully at first, then angrily. Who she was angry at, I couldn't tell. I knew she still blamed herself. I didn't want to press her, didn't want to make her relive it—god knows it wasn't easy to hear either—but the idea of him walking around, living his life, free as a bird, turned the blood in my veins to acid, and it burned. As the pregnancy grew more and more real, it was harder and harder to find a good time to talk to her about it. And then there wasn't any time at all.

I realised, too late, that someone at the funeral might have known him. Might have known what he did, might have seen the bundle of baby and *known*.

I was upstairs, in my parents' room, unable to face the mourners milling downstairs, their pity-filled eyes, their unspoken questions. The baby was quiet, sleeping probably. I sat on my mum's side of the bed, hugging her pillow to my chest, trying to squeeze away the dreadful tearing sensation in the my chest. Her laughing blue eyes shone out at me from the wedding photo on her bedside table. I folded in around the pillow and I pressed my eyes shut.

I heard the front door opening downstairs, the shuffle of shoes and coats and people making their goodbyes. Hurried footsteps down the path. I got up and went to the window, watching black figures disperse and dissipate. And I realised that among the relatives and friends and neighbours were Mum's colleagues, nurses and doctors and porters from the hospital, people who had known her, known him, probably even been at that party. Perhaps Mum had spoken to her colleagues about it; perhaps they knew the truth.

I ran downstairs and out the front door without knowing where I was going. Standing on the damp paving slabs of the path in stockinged feet, I wondered if I was going to start grabbing people by the arm, interrogating them. But what would it achieve? Even if I did explain the story to them, even if they could suggest a name, what would I do with it? Go to the police, report him, track him down? I had nothing to make anyone believe me.

I felt arms around my shoulders and somebody led me inside. They sat me down on the sofa and it seemed very low; I was sinking into the cushions and kept on sinking. Someone placed a plate of food next to me and pressed a cup of tea into my hands, but I barely noticed. There was nothing I could do. There was no way I could bring her back. There was no way I could make him pay.

I wondered sometimes, when I saw Dad watching Robbie, helping him with his homework, maybe, or looking at a picture he'd drawn, what Dad really saw. Did he see Robbie as a son? Or did he see his wife's rapist? His wife's murderer? Sometimes I felt I would like to ask Dad what he thought, to talk about it with him. Did he think about it? About him? About what happened? How it happened? But most of the time, I didn't want to talk at all.

And that seemed to suit. We never spoke of him. We tried to erase him with silence, and we never told Robbie that Dad wasn't his dad.

I should have taken him to the doctor's then, that day we played Frisbee. But it could have been anything. A stitch, dehydration. Ate too much, ran too fast. He recovered in ten minutes, and was back to normal from then on. I forgot about it.

I forgot about it.

He had a check-up six months later. If I think back on it now, the signs were there. He did often seem tired when

I went round for dinner but maybe hadn't slept well or had done a long shift. Maybe once when I put his shoes on, I noticed his ankles were slightly swollen. Or maybe I didn't, and I'm just projecting backwards, inserting things I should have noticed so I can blame myself for being negligent.

The doctor's visit was fairly stressful. Robbie's normal doctor, whom he'd had for twenty-two years, had retired the previous year. This would be the second time he saw this new doctor, Dr Newman, a young-looking woman in a fuzzy purple jumper that was just a little too tight and a prominent engagement ring. Our social worker assured us that she came highly recommended in these sorts of cases, but even so, looking at her made me want to say, *really?* She looked young enough to be my daughter.

Robbie wasn't keen on her either. In normal circum-stances, he might have taken to her, because she was very nice. But with his doctors he was very particular, and he was a creature of habit. The only real improvements we'd made had been in areas like physical therapy, where he'd had the same person working with him on his coordi-nation year on year. We'd been through three or four speech therapists with Robbie when he was growing up, and I believed it was the lack of consistency that slowed his progress. He'd grown used to his old doctor, and he wasn't happy with a new one.

At first, he seemed to have forgotten the change, because he was reasonably happy in the car on the way there. He was playing with rubber bands—*Dad, watch him, he'll cut off his circulation*—and humming to himself. But in the waiting room he remembered. The receptionist said, 'Dr Newman will be right out,' and Robbie knew Dr

Newman was not his doctor. He wouldn't sit down. He tried to leave, and yelled when we wouldn't let him. I stood in the doorway, blocking his exit, politely standing aside for other people, and he began pacing and muttering loudly. Now I think of it, he was out of breath then as well. I put it down to agitation.

We finally got him into the doctor's office by bribing him with the promise of a milkshake. He was weighed and measured—'Going to have to watch those biscuits, Robert' —and with some difficulty we got a blood pressure cuff on him.

'We're a little high here,' the doctor said, frowning. 'Have you been eating nice and healthily? Running around lots?' Robbie gazed at her distrustfully. 'Let me just have a listen here.' She took her stethoscope from around her neck and put the earpieces in her ears. I stood up, expecting Robbie to resist again, but he was interested by the stethoscope so he let her listen to his heart. The frown didn't clear from her face. She felt Robbie's neck, and he wriggled under her fingers.

'OK,' Dr Newman said, settling back at her desk. 'There are some abnormal heart rhythms there, that I think we should just check out. I'm going to send Robbie for an ECG—a heart trace—and maybe an echocardiogram.'

'What is it to look for?'

'Well, I'm not sure at this stage. It may well be nothing serious, but I think it's best we do some tests to make sure. As you know, people with Down Syndrome are at a higher risk of heart complications. What I need you to do in the meantime is keep a real eye on Robert's lifestyle. We need him to be eating right and exercising, to lower his blood pressure and generally reduce the load on his heart. We don't want it to be straining more than it has to.'

I looked at Robbie, who had the stethoscope on and was listening to his chest, his arm, his leg, the wall. I looked at Dad. He didn't look worried; he looked mildly attentive, like a polite onlooker. He nodded. Why wasn't he worried? The doctor kept talking. I wondered if I should take Dad's hand, but I didn't. I wondered if I wanted him to take mine.

'I think he's been having some problems with his ears,' Dad said. 'I've noticed him hitting the side of his head, and I think he's been having trouble hearing, more than usual. Though I don't know, sometimes he just doesn't answer.' The doctor reached out and felt Robbie's forehead.

'Any fever?'

'Not that he's complained of. I haven't really been checking.'

'He's a little warm. Let's have a look at what's going on in here.' She reached for an otoscope and had a look in Robbie's ears. 'We've got a little bit of discharge in here,' she said. 'Doesn't look too serious, probably just a bit of an infection.' She turned back to her computer. 'I'm going to prescribe some antibiotic ear drops for him. Try to avoid getting the ear wet, and if there is a lot of discharge, you'll want to use cotton wool, don't use buds. If he is in pain, you can give him paracetamol or anything like that, that's fine.' She printed off the prescription and gave it to us, along with a referral for the cardiology department. 'See you next time, Robbie,' she said, but Robbie, still wary, didn't reply.

He cheered up as we left, though, chattering happily. Should he get a chocolate milkshake or a banana milkshake? He stopped and held the door open for a young woman with a pushchair. She smiled at him nervously. I glowed at my little gentleman—grown-up gentleman—and said he could choose whatever he wanted.

'Both?' he asked, beaming eagerly.

'Absolutely not,' I said.

I went into Robbie's supermarket after work. It wasn't the one closest to home but I tried to do the shopping there every so often, if I knew he was going to be there, to make sure he wasn't feeding me lies when he told me it was going well.

Also, I was worried about him, since the visit to the doctor's. His job wasn't the most physical of labour, but it wasn't sedentary. Was he putting too much strain on his heart?

I saw him as I rounded the corner of the aisle out of the dairy section. He was stacking packets of crackers, and I pulled back slightly, hiding behind a display so I could watch him. He had his little half-smile on his face. He wasn't a fast worker—I'd seen other stackers throw things onto the shelves at top speed—but Robbie liked to have one thing in each hand, to carefully place each one, making sure all the packets were facing the same way, exactly in a line. Crackers and cereal and things in boxes were his favourite: they tessellated.

A middle-aged man with a basket gave me a funny look, half-crouched as I was behind a stack of Christmas chocolate boxes. I grabbed one of them and pretended to study the ingredients.

Robbie's cart was causing a blockage in the aisle—a

young Asian mother with a little boy in her trolley, and an elderly woman going in the opposite direction. Robbie gallantly hopped off his little stool, wheeled his cart away, and bowed the young woman through. She looked a little wary, but Robbie didn't seem to notice. He winked at the boy as he went past.

I smiled. He was fine. He was the picture of health, and he was happy. I put the chocolates down and went to see him.

'Cammy!' His face broke into a huge smile and he gave me a hug.

'Hi, Robbie. How's it going?'

'Good,' he said.

'What do you have on offer today, then?' I asked, and I walked with him as he wheeled his cart and showed me that ice cream was half price this week.

'Bit cold for ice cream, isn't it?' I said, and he laughed.

'Never!'

'Hey, Robbie,' another one of the store workers called to him as we passed. He was young, probably still a teenager, with a ring through his nose and straightened hair dyed black. 'Keep it real,' he said, raising a fist. Robbie fist-bumped him without missing a beat.

'You're friends with the people you work with?' I asked, and he nodded, waving at a check-out lady too. 'That's wonderful. Are you ready for the hospital on Friday?' We had an appointment for his ECG; I was taking the afternoon off work to go with him and Dad. He looked nervous but he nodded. 'It'll be fine. Piece of cake,' I said, and I kissed him on the cheek and told him I had to get going. He went back to the cracker aisle, humming.

Robbie hated hospitals.

'That's OK, buddy,' Dad said, 'I don't like them either. Nobody likes them.'

We were standing outside the main entrance, surrounded by smokers. Robbie said he just needed a minute. He stared up at the sign, *Main Entrance*, and didn't move. Dad and I looked at each other.

'Are you OK?' I asked.

'A minute,' he said again.

I checked my watch. 'We have five minutes,' I mouthed at Dad, shrugging, so we stood with him and all three of us stared up at the sign. *Main Entrance*. One of the smokers, a huge man with tattoos wearing a hospital gown, spat at our feet on his way back inside. I glared at him, but Robbie didn't seem to notice.

'You ready, buddy?' Dad said eventually. Robbie nodded. I took his hand, and we went inside.

He was actually OK once we were there. He grew very red in the face in the waiting room and I could see him working himself up, so we took his hands and practised some of the breathing exercises we had learnt, all three of us together.

He was fascinated by the ECG machine, and giggled when the technician attached the electrodes.

'You have to stay still now, buddy,' Dad said. 'Remember our breathing.'

'Can you get him to relax?' the technician asked. 'If his muscles are tensed it's going to affect the reading.' I frowned. I hated it when people did that, spoke to Robbie through us, like he couldn't hear or didn't exist. Didn't have feelings. The technician was oblivious to my glowering.

'Robbie, honey, remember the meditation we did? Why don't we try some of that now?'

We had to go back to the GP for the results. My boss was making murmurs about the amount of time off I'd had recently, so I told Dad he'd have to take Robbie on his own and I'd come over to the house after work.

'How did it go?' I said, before I'd even got my coat off. Dad sighed.

'Same things, really. Irregular heartbeat, they want to do more tests. They want to send him for a chest x-ray.'

'An x-ray? What do they think is wrong with him?'

'She wouldn't say, not really.'

'He's not going to like that.' Dad sighed again. He was rubbing his hip. 'Still causing you grief?' He nodded.

'The doctor prescribed me something.' He eased himself into a chair. 'Robert's not a fan of those ear drops,' he said.

'He'll get used to them. I don't think they're very nice either.'

'I can't get him to keep still. I think I'm going to have to pull the tablet trick again.'

'Where are you going to find fake ear drops?' I said. A few years ago, when Robbie had had a respiratory tract infection, we'd had to buy some sugar pills for Dad and me so we could all take our pills together. Otherwise he'd flatly refuse his medication.

'I reckon I can get a bottle from a pharmacy and fill it with water or something.'

'Do you have anything in for dinner?'

'Do you know, I completely forgot. I was going to nip to the shop before I picked Robbie up for the doctor's but I think I just got caught up doing something.'

I caught his eye. 'You know that excuse only worked when you had a job.' He grinned guiltily, and I got up. 'Let me see what I can whip up. You just sit there with your feet up, let me do all the work. I don't even live here anymore.'

'You're a star, darling,' Dad said, sipping his tea and leaning back. I shook my head.

'You planned this all along.'

Dad opened the paper.

'Don't know what you're talking about,' he said.

It was a different shape, a different colour, but it was just another Bad News Room. Dr Newman sat slightly away from her desk, facing us. Connect with the patients, build a rapport. The carpet was worn and purple. I'd never been in a medical facility that had a new carpet. I could map my adult life out in pictures of my shoes against threadbare carpets.

'Aortic valve insufficiency.' She was leaning forwards, forearms resting against thighs, hands clasped. I wished she'd sit up, I was sure Dad could see right down her shirt. 'The aortic valve is the last valve the blood passes through when it goes from the heart to the rest of the body, and when it doesn't work properly, it leads to something called aortic regurgitation. The valve doesn't close properly,' she indicated with her hands what this might look like, 'and blood goes backwards, back into the heart. So the left ventricle, receiving all this extra blood, has to work extra hard to get enough blood out of the heart to the rest of the body. Make sense?'

We nodded.

'The wall of the ventricle can then become enlarged and thickened; we call this hypertrophy. This can cause dizziness or chest pain, because of reduced blood flow to the coronary arteries.'

'So what do we do?' Dad said. The news settled on me like a weight. It felt like I was always doing this, always hearing bad news, always knowing that I was going to have to deal with it. I was tired of bad news, tired of dealing.

'It doesn't seem to be serious at the moment. Severe regurgitation can mean we need to replace the valve with surgery, but I don't think that's necessary. You should be able to manage Robert's symptoms with lifestyle changes. Healthy eating and exercise are important, to keep the blood pressure down, but obviously you don't want to overdo it. If he's breathless or in pain, stop immediately. Moderate exercise is probably best, go for walks, things like that. We will keep a close eye on him, because heart failure can develop.'

'Heart failure.' Dad did this, in these situations, repetition. A hollow echo.

'Yes. There is medication we can prescribe in that situation, diuretics for breathlessness, ACE inhibitors to reduce the amount of work the heart has to do.'

'But he might have to go for surgery.'

'Yes, if things worsen significantly, we will have to consider surgery.'

She stopped. Her spiel was over.

I stared at the toes of my shoes. I knew she was expecting us to say something, but I had nothing to say. It was what it was. Like it or lump it.

'Do you have any questions?'

Dad shook his head. 'Is there anything we need to do now?'

'Just keep an eye on his symptoms. If things seem to be getting worse, let us know straight away. Try getting his weight down a bit, keep a generally healthy lifestyle. How are his ears?'

'Clearing up, I think.'

'Great. Well, if you have any questions whatsoever, do let me know.' She sits up—finally—and swivels back towards her desk. It's over now. She's already thinking about her next appointment. Time for us to leave, time for us to deal with it.

I stood up. I ground my heels into the carpet as I walked out.

'Well,' says Eamonn, clapping his hands. 'The end of an era.'

There's still half an hour to go, but people are beginning to stand away from their finished paintings, giving one last critical eye to the final product. I feel the first flutterings of nerves. My painting doesn't look fantastic, but it's about as good as it's going to get.

Niall is still very close to his canvas, doing something with a very fine brush, the tip of his tongue between his teeth. Morris is just touching up the edge of his picture, Allie is sitting back on her stool looking satisfied. Becca is already washing her hands.

'It's going to be weird not coming every week,' she says brightly. Eamonn lays a hand over his heart theatrically. He's in a playful mood.

'My life will forever be emptier,' he says. Morris laughs. 'No, really, I feel we've taken this journey together, I've watched you come so far, I've really gotten to know you, and now you'll fly away and leave me bereft.' Allie is smiling indulgently, secretively. Rosaline looks grumpy.

'You're seeing us all next week anyway,' she says.

'Yes indeed! Next Thursday, seven o'clock, I want you all here in your glad rags for the first night of my brand new art exhibition, featuring the best new talent in town! Plus ones and twos and threes and fours are very welcome.'

'Are you ready for the show?' I ask Morris as he wipes his brush off.

'Yeah, I reckon so. It'll be good to see what everyone's been working on.' We've all been very secretive about our projects. 'What about you?'

'Oh, as ready as I'll ever be, I suppose.' I sigh. I can't help it. I feel like it had such potential, but I just wasn't good enough to bring it out. Eamonn comes up behind me.

'I can hear that in your voice, Ms Addison,' he says conspiratorially, 'and I want it gone. It's good, you know it's good.'

'You don't think it's a bit—infantile?'

'Not at all. Even purely in execution, it's admirable. So much more accuracy and delicacy than when you first started, it's really a very subtle piece. There's real skill in there.' His words mean a lot to me, though I can feel my face is still unconvinced. He claps me on the shoulder. 'Don't tell me you're scared of showing off, Camille. Afraid of the public eye?'

I stand up, decisively. It is finished now.

'Not at all,' I say, though in truth I am a little nervous. 'Bring it on.' I smile, and Eamonn smiles back.

He carries on circling, offering final comments to everyone. I *am* nervous about everyone seeing it, but as I eye my painting, there's an unmistakable swell of pride in my chest. My smile doesn't fade. Bring it on.

'Scared, Cammy.'

Robbie wasn't smiling, he wasn't humming, he wasn't playing *itsy bitsy spider* with his hands. He was just sitting, arms limp by his sides, staring at me. His leg wasn't jiggling, his eyes weren't jumping around the room. He looked so helpless. And pale.

'I know, darling.' I sat on one side of his bed with Peter; Dad sat on the other side. Peter was doing the crossword. Dad was craning to look out of the door at the nurses passing back and forth. There were two bunches of flowers on his bedside table—one from me, one from Sarah's family—and a card from everyone at the supermarket.

'They said two-thirty.'

'I know, Dad.'

'What's the hold-up?'

'I don't know, Dad, they haven't told me.'

'No food?' Robbie said, checking.

'That's right, darling, you can't have food right now,' I said. 'I know you're hungry. But as soon as you're out of here we can go anywhere you like and eat as much as you possibly can. Are you hungry?' He shook his head. He looked down at the sheets of his bed, and the best word I could think of to describe him was "glum". A thirty-three-year-old man with the vulnerability of a five-year-old. Sad and scared and not knowing what was going to happen.

'It'll be fine,' I said, smoothing the bed covers. 'Everything's going to be fine. They're going to pop a new heart valve in there, and then you'll be up and about and playing footie again in no time, drinking chocolate milkshakes and eating Smarties.' I looked from Peter to Dad, but they didn't say anything, they didn't back me up. I crossed my leg and tapped the toe of my foot in the air in frustration. Couldn't they see we needed to reassure him?

When they wheeled him away, I walked with him as far as the doors of the operating theatre. He didn't say anything, just lay flat and kept his eyes on me, and when I had to stop walking he didn't move his head, just stared blankly at the ceiling.

'Good luck, darling!' I called down the corridor. 'I'll be right here waiting for you when you wake up!'

So, as it turns out, the last thing I ever said to him was a lie.

The Show

It's the last week of my art class and I'm making lasagne for dinner.

The world outside the kitchen window is black, and has been for over an hour already; it's the beginning of December and the darkness closes in by four. I miss the summer, when I can see Peter pottering about in the garden as I cook dinner. He's upstairs at the moment, I think, sorting through some bank papers. Every so often I can hear him moving about.

I slide the lasagne into the oven and straighten slowly, stretching my back. My whole body creaks these days, except it's pain that leaks out, not noise. I lean one hand on the counter, the other on the small of my back, watching the reflection in the darkened window. Phantom lights, speckled by the rain. Solitary figure in a bulky cardi.

Last week was technically the last week of class, the twelfth of twelve sessions. But Eamonn has invited us all— plus guests—to a mini art show so we can see everyone's projects. I'm mildly interested to have a look, powerfully curious about seeing Allie's, and horrifyingly nervous about showing my own. Strangely, the person whose opinion I'm most scared of is Eamonn, and he's seen it loads of times, in all stages of creation. But it might be different in the stark context of a show, as opposed to a class. Next to all those others. *Inferiority complex?*

Peter's coming with me tonight. I didn't even have to invite him, he just asked one day, about two or three weeks ago, through a mouthful of sea bass,

'When's the show, then? I'm looking forward to it.'

I was surprised. I'd told him about my class but I didn't think he'd been paying too much attention.

'The 6th,' I said. He nodded, scooping up more white sauce with his potato.

'Think you're going to be ready?'

I'd had a forkful poised and ready, but it hadn't reached my mouth yet. I was touched that he'd taken an interest. He hadn't noticed that my cutlery had frozen.

'I suppose so. I'll have to be. Nobody's expecting perfection—it's a short timeframe and we're all novices.'

He looked up and smiled at me as he reached for his glass. 'I bet yours will be lovely,' he said.

I smiled back at him, suddenly shy, and went back to my dinner.

I slowly stack up the dirty saucepans and chopping board and knives and put away the pasta and the flour. Everything I do is slow these days. I'm half expecting to grind to a complete halt at some point soon. I glance at the clock. I could make myself a cup of tea and go and watch the six o'clock news. I do normally leave the washing up for Peter. But if I don't do it before dinner, it won't be done until we get back tonight, and it will seem all the more exhausting then.

I run the tap, and while I wait for the sink to fill, Peter comes downstairs wearing a tie and his tweed jacket.

'Very swish,' I say, touched all over again.

'Well, it's not every day your wife stars in an art opening,' he says, kissing me on the cheek and going over to investigate the oven. 'Smells delicious.'

'Set the table then,' I say, batting him out of the way. 'And it's not a real art opening, it's just us. It's like show and tell at Primary school.'

'Well I'm proud of you anyway,' he beams, unquashable in his enthusiasm. It's sweet. It's how it's always been, him by my side, propping me up. How it should be. I turn the tap off and look down at what I'm wearing. It is an art show, after all, even if it is only the seven of us. Maybe I should make more of an effort.

After dinner, I go upstairs to change. The sun glints off a photo frame on an eye-level shelf in the bedroom and I pause. I bend down to the shelf below and pick up the dusty velveteen case that holds my mother's pearls, painstakingly and lovingly restrung all those years ago. The case resists briefly as I open it. I don't wear them anymore—I don't want to draw attention to the folded crepiness of my neck. I run a thumb lightly over them, smooth and cold and resting carelessly on their faded plush bed. I wonder what will happen to them after I'm gone.

I close the case again, gently. I don't want Lucy to have them. She never knew how they looked against my mother's dark curls, below her red, laughing mouth, how they shone as she danced in the yellow glow of the kitchen while the rain beat black against the windows.

She probably wouldn't want them anyway, I tell

myself, putting the case back on the shelf. She has her own lineage to receive, to treasure, to pass on. *Sorry, Mum*, I think, resting my hands on my thighs and staying there, bent over, feeling the pull in my lower back. Behind the pearls, leaning against the back of the narrow bookcase out of the sunlight, with one corner slightly dog-eared, is a thick, square, black-and-white photograph, two school-girls, in uniform, doubled over against a tree trunk, laughing.

We don't have a lot of photos in the house. Our wedding photo, on the mantelpiece, and my parents' in the hall, alongside my graduation photo. I'm wearing my billowing black gown and beaming at someone out of frame, a ghost that only I can see. A couple of Gabriel and Lucy at various ages in the kitchen, plus a Christmas shot of Peter's extended family. The frame at eye level with me now as I straighten up is Robbie, at a work summer celebration. They held it every year, in a park, families welcome. In the photo, Robbie is wearing his red baseball cap and his wide smile, his attention caught slightly off centre. Tucked into the frame is a smaller print of Robbie and Sarah when they were younger, maybe eleven or twelve. Behind the photo frame is a picture of Sarah at her graduation—I meant to get a frame for it, but I never got around to it, and the photo is bending and curling in on itself.

I change into black trousers and a black top with a few sequins on and a slinkier grey cardigan. I add earrings and a dab of makeup.

'You look lovely,' Peter says as I come down the stairs. I pinch the sides of my lower lip to de-smudge my lipstick.

'Thank you,' I say. He offers me his arm, like he did when we were younger, and we walk out to the car together. He opens the car door for me, and I feel like giggling. So glamorous.

It was the same hospital.

The same hospital, the same news, thirty-three years later.

We were two floors lower, there were television screens on the walls instead of posters, Peter was on my left instead of an empty chair, but the feeling was the same. The waiting. Different doctor, same expression.

I think the lights were brighter. When I think about that day, back when I was twenty-two, I remember darkness. The sky was grey, the lights were dim, it was dusky. Now the lights were painfully bright and fluorescent, they almost hurt my eyes.

It didn't feel the same. I wanted to feel some kind of resonance, but I wasn't young and heartbroken this time, I was aged and beaten down. My dad wasn't a strong and supportive husband anymore, he was an old man and he was tired.

And while nothing—nothing—could come close to the devastation of losing my mum, having her taken from me, this time the emptiness cut that little bit deeper because it took everything from me, everything that had filled my life for the last thirty-three years, and it left me with nothing.

At the studio, Eamonn is standing by the door with a tray of champagne flutes.

'Ah, the star of my show,' he says whenever anyone

arrives. I gave him a humouring smile.

'Thank you *so* much,' I say in the poshest, most refined voice I can manage, taking a glass and raising it to him. 'This is my husband, Peter,' I say, and the two men shake hands.

'You have a wonderfully talented wife, Peter,' Eamonn says with his winning smile. 'Champagne?'

'Thank you,' Peter says, 'and I know.'

Allie is hovering by Eamonn's shoulder. If you didn't know them, if you just wandered into the room off the street, you'd think they were together, the way she touches his elbows, leans in to listen to him, laughs at his jokes. He seems happy with her there, he exudes an easy confidence.

'No Jonathan?' I mutter as I pass her. She shakes her head, the tails of her headscarf flying, her eyes shining. I don't say anything else. I'm glad that she's happy.

The easels and tables and piles of cloths and paints that usually scatter the studio have been cleared to one side, and our projects are positioned in a semi-circle on large display boards, each covered with a black cloth. Very theatrical. We gather in the middle of the circle, clutching our flutes and making small talk. A table to one side has crisps and nibbles and more drinks on it. Like a real art show.

Morris has brought his family—his wife, softly-spoken like him, rather short with very thick hair tied back into a ponytail, and a teenaged daughter with chains on her top and an unexpectedly outgoing nature. She is very loud to be sprung from two such quiet people. Niall has also brought his partner, and to my surprise he is a he. Joe, not Jo, apparently. Quite large, the bulky sort of muscle that makes me nervous, inwardly, and a tattoo peeking out from the short sleeves of his T-shirt. I'm glad he doesn't have a shaven head. It's strange to me to see Niall's large dry hand in the hand of another man, but I quite like seeing it. They look happy.

Becca has a big group of friends with her. She is still noticeably skinny, very angular features. Most of her friends are pierced, black-haired, skinny-jeaned. One is a pleasingly round girl in a purple cardigan with glasses on. I can see the outline of a book in her canvas tote bag, and she laughs and jokes with the rest of the group and hugs Becca like everyone else.

Rosaline is alone. She wraps her arms around herself and makes polite conversation with Becca's friends, but she keeps glancing at the door, and I see her sighing. I wonder if she is waiting for Emmi or for someone else, someone to support her, congratulate her, like we all have. I don't think anyone else is coming.

I wonder if Eamonn is going to make a speech—the setting seems to suggest it, as does his melodramatic nature, but I feel that it would be too much if he does. It's nice to play, to pretend, but let's not make too much of a thing about it. Let's not forget what it really is, an adult evening art class for those of us who forgot our talent or are desperately seeking one to cling on to.

Fortunately, all that happens is Eamonn sets the tray down on the table and, arm casually around Allie's shoulders, glances round at the group and says, normal volume, 'Shall we get on with it then?' Murmured enthusiasm from everyone. Peter squeezes my hand. Morris' daughter stands with her feet apart and her hands holding her upper arms, grinning like she's having a great time. Morris rubs her back.

Eamonn doesn't tell us whose paintings he is revealing, and we weren't there when he set it up, so we have to guess based on reaction.

The first one is Allie's. I know it straight away, and not just because she flushes a deep, deep crimson.

She's painted a story, with colour instead of words. It's a girl, standing slightly down-right of centre. She's painted with excruciating precision. She's almost got her back to us, but she's glancing back over her shoulder so you can see her icy blue eyes, rimmed with thick, smudged black lines, her short-cropped hair, the strip of material encircling her head and draping over her shoulder, the long fringe escaping out from under it. An ebony frame against an ivory background. An oversized leather bag hangs from one elbow, she wears black leather ankle boots, and in her white fingers she holds a piece of paper. A letter?

Around her are lots of people, blurring more and more towards the edges, rushed activity. I decide it's a train station, she's clutching a ticket. Her eyes are staring slightly off-centre, she's not looking back at you. They're shining—tear-filled? Is that a slightly paler streak down her cheek, a tear track? I can almost see the people around her striding, hear the rush of trains and the click of heels, imagine her turn away and carry on walking, head down, shoulders turning to avoid the crowd. Perhaps her tears start to flow freely. I see her swallowed by the crowd of people milling around the train, trailing a wake of unhappiness, of perfume, of the brand of a thousand eyes.

'It's beautiful, Allie,' I whisper, squeezing her arm. She's bashful, coy, giggly. I glance again at the headscarf of the painted girl, and I wonder if she's making a choice

Allie herself never made.

'It's alright, I suppose,' she says.

'I love it,' Morris says out loud, 'you really want to know what her story is.'

'Is it a shopping centre?' asks Morris' daughter. 'I think she's been stood up by someone.'

'No,' I say quickly, 'it's a train station.' And then I stop. I don't want to share it with everyone, what this picture says to me. Allie stays quiet, a mysteriously knowing smile on her face, and I know this is the effect she was wanting. She doesn't tell us what she was thinking of when she painted it, she just wants each of us to see what it says to us.

Eamonn, champagne in one hand, other hand on the small of her back, beams with pride. He can't take his eyes off her. She basks.

The next picture I think is Becca's. But from the way Niall blushes, and his partner grabs him and knuckles his head in an affectionate way, I realise it's his. I'm surprised, I didn't know he was as morbid as that.

It's a very dark background, blacks and greens and browns. Standing in a line, going from forward left to back right diagonally across the canvas, is a row of people. It's the same person over again, in the same pose, facing the same way. The one at the front is a normal man, in jeans and a t-shirt; the one behind him is naked. The one behind that is muscle and sinew; then organs, and the last figure is a skeleton, white-grey, luminous and thin. It's eerie, and I'm not sure I like it. It makes me uncomfortable, and I have a suspicion that his anatomical accuracy could use some tweaking.

'Here,' Eamonn says, making wide, slow circles with

his hands as he talks, 'I think you're making a statement about the inherent narrative of a human being, the layers and the stories that make up a person, viscerally depicted in this stark vacuum.' I wonder how he acquired the ability to spout so many words. He always has the same intonation when he goes into this mode, puts the same pattern of stress on the words; *emphasis*, normal, normal, normal, *emphasis*. Niall nods along with it but doesn't add anything, doesn't comment on his masterpiece. I think he wants us to move on.

The third painting is a delicate watercolour, though in my mind would have been better done in more assertive oils, or maybe even acrylic. It's a desk, quite dark, sort of oldy-worldy, of the sort you'd expect to find quills on, and parchment. There's a book open in the middle of it, in a circle of weak light, handwritten until halfway down the second page, where it stops abruptly. The shapes are slightly out of kilter, not quite true to life, though whether intentional or not I can't tell. It's alright, nothing remarkable. I keep my face polite.

There's a moment of uncertain silence; we're all looking around to find the owner of it. Morris? Not Becca. Not me. Rosaline, at the back, raises a hand, almost guiltily.

'I couldn't think of anything to do with narrative,' she said, 'except a story. It's a story being written.'

'A completely valid interpretation,' Eamonn says, doggedly optimistic. 'I left the scope purposefully broad because things that seem obvious to one person won't even occur to another person, and it's great to see the complete variety that a single word produces. So simple, such a humble representation of narrative. Beautiful.'

I wish somebody had come along to stand by Rosaline. She looks unsure of what to do with her hands.

With each unveiling my nervousness grows, the suspense pounding itself out against my ribcage louder and louder each time. By the fourth, Peter can tell—*am I sweating?*—and he takes my hand, smiling calmly.

The fourth is abstract, bright, aggressive acrylics, and my eyes go straight to Becca. She grins proudly. An underlay of acid green has appeared in her platinum-blonde hair since last week.

Like Niall's, it's a dark background, or foreground, I suppose, purplish-blue instead of his navy-green. Three spots—tiny, small, biggish—placed seemingly at random are bursting through the dark from behind, white spots ringed with red and yellow, as though something behind has burned through layers of wrapping.

'It's supposed to be in motion,' Becca explains, 'a point in the process of ripping through. You're supposed to think that it's just started, it's going to happen, all the top layer will be ripped away.'

I can tell Eamonn doesn't like such frequent use of the word "supposed". *There is no "supposed to" in art.*

Fifth has to be mine or Morris'. I'm sad that Emmi stopped coming. I would have liked to see what she came up with.

It's not mine. It's almost like Allie's, but not quite. Same quiet beauty, this time in muted pastels.

It's a hallway, a wooden side-cabinet, pegs of coats, the open front door at the far left-hand side. A bowl with keys in, a discarded flower-head trailing petals, a scarf draped over the cupboard handle. On the pegs, far right-hand side, a child's coat, pink with fur around the hood. An

adult's coat, bulky, brown. Two pairs of wellies below—
one small and silver, one large and green. On the
sideboard, centre stage, a gold trophy, tiny plastic figure
of a gymnast, upside down, toes pointed, on a golden
pedestal. A pair of headphones dangling down. A piece of
paper or a letter, opened and folding back in on itself. The
open green front door, just a sliver of the outside world, a
leaf or two blown in. Who's just left, and where are they
going? It's such a heartfelt depiction of watching a child
grow up and leave, I would almost tear up if I were the
sort of person to get emotional.

'Beautiful,' Eamonn says. 'Just beautiful. The passage
of time, the ultimate narrative. Really good technique.'
He's obviously genuinely impressed. Morris bows his head
in acknowledgement of the praise, doesn't blush or brush
it off, accepts it. His daughter makes a joking comment. I
wonder if she understands the significance. She must be
sixteen or seventeen, maybe older. Maybe she's already
moved out, already read that letter and gone through that
green door.

It is a good picture—equal in concept to Allie's, though
maybe less skilled in execution—but it throws my mood
off. I wish Eamonn hadn't juxtaposed mine and Morris'.
Mine is about the passage of time too, and nowhere near
as poignantly done as his. I suddenly feel mulish, like a
teenager. *If I can't be the only one, I'm not going at all.*

'Best till last,' Eamonn murmurs in my ear very low as
he squeezes past me to the last veiled canvas. I wonder if
Peter hears. Allie hasn't finished studying Morris' painting.
Peter squeezes my hand. I roll my eyes, pretending I don't
care, it's all stupid.

The material comes down. My painting looks crude

and amateurish compared to the others. I feel angry in my embarrassment. I don't want other people looking at it.

My canvas is landscape. *Like Morris'*. There are four faces on it, in a row, evenly spaced. The same face, blank expression, unremarkable, eyes and nose and lips. The first, on the left, has blonde hair with a greenish tint, locks twisting into vines. The irises are a light, pale blue. Next, the hair is darker, thicker, the eyes brighter, the lips full and juicy-red. Further right, the hair is burning into orange leaves, the eyes are deep denim, the lips slightly paler, the skin slightly darker. At the end, the hair is tinged grey and twig-like, the eyes foggy, the skin lined and shadowed, the lips chapped.

I look at it and drop my eyes to the floor. I don't know if people are looking at the picture or at me or at each other with raised eyebrows, and I don't want to know.

Is the silence longer than for the other paintings? Why aren't people saying anything?

I glance up. Eamonn is beaming at me. *Don't ask me to talk about it, don't ask me to talk about it.*

'I really love this piece,' Eamonn says. 'We've got the passage of time again, the classic narrative, but here Camille has juxtaposed the quintessentially cyclical passage of time, the seasons, with the ultimate in non-renewable time, age. Just wonderful.' His eyes are on me but I keep looking at the floor. I'm not going to look at him, I'm not going to make any facial expression, I'm not going to confirm or deny what he's saying or tell everyone what I was thinking and what it means to me. It's none of their damn business.

'That's so good,' Allie says.

'I love the hair, the way it's all the same shape but made of different things.' That's Rosaline. I look up at

Peter and he's smiling at me.

'It's really good, Camille,' he says, just for me. 'You're an artist.' I pretend to toss my hair like a diva, and feel myself start to breathe again as Eamonn claps his hands and the attention moves away from my painting.

'You've all done exceptionally well,' Eamonn says. 'All of you, you've really picked up the techniques, you've created really unique expressions and so many different interpretations of the theme. I'm so impressed. You've been a pleasure to teach, and I hope you'll all take away if not a long-lasting habit of art, then at least an insight into viewing artworks interpretively. Now I'm sorry to say that this class won't be running next term—'

'What?' says Becca. 'Why?' Her friends murmur in outraged solidarity. Eamonn shrugs apologetically.

'Not enough takers to justify it, economically. I'm quite a luxury, you know.' He winks jovially, like an uncle. 'The university says we need at least twelve per class, to make it viable. I'm a luxury, but I'm a luxury of an acquired taste, it appears.' Allie stands by him, protectively.

Becca and Morris seem upset by the news. Rosaline is checking her phone, apparently not listening. Niall and I take it impassively. It's a shame for the community to lose a nice facility, and a shame for Eamonn to lose part of his job, when he so obviously enjoys it. But I wasn't planning on coming again. I've never seen the point in returning to the same thing over and over again.

'Anyway,' Eamonn says, 'eat, drink, be merry, and bask in your combined artistic genius.' He raises his glass, and turns away to talk to Allie. People start to talk, to wander back around to look at paintings, to reach for nibbles. Eamonn bends his head slightly too close to Allie's neck to whisper in her ear, eyes looking away but fingers stroking her forearm slightly too suggestively. Surely everyone here knows what's going on. But why would they mind?

Peter wanders back over with a handful of mini cheese biscuits.

'I'm so impressed by people who can draw,' he says. 'I just seem to make a mess. It looks so good in my head, and then it comes out on paper all warped.' He shakes his head. 'You're much cleverer than I am, Cammy.' I shrug.

'It's not that hard. I love Allie's, though, that's beautiful.'

'Do you get to keep them?'

'We can keep everything we've painted, but Eamonn wants to do a display of some of them, so I've told him he can have whatever he likes of mine and I'll pick them up when he's done.' Peter gives me a one-armed squeeze.

'I'm so proud of you,' he says. I smile, and give him a small kiss.

'Thank you, darling,' I say.

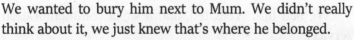

We wanted to bury him next to Mum. We didn't really think about it, we just knew that's where he belonged.

But he wasn't Catholic; he'd never been christened, much less confirmed. We'd never taken him to church, we never spoke about God unless he asked about something he'd heard in school. Mum had been the devout one. Dad married her in church, went with her to midnight mass at Christmas, and said grace with her before our Sunday meal, but not out of any true belief, just because it was the done thing. Because Mum cared about it, and Dad cared about Mum. When she was gone, any faith Dad may have had, left over from his childhood in the dark recesses of his mind, fled, instantly.

I'd long ago given up on the idea of God, finding religion irrelevant and illogical and full of rules nobody could explain to me. So it wasn't even a conscious decision to raise Robbie without religion, it's just what came naturally to us. And now that instinct was going to keep him from his mother in the afterlife, prevent us from doing this one simple thing that we wanted, that we liked to believe she wanted, just that smallest hint of closure.

'Fine,' I said, throwing my hands up. The skin of my face was dry and tight, my hair pulled away from my face too harshly. I stood up, my chair scraping. I'd had enough. I'd had enough of this. I'd spent thirty-three years of my life sorting and dealing and giving up my time and my life when I could have been travelling and exploring and really living. I could have done my Law degree, I could have got a job I loved, like Peter's friends who wouldn't shut up about the exciting things they were doing at work whenever we had them over for dinner. I left, I walked out and let the wind whip the edges of my jacket.

We had him cremated, and a small commemoration service.

I've always had a good memory, even for things I'd rather forget. The phone call in Beijing. The endless flight home. The hospital waiting room. Michael leaving. If I let myself, I can relive in vivid horror exactly the way I felt, exactly how it was to have my world come crashing down around me.

But Robbie's funeral—it's a blur to me. I can't

remember waking up in the morning, or if I ate breakfast. I remember doing up the button on my skirt, and putting the backs on my earrings. I don't remember what was said at the service, I don't remember the sound of the singing. I don't remember what expression I wore or what I said to the people who passed by to pay respects. I remember thinking there were a lot of people—his colleagues and boss from the supermarket, kids and parents from the support group, neighbours. Everybody loved him. Of course they loved him, he was the essence of loveliness. He was kind and caring and wanted everybody to be safe and cared for. He was far too good a person to be born the way he was, to have lived the way he did.

I didn't let myself cry. Peter cried, as he had when Robbie died, but I clenched my fists and my teeth and refused. I got annoyed at Peter, ever solicitous, forever at my shoulder with creased forehead and hushed voice, asking if I was OK, if he could do anything, if I needed anything. I shrugged off his hands and wished he would stop smothering me, felt guilty for it and turned the guilt into anger.

Sarah and her mother sat with us in the front row. She was a beautiful young woman of twenty-nine, working towards a PhD in genetics. Her speech and her movements were slightly thick, slightly blurred, and her face looked out of proportion—small eyes, broad forehead—but she fiercely refused to let it get in the way of her intelligence and her eloquence. She held my hand as we sat there, and somewhere deep inside a wrestling match took place over the pride I felt for Sarah doing so well, and the bitterness that Robbie had been so much less lucky.

I took the urn—small, quiet, lifeless—to visit Mum's

grave. I knelt on damp grass and leant my forehead against the cool, rough stone that was all I had left of my mother. The urn was engraved with Robbie's name and dates. A paltry summary, that utterly failed to express everything that is a person. It referred to Robert but the life it summed up was mine. This was everything I had achieved with my life—this grey, ceramic, premature urn.

I stayed with Dad, in Dad's house, my house, for a while afterwards. Dad had moved his desk into my old room at some point but it was mostly the same. Robbie's room, which we had converted for him from Dad's old study all those years ago, stayed shut.

I didn't talk to Peter. I couldn't. I knew he just wanted to be there for me, to support me, I knew he was upset too and maybe he even needed me, but I couldn't face him. I couldn't see him, I couldn't talk to him, I didn't want him to hold me. When he rang, I ignored it. When he came round, I told Dad I didn't want to see him and I stayed in my room. I could barely even have a conversation with Dad. I was so angry, and all the raging in the world couldn't give me my life back.

After my ten days of compassionate leave, I had to go back to work. My colleagues walked on eggshells around me, staring at me as though I might explode. I was quieter than normal, maybe, terse when I had to speak to anyone. I wasn't interested in small talk or chit-chat by the water cooler, but I hated their eyes on me, wary, not knowing what to say. I would have been the same in their shoes, but I couldn't stop being angry with their incompetence, their lack of understanding. They didn't understand, they couldn't understand. Nobody could.

I had lunch with Peter.

'Darling, how can I help you?' he said, earnestly, reaching for my hand. He was so patient with me, so caring. I hated that I snapped at him.

'I don't know, Peter, if I knew how to make everything better, I would do it. I don't have all the answers.' I enunciated in my anger, almost spitting. He leaned back in his chair, away from me, looking defeated.

'Alright, Camille. Alright.'

He suggested I look for a new job. He suggested we travel. He tried to make me see that instead of resenting all the things I hadn't managed to do, I could start doing them—but I didn't want to hear it. I didn't want to have to start finally living life for myself at fifty-five.

I did think about getting a new job. I considered sitting down and searching my soul, finding out what it was that I really wanted to do, really applying myself to doing it. But I was old. My CV hadn't grown in thirty years. I couldn't learn something new, nobody was going to think I was worth anything. All I could do was grit my teeth—already ground to the roots—and get on with my job until the time came for me not to get on with it anymore.

I worried about leaving Dad on his own. He was seventy-nine years old and hadn't been by himself since before I was born. He was still independent, though he walked with a cane and we'd had a stair-lift installed, and he took pills for his cholesterol but was otherwise in good health. Physically, there was no reason he couldn't live in the house on his own. But if it was me, if I had to suddenly be on my own in this house, the first house he'd brought his new wife back to, the house he'd raised a daughter and later an adoptive son in, a house so full of memories and pain—if I had to face that house every day on my own, I don't think I'd have been able to do it. Even after all he'd managed to do, I was scared the loneliness would crush him. It was hard to go from constantly needed to all alone.

One night after dinner, he knocked on my bedroom door. His head poked around the edge.

'Can I come in?' The same ritual, I had seen him do this a thousand times, right from when I was a little girl. And here we were, almost two pensioners, still going through the same motions. I smiled.

'Of course.'

He sat down beside me on the bed. 'Sweetheart, you have to go home,' he said, taking my hand in his and patting it. I remembered his hands from when he used to pick me up and swing me onto his shoulders. I thought they were the biggest and strongest and safest hands in the world. Now they were papery and folded and veined, and the knuckles were swollen. Mine were halfway there too. 'I appreciate you sticking around and helping your old Dad out, but you have to go back to Peter. He's hurting too, you know, he loved Robbie.'

'I know, Dad.' I leaned my head on his shoulder, even though it made my back twinge. 'Will you be OK on your own?'

'I'll be fine, pet.'

'I miss him.' It had been three weeks since Robbie died.

'I know you do. I do, too.' There was a tone in his voice that I knew only I could understand. Conflict. You could love someone and miss them terribly, and still wish they'd never been born. Missing Robbie only made us realise how gone Mum was, and how much we missed her.

We sat like that for a while, in the fading light.

'I'll go back tomorrow night,' I said. 'I'll call Peter tomorrow.'

'He loves you, you know. You're very lucky.'

I closed my eyes.

'I know.'

I told Peter I'd be home after work, in time to cook dinner. I sat in the car outside his house—our house—for a while with the heater running, staring straight ahead. I didn't know why I was making such a big deal out of coming home. I'd lived there with Peter for years; nothing about our situation had changed. It just felt like as soon as I went back in there, I was officially starting my life without Robbie. And when Robbie had been my focus, my purpose for so long, I wasn't sure I really knew how to lead a life without him.

The front door opened, and Peter came out. He walked casually over to the car and leaned on the roof. I rolled the window down.

'You coming in?' he asked nonchalantly, looking out over the hood of the car.

'I suppose so,' I said.

'There's a surprise for you in the living room,' he said. His words were unexpected—surprises weren't something we did; as a general rule, they weren't something I liked. Against my will, he had piqued my interest.

I went inside, and pushed open the door to the living

room. She was sniffing around the bottom of the TV stand, intensely curious. A gorgeous golden retriever, only a puppy, all paws and ridiculously outsized eyes. She looked up at me when I came in, tail wagging ten to the dozen, and stuck her tongue out and panted at me.

I melted at the sight of her.

'Aren't you gorgeous,' I breathed, dropping to my knees. She came bounding over and put her front paws on my legs, reaching up to lick my face. I scooped her up and kissed her, marvelling at her soft fur, her puppy smell, how completely she had me enraptured. She wriggled delightedly and I held her to my face and finally, finally, all the tears came out, and I sat on my floor, slumped against the sofa, and held the dog to me and cried and cried.

I don't know why I look at my phone. It's not like I'm the kind of person who's constantly glued to it, feel lost without it—I can go days without remembering to check it, by which time it's dead, and when I revive it, it glows blankly up at me because the only people I know who'd ever call me always try the landline first.

Maybe I'm feeling more self-conscious than I realise, standing around making chit-chat without the safety of a canvas to hide behind and a brush to busy my hands with. Maybe it's because I see Rosaline, standing precariously with her legs crossed and her phone in her hand because it doesn't look like she has any pockets. She's wearing an insubstantial ditsy-print dress and a chunky cardigan the same length, from which her slim legs seem endless, wrapped around each other and ending in insubstantial, battered plimsolls. The way she's standing makes her feet collapse over to the side, and I wriggle my toes in my shoes—practical, sturdy—just to reassure myself that I have solid contact with the ground.

Becca is wearing chunky black boots with silver buckles, resting her weight heavily on one hip with the other foot jutting out carelessly. I am surprised to notice that Allie is wearing peep-toed heels, and her toenails are painted.

With a jolt, I bring myself back to what Morris' wife is saying, and I feel my face heat as I realise I haven't been listening, and I don't know what to say. I nod my head and try to smile in a way that implies agreement or concentration, but not necessarily happiness, in case she's talking about something grim. My hands, desperate for something to do, reach for the clasp of my bag, dig inside, find my phone. I draw it out, and my face reddens further because it annoys me when people look at their phone in the middle of a conversation with someone else, but I glance down at it anyway and am taken aback to see a voicemail message is blinking at me gently. It's Dad's care home.

I frown, forgetting my embarrassment. I excuse myself from the group—Peter effortlessly smooths over the gap— and raise the phone to listen. The high walls and bare floorboards make the room echo, and I struggle to focus on the tinny voice in my ear. I slip out of the wide double doors, and down the corridor. I don't have my coat but the outside looks dark and cool and calm, so I go out of the main door too and let the frosty air gently prickle my cheeks.

I fold one arm across myself and squint down at my

phone in the other hand, trying to restart the message. I'm distracted by an orange glint—a cigarette glowing at me from the blackness. It's Emmi, leaning by the main door, head thrown back against the wall. I'm so surprised to see her, I forget the phone message.

'Emmi,' I say. 'What are you doing here? Why don't you come in?'

She drags dramatically on the cigarette, pauses, and exhales a cloud of smoke. I frown, but I don't say anything. She's old enough to know what smoking will do to her, and she's old enough to decide if that matters to her or not. She looks at me sideways without taking her head from the wall.

'Too embarrassed,' she says. I can't tell if she's been drinking or not. 'I've really screwed up.' I put my phone away so I can fold my arms and bury my hands in my elbows to keep them warm.

'Rosaline would love to see you,' I say. Emmi shakes her head slightly, sadly. I sigh, too. 'What *is* going on between you two?'

'I made some bad decisions,' she says evasively. 'And I've screwed up everything—my degree, my friendship with Rosaline, my fucking sanity.'

'Over a boy?'

She screws her face up, turning away from me, and I regret the choice of word. I didn't mean to trivialise.

'OK look,' I say. 'I don't know what's going on in your life. I don't know if things are really as drastic as you make out, or if it will all look small and petty in the morning, but whatever it is, believe me, you can cope.'

'My troubles will make me stronger and one day I'll look back and be thankful for everything I went through because it made me who I am?' She heaves herself from the wall, drops the cigarette butt on the ground and grinds it out with her shoe.

'Not at all.' I frown again at the smouldering smudge on the floor. 'You don't have to be thankful for everything that happens to you, you don't even have to like it.' I take a deep breath, and feel the cold chill my lungs. 'Sometimes shit things happen and they're shit and that's it, and everything would have been better if they hadn't happened.'

Emmi pulls her coat tighter around her and shivers. 'That's not the most inspiring of pep talks.'

I smile wryly. 'I'm not the person to give motivational speeches. There are plenty on the internet, I believe, if one knows where to look.' She nods at her feet. 'If it helps, I do think most shit things can be dealt with. You can cope with them, even if you don't like them.'

'Is it only shit things though? Is it just—coping, until I die?'

I blow out through my cheeks and squeeze myself tighter. 'There are good things buried in there too,' I say. 'Sometimes they're just hard to see.' I wonder if I should hug her, but instead I just reach out and touch her shoulder. 'You don't have to go in there,' I tell her, 'but text Rosaline. Buy her a drink. It sounds like you need a friend, and I suspect she does too.'

Emmi screws up her face ruefully. 'Is this the wisdom of age speaking?' she says.

I take my hand back. 'Something like that.' I shiver slightly. My face and my nose are beginning to hurt from the cold. I turn to go back inside, reaching for the door. 'There's an ashtray just there,' I say to Emmi over my shoulder, nodding at the bin by the door.

I walk briskly back down the corridor. I suddenly desperately want a mug of tea to wrap my hands around. Back in the studio, I stand close to Peter and slip my hands through the crook of his elbow. Morris' wife is still talking.

When I retired, we went to Mauritius.

I think Peter would have wanted to surprise me with it, meet me outside work on my last day and present me with plane tickets out of the blue. But he knew me too well. He told me over dinner a few months beforehand that he was thinking about a holiday, and asked if that was something I would be interested in and where I might like to go.

I looked at him over the water jug, chewing. I thought about it, carefully. I swallowed.

'That sounds lovely,' I said. 'Let's go on holiday.'

I liked the sound of Portugal, but I wanted to go as far as possible, and Europe just seemed too close to home. I wanted South America or sub-Saharan Africa, but we agreed that we were too old to play dice with cocaine gangsters or Russian roulette with our digestive systems. Peter wasn't very good with spicy food, so I said we probably shouldn't do Asia. I vetoed Australia as well, so we ended up with Mauritius.

I was surprised how much I enjoyed planning the trip. And then I felt guilty for enjoying it, for looking forward to something and being happy about something, even though it had been so long since Robbie's death.

We blew a lot of our savings on it. It was strange, being

in an airport, getting on a plane, not having to keep one eye on Robbie, not having to worry about anything but what I was doing, not getting anxious in public places or around people, not constantly checking around me or running through a million things in my head. I didn't know how to not have anything to do, not to have anything to worry about. We read books on the beach and went for walks and had long, leisurely lunches in restaurants. The island was beautiful, the weather was gorgeous. It was a perfect trip, it just felt... empty. The hotel room was clean and lifeless. Without constant logistical organisation to busy myself with, I found myself struggling for conversation. Peter smiled and took my hand and seemed content, so I didn't mention it to him. I lay back with my legs in the sun and my hands folded on my sagging belly and stared at the blue, blue sky.

'Let's go away for Christmas,' Michael said.

We were navigating the labyrinthine alleys behind the school where I taught English, side-stepping potholes and mud puddles. Rickshaw drivers careered wildly around us and wizened old men squatted by walls chewing betel nuts. I'd learnt to keep about a foot of distance between the two of us when we were out in public, which usually meant he was walking ahead of me and often made conversations difficult.

'What?' I said, skipping over a pile of manure. 'You've only just got here, and already you want to leave?'

'We could go somewhere warm,' he said pointedly. We'd been in Beijing for about a month, and October was bringing a chill with it. 'Bangkok. Kuala Lumpur. Sydney. Fiji.' I stopped to check the directions I was clutching in my hands. We were on our way to dinner, at the house of a timid young woman who taught at the same school as me. Her English wasn't great but she was fascinated by me and my stories of life back home, and particularly my thick hair, so wiry compared to hers. Michael had been thrilled at the invitation.

'Everything at the embassy is so English,' he'd said.

'OK,' I said. 'Let's take a holiday from the holiday.'

'This isn't a holiday, we've both got jobs,' he said. 'This is life. We're both grown-ups with jobs, doing life. In Beijing.' He grinned. 'We could go away for two weeks and come back in time for the Spring Festival.' He swung his hand, and I longed to grab it. 'Come on, Millie, I want to explore the world with you.' He held my gaze, and I almost stamped with frustration at not being able to kiss him.

'Can we afford it?'

'Of course we can. I'll lend you the money for the ticket if I have to.'

I laughed as we turned through a gate into a front yard. 'OK, let's go!'

I squeezed my arms to my side and felt the flutter of anticipation in my chest. So much to look forward to. Real Chinese hospitality, Christmas in the sun, the Spring Festival, exploring the world, doing life. With Michael. Side by side but not touching, we shared a smile. The world was our oyster.

'Now, so help me god, if I see you cross your chopsticks again I will disown you,' Michael muttered as he knocked on the door. 'You're an embarrassment to be seen out with.'

'I'm a delight,' I said, outraged. I elbowed him in the ribs, rather harder than I intended, and as the door opened we both had to bow low to hide our laughter.

⁓

Peter and I walk hand-in-hand across the dark car park. The students have gone home for the Christmas holidays and it's eerily quiet. Frost whispers in the air. I look around for Emmi, but I can't see anyone. Rosaline slipped out very early, eyes glued to phone once again. I feel slightly piqued she didn't say goodbye.

We wave to Morris and his wife and daughter as they get into their car—I can't quite see the make but it looks curiously small for Morris, who's well over six foot. He almost has to fold himself inside.

Niall, his partner, Becca and her friends have gone off to the pub together, a band of coats and hunched shoulders and hands in pockets retreating into the darkness. Allie and Eamonn are still in the studio, and when we left they were making no motions towards leaving.

My shoes sound on the concrete. Peter shivers, pulling his jacket closer to him with his free hand.

'Going to have to start thinking about Christmas shopping,' he says.

'And the cooking,' I say. 'I'll get the lights down from the loft on the weekend.' Peter nods, reaching in his pocket for his car keys.

'It's a shame they won't be running your class anymore,' he says. 'Just when you'd started something so promising.'

'I'm too old to be starting anything,' I say. 'I'm just

killing time at this stage.' Peter frowns as he reverses—he doesn't like it when I speak like that. 'Don't worry,' I say, 'I'll find something to amuse myself with. I can keep painting, even if there's no class.' Peter seems mollified by this, but I'm not just saying it for him. I will keep painting. I press my back into the seat, stretching my legs out slightly. 'Do the bins go out tonight?'

I keep my eyes on the window as we drive through the darkness, and I watch the streets go past as I've watched them for years, and I wait for home.

Acknowledgements

Immeasurable and eternal gratitude to Mum and Dad for all you put up with from me, for providing tea, hugs, Whats-App chats, walks round the lake, and general emotional buttressing. Equal thanks to Adam for helping me out so thoroughly and enthusiastically with something so un-Adam-like, just because it's important to me.

Special shout-out to Arran, Rob and Eddie: thank you for your time, feedback and encouragement—it really does mean the world.

About Atmosphere Press

Atmosphere Press is an independent, full-service publisher for excellent books in all genres and for all audiences. Learn more about what we do at atmospherepress.com.

We encourage you to check out some of Atmosphere's latest releases, which are available at Amazon.com and via order from your local bookstore:

Á Deux, a novel by Alexey L. Kovalev

What If It Were True?, a novel by Eileen Wesel

Solitario: The Lonely One, a novel by John Manuel

The Fourth Wall, a novel by Scott Petty

Knights of the Air: Book 1: Rage!, a novel by Iain Stewart

Heartheaded, a novel by Constantina Pappas

The Aquamarine Surfboard, a novel by Kellye Abernathy

A Very Fine House, a novel by Rose Molina

White Birch, a novel by Paul Edmund Lessard

Saigon, a novel by Ralph Pezzullo

Melody Knight: A Vampire's Tale, a novel by Tony Lindsay

Staged, a novel by Elsie G. Beya

A Grip of Trees, a novel by Phillip Erfan

About the Author

Alanna (rhymes with Hannah) was born and raised in Nottingham, England. She holds a Bachelor's degree in Classics and a Master's in International Relations, and currently lives, works, and salsa-dances in Barcelona.